MW01120425

Season

Amanda C. Thompson

authorHOUSE®

AuthorHouse™
1663 Liberty Drive, Suite 200
Bloomington, IN 47403
www.authorhouse.com
Phone: 1-800-839-8640

First published by AuthorHouse 10/29/2007

ISBN: 978-1-4343-3572-2 (sc)

Printed in the United States of America
Bloomington, Indiana

This book is printed on acid-free paper.

Dear Reader,

There are so many things running through my head about this book. First and foremost: If you are reading this book, chances are, you've also read Millennium Girl. Looking back, that seems so juvenile. I was just a middle school kid writing about her middle school friends and how she wished her life could be. But as time passed, I felt that the story was not over yet, and I committed myself to writing a sequel. The story I wanted to tell this time had an even more important message, and I felt it had to be said, but in order to say it, I had to allow the characters to take on lives of their own and grow away from the people I based them on way back in middle school. Are they the same characters you read about in Millennium Girl? Yes, they are, but they're growing up, just like I have since then, and just like my audience has.

I guess what I really want to say is this: the people in my first book were, for the most part, people I knew, with some adjustments here and there, but they've grown into people quite unlike their real-life counterparts. And so, for all my awesome friends who think they may see themselves in this book but can't understand how I got such a twisted impression of them – that isn't it at all. And if you think you belong in this book but don't see yourself, once again, do not take personal offense. I have now had two editors tell me that I have too many characters. I love you all dearly, and if anything I've said (or not said) here in this book offends any one of you, I'll probably go cry. I'm not passing judgment of any sort, nor am I saying that you are still the people I'm talking about in this story. In fact, some of our true stories are probably even stranger than fiction (to use a platitude). Thank you to all those wonderful friends for the fun times and struggles that inspired me and for being crazy, awesome, talented and beautiful, even if you don't think you're any of these things, because you are.

I hope that Season can act as a tribute to all the years we spent together studying, playing, traveling, rocking out – you know, those "golden years" we're all going to talk about when we're seventy years old. We're all moving on to our different futures in different places around the globe, and who knows where life will take us? Through it all, I promise I won't ever forget you, and please don't forget me. Keep in touch, call often – I'll pay the long distance charges! (I say this now, but just wait until I'm trying to pay bills with the meager earnings I make off of whatever I publish next…). But really. We've been through so much together. I know there's so much more ahead of us, and I want to be there to celebrate with you in the good times and help you through the tough times. I love you always and forever!

To those with objections to content and form in this story, I extend my deepest apologies. All that I ask is that you bear this quote in mind: "I must go through the valley to stand upon the mountain of God" (Tai Anderson). Life is filled with challenges. It's up to us how we handle them. Like all of us, Carolyn is finding her way.

Infinite thanks to Wendy Simeone for her spectacular editing, to my supportive family and friends, and to my Lord Jesus Christ, the greatest inspiration of all.

God bless!
Amanda C. Thompson
May 29, 2007

PART ONE

IT WAS THE BEST OF TIMES, IT WAS THE WORST OF TIMES, IT WAS THE AGE OF WISDOM, IT WAS THE AGE OF FOOLISHNESS, IT WAS THE EPOCH OF BELIEF, IT WAS THE EPOCH OF INCREDULITY, IT WAS THE SEASON OF LIGHT, IT WAS THE SEASON OF DARKNESS, IT WAS THE SPRING OF HOPE, IT WAS THE WINTER OF DESPAIR, WE HAD EVERYTHING BEFORE US, WE HAD NOTHING BEFORE US, WE WERE ALL GOING DIRECT TO HEAVEN, WE WERE ALL GOING DIRECT THE OTHER WAY...

~CHARLES DICKENS,
A TALE OF TWO CITIES

Chapter One

Getting dragged out of bed by her baby brother Jimmie had not been Carolyn's plan for the morning of January 1, 2000, but that was what happened. After the party the previous night – and, most importantly, her and Matt's private fireworks celebration around midnight – she lingered in a state of ecstasy and drowsiness, and would have gladly stayed in bed far past noon, reminiscing over Matt's kiss. Her very first. She smiled hugely just at the thought.

"You look like a baboon when you grin like that," Jimmie taunted.

"You look like a baboon anyways," she shot back cheerfully, rolling out of bed and looking at the bright red digits glowing on her alarm clock. "What got you out of bed so early?" She tugged on a bathrobe and ran a comb mindlessly through her hair.

"We have the *greatest* birthday present for you!" Jimmie practically shouted, fidgeting. "I couldn't go back to sleep because I was so excited to give it to you!" *That is SO cute,* Carolyn thought, smiling down at her brother's glowing face. He was acting as if it were *his* birthday, not hers.

"Oh, really? So what is this present?" she wheedled, still stroking her already smooth hair with the comb. She already had everything in the world that she could possibly want.

"I can't tell you!" Jimmie said exasperatedly. "Just come on, Mom and Dad are already waiting in the living room!" He took her by the wrist, causing her to drop the comb, and dragged her through the hall, down the stairs, and around the Christmas tree to where their parents waited on the couch with two sizable gifts on the floor in front of them.

"Morning, Lynnie," said her mom, ever-cheery and oblivious to Carolyn's antipathy toward the pet name. She rose to wrap Carolyn in a hug. "Happy birthday!"

"Thanks," Carolyn replied into her shoulder, hugging back and trying to remember when she'd grown to be taller than her mother.

"Happy birthday, Skiblink," her dad threw in, his face glowing with her favorite lopsided, genuine smile. Carolyn kind of wished he wouldn't call her that, either – she was thirteen now, for crying out loud – but she let it slip for the day.

"Morning, dad," she responded, giving him a hug, as well. "Jimmie says you got me the best birthday present ever."

Dad chuckled. "I'll leave that to you to decide," he said.

"She's gonna *love* it!" Jimmie exploded, barely containing his excitement. "Open it, open it, open it!"

Carolyn looked at her parents. "Go ahead, Lynnie," mom urged. Grinning, Carolyn bent and tore the paper off the long, awkward package, and inhaled sharply when she saw what it was.

"A… guitar?" she asked in astonishment. Her parents seemed pleased by her reaction. It was true that she hadn't been able to decide what to put on her birthday list after having a wonderful Christmas just last week, and the idea of taking up guitar hadn't so much as crossed her mind, but the moment she laid eyes on the frosty blue electric guitar in all its sparkling-new splendor, she realized what a perfect gift it was.

"Doyoulikeit? Doyoulikeit?" Jimmie asked, bouncing all around.

After a moment of dumbstruck silence, she answered, "I *love* it! You guys are the greatest!" and gave them all hugs, saving the biggest one for her "annoying" little brother.

"I picked out the color," he announced proudly.

"And you did an excellent job, Jimmie," Carolyn assured him. "It's perfect."

Positively beaming, Jimmie insisted that she open the rest. Carolyn smiled some more. "I'd like to take enough time to enjoy each one," she explained. "If I open them all at once, how am I supposed to enjoy them?"

Patience was not a virtue Jimmie had mastered quite yet. "You can enjoy them *after* you open them all," he said, looking at Carolyn as though she were nuts for still having another bulky present still fully wrapped by her feet.

"Okay, okay. How about this one next?" she suggested, already taking the wrapping paper off. Inside was an amplifier, large enough to reach her knees in height, but small enough to tote around by herself. Carolyn grinned deviously and said, "I bet you guys will regret buying me this... but thanks!"

Her parents smiled at her and at each other in satisfaction, sensing that her enthusiasm was genuine. Mom passed her a card, and Carolyn slit it open as carefully as she could while Jimmie bounced on the couch that she was leaning against. "Where is all that energy coming from?" she asked him. She was still groggy and reminiscent, and had the feeling she would be that way for awhile.

"Idunno," Jimmie said, still bouncing. "Now you have to open the one that I picked out all by myself. I even bought it with my own money!" He swelled with pride as dad passed her a smallish package with a home-made construction paper card taped to the top. Seeing her brother's delight, she told him the card was beautiful, and tore off the wrapping paper as violently as Jimmie himself would have. She uncovered a black guitar strap patterned with blue moons. "Wow, Jimmie, this is awesome!" she said, and meant it. She definitely preferred this sweet, generous version of her brother to the gnat he usually was. Jimmie's round face flushed with pride.

"Gram and Gramps sent these for you," said mom, producing a box that probably contained some sort of jewelry and a small but heavy package. *At least they didn't send socks.* Carolyn opened the heavy, irregular gift first. This one, a Swiss Army knife, came from Gramps. *Very useful,* Carolyn thought sarcastically, but she acted excited as she moved on to Gram's gift. She secretly hoped it would be a pair of earrings, since she had recently lost one of her favorite pairs.

When she opened the box, what she found was a necklace, and a very pretty one, at that. Silver inlaid with garnets, her birthstone, it looked very expensive, and Carolyn probably would have worn it with pride if it hadn't been a cross. The problem was that she didn't want to walk around advertising that she was a part of some organized religion, when almost the opposite was true. Although Leah, her best friend from before the move to California, had been big on church gatherings and such, those things had never been Carolyn's scene. She always felt so... restricted, cramped; as though every critical eye were just waiting for her to make a mistake so they could send her off to confession or something. As beautiful as the necklace was, Carolyn guessed she would probably use the Swiss Army knife before she wore *that*. She feigned excitement again, though.

"It's really pretty," she got out. Mom looked over her shoulder and admired the sparkling cross as it dangled from Carolyn's fingers on its delicate chain.

"It's beautiful, Lynnie! Do you want me to help you put it on?" she offered, and Carolyn could tell that her mom's appreciation was unfeigned.

"Um… not right now," she answered, trying not to offend her mother. She replaced the necklace and capped the box. "Maybe when I get dressed." *But don't count on it,* she added silently.

Chapter Two

"Can you believe my parents got me a guitar for my birthday?" Carolyn mentioned to her friends as they browsed through the mall. "It was so random... I don't know what made them think to get me one."

"That's so cool, Carolyn! I'll bet you're going to be a rock star now..." Molly said excitedly.

"Chyeah, right," Carolyn laughed skeptically.

"Yeah! You and Molly could have a band and stuff!" Margo piped up.

"Huh?" Carolyn hadn't realized Molly played an instrument. "What do you play?"

"The drums, of course," Molly stated. "Where were you all last night when I was yammering on about the drum set my parents got me for Christmas?"

"In space," Tori answered for her. "You were more than a little out of it all night."

"I guess..." Carolyn said slowly, wondering what to tell her friends. "Maybe I was just overly happy that Matt is back on his feet again," she invented, and immediately berated herself for bringing Matt into the picture at all. Blushing, she turned to look at a pair of red Chuck Taylors in a store window to hide her embarrassment. She knew it would only be a matter of time before they figured out that something had happened between her and Matt, especially if she kept blushing at the mention of his name, but she couldn't help herself. She wished she could keep her little secret to herself just a little longer so she could treasure it in her heart, but evidently, that wasn't going to happen.

"Heyyy…" Tori said, turning on Carolyn. "Speaking of Matt, where did you two disappear to last night?" *Why does she have to be so* perceptive? Carolyn thought. She grimaced at the Chucks before turning around.

"Hey, yeah, that's right," Molly chimed in, eyeing Carolyn suspiciously. "I saw you guys sneaking off. What's up with that?" Carolyn realized there was no way around her friends, and resolved to tell them the truth. They kind of deserved to know anyway, after all she had gone through with Matt since she'd moved to Long Beach.

She took a deep breath and mumbled, "welldonttellanyonebutmattkisse dme," all in a jumble. Her friends leaned in. She repeated, more slowly this time. "Matt kissed me." Margo squealed.

"Ooooh!" Molly teased, winking and giving Carolyn a nudge in the ribs.

"It's about time!" Tori said, just loudly enough to attract the attention of the rest of the girls who had joined them.

"What happened? What'd I miss?" Ashe asked excitedly.

"Matt kissed Carolyn last night," Tori blabbed.

"Tori!"

"*What?*"

"Omigod that is so great!" Ashe bubbled. "You guys! You guys," she said, turning to Anne, Kate, Erin, and Shawna. Carolyn knew that as soon as *they* heard about it (not so much Anne, but the others), it would be all over the school, but before she could protest, Ashe had announced, "Matt kissed Carolyn last night!"

"Aww! I always knew you two were right for each other!" said Kate.

"That's so sweet!" Shawna added. Erin remained silent – she was still trying not to copy Shawna, who she had shadowed and imitated for most of her life.

"Well, now, is there anybody else we forgot to tell?" Carolyn muttered. "Let's ask if we can borrow the loudspeaker: 'attention, all shoppers…'" Her friends laughed.

"That's, like, so cool, Carolyn," Erin said. "Now you're, like, a *real* Millennium Girl. So, like, what's it feel like?" Carolyn had never realized how many times Erin used the word "like" in one sentence until that point, and suddenly it really irked her.

Carolyn shrugged. "Cool, I guess. Anybody up for fries and a shake?" she proposed, hoping to change the subject.

"You're not distracting us *that* easily," Anne said. "You have to give us *all* the details."

"I'd rather not," Carolyn mumbled, her blush deepening.

"Oh, come on!" they urged.

"I've never been kissed, so I don't know what it's like," Ashe pleaded.

"Me either," Erin added. "Is it, like, as great as everybody thinks it is?"

"I think," Carolyn said sagely, "that you guys just need to find out on your own when the time is right."

"None of that 'young grasshopper,' 'wiser-than-thou' crap," Molly insisted. "Just tell us a little bit?"

"What do *you* want to know for? Chris kissed you forever ago."

Molly looked a little hurt by this, and Carolyn promptly apologized. "Hey, I'm sorry… I didn't think that would hurt your feelings… It's just," she whispered, "I really don't want to tell all of *them* about it, y'know?"

"Oh, it's not *that*…" Molly assured her. "It's okay," she continued, sounding slightly insincere. "It shouldn't have hurt my feelings. It's just, well…" Molly bit her lip, and Carolyn saw tears welling up in her eyes. "I'm sort of sensitive right now because…" she tried again, but she seemed incapable of finishing.

Margo jumped in. "She and Chris broke up over Christmas break," she whispered, her breath tickling Carolyn's ear. "Not exactly the best Christmas present, you know?"

Stunned, Carolyn looked to Molly for confirmation of this momentous news. Molly and Chris had been The Item last year. But it seemed that they no longer were, since Molly sadly nodded 'yes,' tears balancing on her lashes, ready to fall. She stared at her tattered blue Chucks, still unable to speak.

"Aww… that was dumb of him," Carolyn comforted. "We'll pick you a better boyfriend next time."

Far from comforting or cheering her, this statement only increased Molly's distress. "No!" she cried. "I… I don't want another boyfriend… I only want Chris. I *really* like him, I can't even describe it. I'll get him back! I don't want anybody else," she declared. Her eyes still shone, but the tears seemed to have receded just a little.

"Not even that guy over there with the awesome purple Mohawk?" Margo asked with a giggle. The corners of Molly's mouth twitched a little, but she refused to smile.

"I don't get it, though. If he dumped you, why would you go back to him? He's not worth it," Carolyn reasoned.

"People make mistakes, Carolyn," Molly retorted. "He'll figure it out." With that, she closed the conversation, leaving Carolyn to wonder how someone could be so faithful to a guy who didn't even like her anymore, and whether she would do the same for Matt.

"Can I see your new drum set?" Carolyn asked Molly as they rode home in awkward silence. Molly was still moody, to say the least, and the tension in the air was thick enough to choke on.

"Sure, whatever," Molly replied with an apathetic shrug, turning more towards the window and pulling her knees up to her chest. Carolyn desperately wished to break the barrier that she had inadvertently erected between herself and her best friend.

"Cool," Carolyn said timidly, not expecting a response – so she wasn't disappointed when she received none.

"And *I* wanna see *your* guitar," Margo demanded. Her enthusiasm felt out of place, but Carolyn latched on to it in hopes of bringing some more cheer to the crushing weight of the air in the minivan.

"Sure! It's so cool! …I only wish I had a clue as to how to play it. I guess I could always teach myself… I've heard of a lot of people who are doing that these days…"

"Yeah! Finn was trying to do that… back when, you know, we were going out," Tori explained.

Carolyn raised an eyebrow. "You're not anymore?"

"Well… it was sort of on and off…. He thinks I flirt too much with other guys, but I don't mean to," Tori said sheepishly. Carolyn nodded in understanding. Tori did seem to have some sort of radar that pinpointed the most attractive male in the vicinity every time she entered a room, and she almost always hunted him down and started a conversation with him. She had the hair-toss down pretty well, too. Carolyn never "tossed" anything – her hair was just too heavy for that, and she never felt like treating it specially just to make it flippable. "We were pretty short lived. We never even kissed. Well, except for that one time that I tried to kiss him at the movies…. I think *that* was why he broke up with me, actually…

"But anyway… that wasn't really the point," Tori continued. "He managed to teach himself enough to join up with some other guys and start a band.

Have you heard them yet? I think they're supposed to play a short set at some party next week…"

"No, I haven't," Margo confessed. "I didn't even know he was in a band! But I can't wait to see him and his buddies make fools of themselves next week." She smirked.

"Actually, they're pretty decent," Tori defended. "Just wait and see."

"Well, if worst comes to worst, I could always make Finn teach me," Carolyn proposed.

Mrs. Gilman pulled up to the house, and everyone clambered to be first out of the car. Molly trudged along behind. "Come on, Molly!" Tori called from up ahead. "Show us your drums!" Molly plastered on a happy face and obliged, which seemed to satisfy the others, but Carolyn could see right through her hollow smile. This breakup was really killing her. Carolyn's heart went out to her. *If only I could make it better….* That was her aptitude: making things better, helping her friends out of rough spots. Now, when she needed it most, would her talent abandon her?

Molly burst through the door to her room and indicated a shiny new, black Pearl drum set. "Here it is," she said with forced enthusiasm.

"Wow!" Aisling exclaimed. "That's a *really* nice drum set, Molly!" She cautiously ran her fingers along the smooth and shiny surface, eyes sparkling.

"Thanks."

"Can I try it?" Anne asked longingly.

"Yeah, sure, why not?" Molly agreed, producing a pair of drumsticks from a nearby canvas bag, which tipped over, spilling its mass of drum tabs all over the floor.

"Wow, someone's been busy," Carolyn commented, stooping to help stack the wide-strewn papers. "Can you seriously play all of these?"

Molly shook her head. "Mom's getting me some lessons with some crazy ex-rock-star guy."

"Really? Who?" Tori asked.

"I dunno. He wasn't exactly famous, he just played in some hardcore local band or something like 30 years ago."

"...I see," Carolyn said, shoving the mess of papers into the bag.

"Yeah, he works at a music store a couple towns over," Margo explained. "His hair is probably as long as Anne's, only greyer." They all looked past the drum set at Anne, whose blonde hair, even in a braid, reached most of the way down her back.

"Wow," Anne commented, fingering a lock. "That's shady." She clanged a cymbal. "Why don't you just have my big bro teach you?"

"You have a *brother?*" Carolyn asked in astonishment. "Who *knew?*"

"I did," Anne said with a grin.

"Yeah, he's still in high school, but he got a scholarship to spend the semester abroad, so I haven't seen him in forever. He was in Europe all this summer, and he's been attending a French school since August. And now... he's back. Joy of joys." She rolled her eyes.

"How come you never mentioned him before?" Carolyn asked. She supposed the others had known, and Anne had just assumed that Carolyn didn't need to be told.

Anne shrugged. "You never asked?"

"Hey, I forgot about him! He used to be pretty cool I think," Margo said. "When we were younger..."

"I don't believe I've had the pleasure of meeting him," Tori, who had a particular fondness for older boys, said eagerly.

"It's no pleasure, I assure you," Anne promised.

"All the same, is he home now?" Tori pressed.

"I dunno, I guess."

"Let's go see him, then!"

"Well, if you really want to-" Anne started. Tori was already halfway out the door. "I do!" she called back.

"You guys go," Molly said. "I'm kind of tired... I'll meet him another day."

"But Molly! We're going for you!" Tori clarified, popping her head back in the door. "You're the one who needs drum lessons. Come on, it'll be fun!"

"I dunno... I think I'm just going to stay here and rest..."

Carolyn was incredulous. Molly: the cheerful, hyperactive, happy-go-lucky girl who had eagerly stepped up as Carolyn's best friend during that awkward first week in a new town, the one who always found something to laugh about simply because she loved to laugh – "tired?" Sad? Depressed? It was acceptable (and even expected) that she would be rather blue for a few days or weeks after such a breakup, but Carolyn couldn't quite understand why Molly preferred the solitary sadness of her room to an evening with friends who only wanted her to be happy. "I really think you should come," she said carefully, avoiding any allusion to the situation with Chris. "We have to go back to school tomorrow. Do you want to spend the last day of your vacation alone and bored?"

"Well..." Molly remained reluctant, but consented at last. "Just for a little while, though."

Everyone borrowed some form of wheels from the Gilmans' garage – bikes, scooters, roller blades, and in the case of poor Tori, a skateboard, which she wound up trading to Margo, who surprisingly had some skills at skating. Of course, "skills" in Carolyn's book meant being able to stand on the board for more than a second without landing on her butt, since she couldn't skateboard at all. They hurried to Anne's house before Molly could change her mind.

Barging through the door into the kitchen, Anne shouted, "SKITT! ARE YOU HOME?" As she followed Anne into the meticulous living space, Carolyn realized that in spite of all the times she and Anne had hung out in the past, she had never been in Anne's house until now. She looked around. The kitchen was a traditional blue with vintage-looking porcelain plates, teacups, and salt-and-pepper shakers decorating the room. It appeared that either Mr. or Mrs. Donahue had a fetish for salt-and-pepper shakers, since countless shakers ornamented not only the kitchen, but the dining room as well – a procession of exotic shapes and colors balanced delicately on the trim of the room to the right of where they stood. The door directly across from the entrance they'd used led to an equally immaculate living room, which was utterly devoid of the books, magazines, and trinkets that littered her own living room. A collection of shoes beside the door greeted anyone who happened to enter, reminding them to take off their own footwear. The house seemed *too* nice, and Carolyn was reluctant to breathe for fear of knocking down one of those precious shakers. She couldn't picture anyone playing drums in a house like that.

"*SKITT!*" Anne hollered again.

"Yah! Whaddaya want?" The deep voice drifted down a flight of stairs that must have been off to the side of the living room, just outside her line of vision.

"I brought some of my friends over!" Anne called, only minimally more quietly than before. Apparently she and Skitt enjoyed yelling across the house at each other, but it made Carolyn uneasy. She was certain that at any moment, one of those shakers would fall to the floor and shatter into a billion tiny pieces.

Skitt didn't reply, but a minute later, he appeared in the living room door, just pulling a shirt over his head of wet hair, exposing a toned six-pack. Carolyn tried not to blush as she realized he had just been in the shower, but Tori stifled a giggle behind her, and a chain reaction had all of them in stitches in moments.

"*Okay*, Skitt, stop showing off to my *eighth-grade* friends," Anne said irritably. It didn't take Carolyn long to realize that he hadn't been showing off for *them* – he'd been showing off for the heck of it. He was just a big flirt. Someone had probably told him how devastatingly handsome he was, and he'd gotten a swollen ego, and that was the end of his bashfulness. And he *was* handsome: towering well over six feet tall, his longish, dirty-blond hair was still mussed from his shower, his eyes flickered hazel behind long eyelashes, and his grin was stunningly straight and white.

Carolyn mentally berated herself. She had finally – *finally* – scored Matt, and no one could be better than him. Besides, all she knew about Skitt was that he played the drums, liked to flirt, and was in high school (and therefore, was probably too old for her anyway).

"Eighth grade? I would have guessed you were at least sophomores," he teased. Carolyn told herself she was imagining it, but it seemed that those hazel searchlights had locked on her when he said this. She pretended not to notice. She knew that he was nothing more than a flirt, and that it probably came naturally for him to tease and mess around, but she also knew that if she let herself, she could easily find herself falling for him. *And just when you finally got somewhere with Matt!* She scolded herself. *You need to wash your brain out with soap! What* loyalty, *what* dedication! *I guess it's true that we only want something as long as we can't have it.*

"Skitt," Anne said loudly, warningly, "this is Molly, Margo, Carolyn, and Tori. And you know Ashe. Everyone... my brother – SCOTT." Skitt seemed miffed by this, and Anne grinned smugly at him. "Scotty hates it when we call him by his *real* name," she cooed.

Skitt brushed it off. "Hello, ladies," he said, smoothing his hair.

Anne threw up her hands in defeat. "Molly got a drum set for Christmas," she informed him. "Do you think you could teach her to play?"

"Of course," Skitt agreed readily. "Uhm... which one did you say was Molly?" Everyone laughed a little at that, and Molly stepped forward a teeny bit. "Nice to meet you, Molly." He politely held out his hand for her to shake, and Molly uncertainly grasped it for a fraction of a second, warily watching Skitt's face. "Shall we go up to the attic and begin our study of the fine art of drumming?" he offered with a charming grin.

"*Now?*" Molly asked in surprise.

"Sure, why not?" Skitt agreed.

"But, …well, I… I… guess," she stammered.

Anne glared at Skitt, but addressed Molly. "If you're worried that Skitt is going to make a move on you, don't be. He flirts a lot, but he's harmless." It sounded like she was talking about a puppy whose bark was worse than his bite. Anne shoved her face into her brother's. "Skitt, Molly has a *boyfriend*, and it's not you, so don't you pull anything on her, hear?"

Suddenly, the door slammed. Carolyn flinched, waiting for the sound of a shattering pepper-shaker, and sure enough, one of the shakers smashed loudly on the linoleum behind her. Shocked, everyone spun and faced the door, exchanging puzzled looks as they watched Molly speed away on the skateboard.

"What did I do?" Skitt asked, sounding genuinely sorry that he had caused such a reaction, and confused as much as any of them. "She wasn't *really* worried about that, was she?"

"Nonono," Margo reassured him. "It had absolutely nothing to do with you. Trust me, I'm her sister; I know these things."

"Then what was that all about?" Anne asked, opening a closet to get a broom and a dustpan.

"I'll get it," Skitt hastily volunteered, and left the girls to their discussion. *How perceptive of him,* Carolyn thought.

"So?" Anne prodded in a hushed voice. "What's the matter with her?"

"It has to do with Chris," Margo replied vaguely, not wanting to betray Molly's trust by giving too much information, but hoping to explain her behavior.

"Aha! I thought it might," Anne said smugly, sitting back. "She left right when I told Skitt she had a boyfriend. Did they… break up?"

Margo nodded hesitantly, and told as much as she knew. "She used to tell me everything. We were best friends. But ever since Chris came along, we've been growing apart. He's all she's cared about ever since they started going out." Her eyes were downcast, and with what seemed like an immense effort, she lifted them to look at her friends.

"It's that bad?" Carolyn asked. Margo nodded sadly. "You know, Chris seems like a cool kid... as a friend. But... he seems like a bad influence on Molly... when they're dating, I mean. He's pulling her down." She watched Margo carefully for her reaction, in case she'd said something offensive without meaning to, but Margo nodded in agreement.

"Tell me about it," she sighed, throwing herself onto the couch in frustration. "I just... wish I knew what to do for her." She clenched her fists and set her jaw, but a tear escaped her eye and ran down her cheek.

"We all do," Carolyn comforted, sitting next to her and patting her shoulder sympathetically. Anne and Tori joined them on the couch for a group hug. Margo sniffled and thanked them. By the time Skitt returned, she had regained her composure.

"Everything all right, ladies?" Skitt asked with that trademark grin of his.

"For now, anyways," Tori replied.

"I might know just the thing to cheer you all up," Skitt mentioned.

"Yeah, what's that? Play Nintendo for a few hours?" Anne teased.

Skitt chuckled. "No. I was thinking more along the lines of, 'I know someone who's having a party tonight, and maybe a night out would take Molly off your minds for a little while.'"

"I'm guessing this isn't a birthday party with a clown and balloon animals," Carolyn said. "I'm pretty sure my mom would kill me."

"Same," said Tori.

"I've been to one of Skitt's friend's parties," Anne said. "It's actually pretty fun; nothing bad has ever happened to me. You should come."

"I'm in," Margo announced. Carolyn stared wide-eyed at her friend. She hadn't expected Margo to want to go. She wasn't even sure *she* wanted to go

– hence the "my mom would kill me" excuse, which was at least partially true. But *somebody* had to go with Margo.

"I'll go too," she said quickly.

"*You're* going?" Tori asked incredulously. "I thought you said your mom would kill you."

"My mom doesn't have to know. I'll say I'm going to the movies with Margo and Anne," Carolyn said rebelliously. *My god… did I just say that? Since when have I been a liar?*

"That's the spirit!" Skitt said. "So… how about you guys come back here by eight and I'll drive you?"

"Sounds cool," said Margo.

"I'm in," Tori muttered.

"See you then." Skitt turned and disappeared down a set of stairs. Moments later, they heard artificial gunfire, and Anne shut the basement door, rolling her eyes. "His stupid Nintendo. Carolyn, I still want to see your guitar. Let's go."

Chapter Three

"It's soo pretty, Carolyn," Margo commented, fingering the neck of the guitar. "Can you play anything yet?"

"I wish," Carolyn answered.

"Try," Anne insisted. "Just make something up."

"Well… I guess," Carolyn caved. She started to play, but the noise that came from the guitar could not exactly be called music. *And that is why I do not plug it in,* she thought to herself.

"Ouch! Aw, crap," she said suddenly, shaking her hand. "Those strings hurt like crazy. And I think I just broke a nail." She put her fingers in her mouth and gnawed on the broken nail. "I can tell I'm going to be an awesome rock star one day," she said around her fingers. Her friends laughed.

"Hey, it takes practice," Anne reassured her. "Once you learn some basics and get used to the strings – who knows?" Carolyn smiled and thanked her without removing her fingers from her mouth.

The bedroom door suddenly banged open, and Jimmie appeared in the doorframe. "Mom says it's time for dinner," he announced, and left before Carolyn could yell at him for forgetting to knock.

"…Okay, that was weird," Carolyn said. "I guess that probably means I have to kick you out now." They all started down the stairs.

"Let's meet at the corner at quarter of 8 and walk to Anne's from there," Tori said to Carolyn and Margo, who nodded in agreement.

"See you at 7:45!"

Carolyn opened the door for them. *"For the movie,"* she added for her parents' benefit.

"Bye," her friends replied with a giggle as Carolyn winked and shut the door.

"Carolyn! Come eat!" her mom called impatiently, just as the phone started ringing.

"I'll be right there! I'm going to get that!" she shouted, and dove for the nearest phone, nearly falling over Buddy in her hurry. "Hello?"

"Happy birthday to you…" sang a voice that she immediately recognized as Matt's.

"Hey!" she said excitedly. "Thanks!"

"Anytime. Have a good day, birthday girl?"

"Yeah!" She recalled Molly's gloom and added, "Well, except for one thing-"

"Carolyn! Dinner! Now!" her mom called again, sounding even more impatient.

"I'll be there in a minute!" Carolyn retorted exasperatedly.

"Everything okay?" Matt asked.

"Yeah, my mom is just being annoying… I guess I'll have to talk to you later. Hey, uhm, I'm going out with Anne, Tori, and Margo tonight, wanna come?"

"Well… I was going to invite you to the pizza place downtown…"

20

"Oh! Well, I would have loved to go, but-"

"It's okay," he assured her. "Where are you going tonight?"

"*Carolyn!* I'm not going to ask you again!" her mother shouted from the next room.

"I'm sorry, I really have to go. Meet us on the corner at 7:45, okay?"

"I- okay, see you then," Matt said in a rush.

"Cool, bye." She hung up, feeling guilty for being so abrupt, but she didn't want to get on her mom's bad side – if she wasn't already. Carolyn wondered what was bothering her so much, but deemed it safest to keep quiet.

"Sorry, I'm here," she apologized sweetly, slipping into her seat next to Jimmie. She eyed the heap of what looked to be meatloaf and opened her mouth to complain.

"Eat it," her mother ordered. Carolyn quickly shoveled some onto her plate and squeezed ketchup all over it.

"Now, don't take it out on Caro," her dad said. Carolyn looked up in surprise – her dad usually called her something silly and embarrassing, such as "Skiblink" when she had first chosen that as her web address. She was thirteen now – old enough to go to a party with her friends. She wasn't a little girl anymore, and she appreciated the change to a more mature nickname than "Skiblink." She tried to meet her father's eyes in a way that conveyed that feeling, but he seemed not to notice.

"I'm not taking anything. Out. On. Anyone." Carolyn's mom angrily dished vegetables onto her plate, accentuating her syllables with the clanking of the serving spoon. Buddy crouched nervously in the corner, watching the food as it was served but not waiting under the table for a morsel to drop like he usually did, and Carolyn knew something strange was going on. Animals could always sense those things. She looked at Jimmie in confusion.

They had a fight, he mouthed. Carolyn's stomach seemed to fall out of her body entirely, and she lost what little appetite she'd had left after surveying the singed meatloaf. *A fight? My parents don't fight. What could they have fought over? It can't have been money. We've never had money problems before.*

"Carolyn, eat your supper before it gets cold," her mother insisted, trying to sound tender and maternal, but only achieving a bossy tone that made Carolyn want to plug her ears and sing loudly, "*I'm not listening! I'm not listening!*" Carolyn started cutting the food and pushing it around her plate, but she couldn't bring herself to take a bite.

"I have to meet Margo and Tori soon," she announced suddenly, her voice sounding too loud in the awkward, tense silence that had settled over the kitchen while they ate. The clock on the stove told her she still had upwards of half an hour before she actually had to be somewhere, but the weight of the air made it impossible to breathe. Jimmie gave her a look that said, "You're *leaving* me here? With *them?*" Carolyn wished she could do something for him, but she certainly couldn't bring him to the party with her. "Sorry, Jim, you can borrow my video games or whatever you want," she said, feeling generous – or maybe just desperate to get out of the house without incident.

"When will you be back?" asked her mom, clinging to that maternal image.

"I don't know, like ten or eleven." She braced herself. They weren't going to let her go. As much as she didn't want to be at the party, she'd take anything over spending the night at home.

"That's late, Caro," her dad said with concern. "Where are you going? Who will you be with?" She could tell from his smug expression that he felt he'd one-upped her mom in parental responsibility, and at that moment, she bitterly hated both of them.

"The movies with Margo, Tori and Anne," she replied in a rush, leaving Matt and Skitt out of the picture just to be safe. "Gotta go, see you tonight."

"Take my cell phone with you," her mom demanded.

"Okay." Anything, *anything* to get her out of there, and fast. She ran upstairs, snatched the phone from her mom's room, whipped on some night-out clothes for the party, and darted out the back door. Free.

She had ages before she would have to make her way to the corner, so she stole away to her favorite boulder in the woods – her "thinking spot" – to ponder this situation between her parents.

It's probably nothing. Lot's of kids' parents fight all the time. I'm lucky that mine don't. She had already ruled out money. People who were short on money did not buy their kids electric guitars for their birthdays when they hadn't even asked for one. Had she and Jimmie done something wrong? As far as she knew, both of them were easily making the grade. They both had plenty of good friends and plenty of good, healthy extracurricular activities, but she couldn't come up with any more ideas. *Maybe it really is nothing. God, if you're even real, don't let this come between them. Make everything okay for them... for all of us.* Then resolution took the place of hopelessness. *Whatever's wrong, I'll fix it. That's what I do.*

Without realizing it, Carolyn had started pacing, but at that moment, she heard a rustling in the woods that sounded too large and clumsy for a squirrel. She stopped and listened – there it was again! It wasn't dark, but twilight was setting in, and Carolyn was getting creeped out.

"Who's there?" she asked, and the words felt bold until she heard them squeak out from between her lips.

A sudden rustle indicated a surprised jump from whoever was out there. Apparently he or she hadn't known Carolyn was there. She relaxed just a tiny bit – at least nobody was intentionally stalking her. "Who's that?" the person – he – said.

"Who's *that*?"

"Is that – Carolyn?"

"*Matt?*" Carolyn saw his sunny hair bursting through the foliage and felt her heart resume its normal activity of beating. "You know, you scared the crap out of me," she accused.

"Aw, geez, I'm sorry," he mumbled.

"Boy, am I glad it's you and not some creep," Carolyn admitted.

Matt smiled. "What're you doing back here?"

"Oh, I just come back here to think sometimes. Things are weird at home tonight. I wanted to get out," she confided.

"Oh. I'm sorry. I'm kind of here for the same reason."

Carolyn remembered how hard it had been for Matt when his mom passed away in October. "Yeah?" she pressed.

"Well... now that grandma's officially moved in and is a 'legal guardian' or whatever, she's coming up with all these really annoying rules. We've been avoiding each other this week, but we sort of blew up at each other today."

"What sorts of rules?"

"Let's just say the lady is a little obsessed with church," he began. "She brought us to the late service on Christmas Eve, dragged us out of bed for the early service on Christmas, and this morning she had us all up at 6:30 for what she called a 'family breakfast' before the 8:00 service. I've only just escaped the evening service, and that was *after* her 'family supper.' She's like, a let's-be-a-happy-religious-family nut or something. And that's just Sundays." He sank down on the rock, looking, Carolyn had to admit, like he'd been up since a lot earlier than 6:30 – more like he hadn't slept in days. How had she missed this in him the night before?

"Wow. I had no idea she was such a fanatic. I wish I had some advice for you." Carolyn joined him on the rock. "How are you coping? With...." *Your mom not being there,* she said silently, and Matt understood.

"I just keep expecting her to walk in the back door, covered in dirt after an afternoon of gardening, or call us to dinner when we're already halfway there because whatever she's cooking smells so delicious." Carolyn had to lean in to hear because he was speaking so quietly. The still-raw pain was evident in his tone. She took his hand, wishing she could magically erase it all. Matt shook his head hopelessly. "And it makes me wonder: What's life coming to? We're all headed in the same direction, aren't we? What I want to know is, where is she now? What happens next?"

Unable to come up with a suitable answer, she admitted, "I dunno. Maybe nothing."

"But if there's nothing else, then what's the point of living? Money, success, friends – they don't come with us."

Carolyn thought about what mattered the most. "Well... I guess to leave your mark on future generations. To fulfill your dreams. To be happy."

"So... you don't really know," Matt clarified.

"Yeah, nope, I have no idea. Sorry." They sat in peace, fingers entwined, for what seemed to be a very long time. Dusk settled over them, carpeting the clearing with silky silence. Carolyn shivered slightly in the waxing night, but Matt was too absorbed in thought to notice.

With a sigh, he fell back to his original rant, visibly relieved at the opportunity for a change of subject from that of his mother's untimely death. "Grandma sets all sorts of crazy chores for us. Says it 'builds character.' She doesn't do *anything*. It's driving me crazy! Well, except sometimes she still cracks out the old roller skates..." They both laughed a little at the comical memory of Mrs. MacMillan roller skating around the house, tossing grapes in the air to catch with her mouth – but missing most of them, and running over them seconds later. "Just don't make me go back! I hate being Cinderella! The mice won't talk to me."

Carolyn laughed again, breathing more easily in the lightened atmosphere. "You always cheer me up," she told him.

"Just being with you cheers me up," he replied. Carolyn's insides melted, slowing her brain's processing activities almost to a halt. "So... are you going to let me in on what we're doing tonight?" Matt prompted. "You hung up so quickly earlier."

Carolyn snapped out of her fantasy as best she could. "Huh? Oh, well, I'm going to a party with Tori and Margo and Anne. We're looking out for each other."

Matt nodded slowly. "What kind of party?" he wanted to know.

Carolyn shrugged. "One where we might *need* to look out for each other, I guess." Matt grimaced, and she quickly added, "It'll be an adventure! A 'yay, I'm finally a teenager!' sort of adventure."

"All right," Matt agreed grudgingly. "But I'm only going because you are."

"Thank you." She wrapped him in a hug, which served the dual purpose of expressing her gratitude and warming her bare arms. It took her by surprise when she found Matt's lips pressed against her own. And that was it – all rational thought ceased entirely. She kissed him back, and that was all that mattered. She left her worries about her family and about Molly behind her, and her world exploded into bliss.

Without breaking the kiss, Matt grabbed her hand and held it up so he could read the watch. He pulled away, and Carolyn reluctantly sat back. "What time were we supposed to meet the gang?" he asked.

"7:45, why?" She took her hand back and looked at the watch. Thirty seconds to make it to the street corner. "Crud."

"Let's run," Matt suggested, and took off, leaving Carolyn with no choice but to follow at a sprint, since he had taken her hand again. They made it to the corner three breathless minutes later, and Carolyn dramatically fell to her knees. Running had never been her strong point.

"Hi… everyone…" she panted out.

"Oh, give it up," Tori said, nudging Carolyn with her foot.

"Don't make me carry you," Matt taunted. At that, Carolyn fell completely over and smiled innocently up at him. He rolled his eyes and bent over.

"You aren't seriously going to—Carolyn, you wuss," Margo teased, pulling her constant companion, her camera, out of her bag. "This one's going on my blog," she said as the camera clicked, blinding all of them with its flash and immortalizing the moment when Matt held Carolyn in his arms, just before he half-dropped her.

"Ow! What was that for?"

"That was a reminder to me that I need to hit the gym," he winced. Carolyn stared at him in complete shock, trying to decide whether she should be offended. Then he winked. "Just messing with you. I could carry you all the way to Anne's if I wanted."

Ego, ego. "Then do it," she dared him.

"I said 'if I wanted!'" he protested as Carolyn tried to clamber onto his back, and Margo snapped pictures until none of them could see a thing. Blinking, Matt said, "You seem to have your energy back. Walk."

Turning, they caught Tori trying to catch a piggy-back ride on Margo's back, but Margo broke free and ran for it, the rest of them doing their best to keep up until they made it to Anne's house.

Anne opened the door for them. "Hey, come on in, we're just about to leave.… Anybody want a snack?" she offered. Carolyn could feel her stomach's growling echo through its emptiness.

"Food would be awesome," she said.

"Cool. I made brownies," she said, revealing a plate of brownies that were still emanating heat from being baked. Carolyn's mouth watered, and she gratefully took three.

"You're my hero," she said around the delightful fudginess in her mouth.

"No prob. So… Matt. What inspired you to come?" she inquired conversationally.

"Carolyn," Matt replied, with a smile in her direction. Anne nodded approvingly and offered the plate of brownies to the rest of the gang, but they were all full from dinner.

At that moment, Skitt made his entrance, clad in the same casual outfit he'd been wearing earlier. Carolyn suddenly felt self-conscious in her mini-skirt and low-cut top, and the feeling was only augmented by the brownies she held – one in each hand – as she swallowed the first. She looked at the brownies, and then at Skitt. "Hi Skitt. Wanna brownie?" she offered. Out of the corner of her eye, Carolyn thought she saw something that resembled jealousy flit across Matt's face, and she mentally kicked herself yet again. *At this rate, my brain is going to need some shin-guards...*

"What'd you do, drop it on the floor? No thanks. Come on everybody, in the car," Skitt said.

Matt looked surprised. "You're driving?" he asked suspiciously.

Skitt stopped at the door and turned. "Of course. And you're..."

"Matt. Carolyn's boyfriend," he specified, and the possessive note in his voice was evident to her. Carolyn glanced at Skitt, who shrugged and continued out the door, but she was almost certain she had seen his face fall – just infinitesimally.... But maybe she'd only imagined it. Of course she'd imagined it. She followed her friends to the car. Anne called "goodbye" to her parents.

"Where exactly *are* we going?" Carolyn asked as the four girls squished into the back of the car.

Skitt looked at a piece of paper. "42 Pleasant St.," he recited. That didn't exactly help, since Carolyn had never been on a Pleasant Street since she'd moved to California. But she left it at that, and trusted Skitt to get them there and back again in one piece.

CHAPTER FOUR

Even from the end of the street, it was obvious which house the party was at because of the multitude of cars parked along the lawn and the volume of the music, which reached their ears through closed windows and the car stereo, which was blasting some sort of alternative rock, before they even parked. Tori said something that Carolyn couldn't hear, and she and the other girls shouted "WHAT?" over the noise.

"I said, 'We're going to be deaf by the end of the night!'" Tori screamed. Skitt parked and cut the music, and Carolyn, ears ringing, whimpered, "I think maybe we already are."

They tumbled out of the car, and Matt pulled Carolyn aside before they went in. "Do you really want to be here?" he pleaded.

Carolyn just shrugged. "We're here now. There's not a lot we can do about it. Let's just go in and have some fun. Forget about our crazy parents for a little while, right?"

"Right. Sure. Just, stay with me so I know you're safe."

"Where else would I go?" Carolyn said loyally. They rejoined the others at the front step. The music hit them like a wave as they crossed the threshold. It was as though the entire house gyrated to the beat, and that included the people. Carolyn was shocked at how some people were dancing – if it could even be called that. Skitt went off to party with his older friends, and Carolyn began to feel very vulnerable. She clung to Matt's arm as she desperately searched for someone she knew, and was relieved to find a few familiar faces amid the sea of strangers. Her once-enemies Kate, Erin, and Shawna were there. Carolyn was dismayed to see that her current nemesis, Paul, was also there – *but I should have known he would be.* He was dancing with Shawna, which meant that his romantic relationship with Kate must have been very short lived. It appeared that Kate had ditched him for his gangly high-school friend, Mark. Poor Erin had gotten stuck with rat-faced Jason, which she actually didn't seem to mind, judging by the fact that they were passionately making out right in the middle of the dance floor. Carolyn couldn't watch. She uncomfortably tugged at her low-cut shirt and adjusted her skirt, wishing she had gone for pizza with Matt instead.

Then the hordes of people swept the innocent victims into their ranks, and it was all they could do to stay together amidst all the sweaty shoving. Carolyn wrinkled her nose at the sticky odor of too many people crammed into too little space. Some of the high-school kids looked at them hostilely, but Anne ignored them and started to dance, shouting something about a mosh pit. Carolyn goggled at her.

"What's gotten into you?" she asked. "I've never seen you like this! I didn't even know you *went* to parties!"

"Just go with the flow!" Anne said, but that didn't really answer Carolyn's question.

"What's that supposed to mean?" Carolyn asked, peering through the shoulders of much older, taller people.

"If you're in study hall, study hard. If you're on the sports field, play hard. If you're at a party, party hard," she reasoned. Something about that didn't ring quite true to Carolyn, but Anne got swept away, grinning. Carolyn turned back to the rest of her friends, to find that Matt was the only one still there – and that was probably only because they were desperately clutching each other's hands.

"Where did the others go?" Carolyn asked. In spite of herself, she was finally starting to feel like dancing, and Matt seemed to be warming to the music as well.

"Tori was thirsty, so they went to find something to drink," he explained.

"Okay." She and Matt moved together naturally, and it wasn't long before they were dancing just like everyone around them. Carolyn twisted awkwardly to make sure he heard her when she said, "This isn't so bad after all."

"No, it's not," Matt agreed, planting a kiss on her mouth. Electricity sizzled through Carolyn's brain. She loved it when he caught her by surprise like that. She wondered what Kate, Erin, and Shawna would have to say about it – she remembered their jealousy when Carolyn and Matt had danced together for the first time. Fortunately for her, it seemed they had all moved on, and she was sure none of the high-schoolers cared at all. They pulled apart, and Carolyn smiled up at him, leaning against him for support as the rest of the crowd continued to press in on her. She drank in the sparkle of his icy clear eyes, basked in the warm glow of his strawberry blond hair and gentle features combined. She was safe here in his arms, which were not too shabby for someone who had just confessed he needed to hit the gym. *I must be the luckiest girl at this entire party.*

They had no idea how long it had been, but suddenly Margo came shoving through the masses – earning herself some very nasty glares – looking small and scared amid all those older kids. "You've got to come quick," she begged urgently.

"What's the matter?" Carolyn asked, already following Margo.

"Tori's a mess," Margo said over her shoulder. "We were hanging out at the refreshments table because it seemed safer than *this* mess, but... she feels really sick and dizzy. I think she needs to go home." Margo seemed panicked. They broke free of the crowd, and Margo dragged them out to the kitchen, where Tori drooped on a stool, slumped over with her head on the counter. Other students hung about, talking and laughing loudly as Jason danced energetically on the kitchen table. The onlookers were mostly high-school kids, but even Kate, Mark, Shawna and Paul had joined in, clapping to keep the beat and encourage Jason. Erin lingered on the fringes of the crowd, apparently waiting for Jason to finish showing off.

"How much punch did she drink?" Matt asked suddenly and forcefully.

Margo's eyes widened. "You don't think she's... *drunk*... do you?" Carolyn felt the blood leave her face. *No way. No* way.

"How much did she drink?" Matt repeated.

"Well, one right off the bat, then another after she stuffed a bunch of goldfish she found in the cabinet in her mouth... and she's been sipping away the whole time we've been out here avoiding the chaos, so maybe.... Four?"

"I'll bet it was spiked," Matt said angrily. Carolyn's stomach plummeted. *Her* friend had had a spiked drink? What were the older kids thinking, serving spiked drinks to younger partygoers – and without even telling them? What were they doing serving spiked drinks at all? That explained the noisy, exaggerated laughter coming from the crowd around the table.

Tori groggily lifted her head as they approached, and looked at them with half-closed, unfocused eyes. "I'm gonna hurl," she groaned, pushing herself away from the table. *Just grand,* Carolyn thought. She and Margo each took Tori by one arm and supported her to the bathroom, but there was a line outside, and Carolyn suspected Tori couldn't wait much longer. "Let's take her upstairs!" she shouted to Margo. "There must be another bathroom upstairs. Matt, we'll be right back." Matt nodded and found a nook near the stairs where he wasn't likely to be swept away by the crowd. Carolyn and Margo assisted a pale and trembling Tori up the stairs and down a dim hallway lined mostly with closed doors until they finally came to the open door of the bathroom. Tori gratefully rushed in. Carolyn couldn't watch.

"I can't handle this," she said weakly, almost gagging at the rank smell already emanating from the small room. "I want to go home."

"I'll take care of her," Margo offered bravely, following Tori into the bathroom. "Wait here." She shut the door.

Carolyn leaned on the nearest wall and closed her eyes. How did she ever get into such a mess? She sank down on the floor and put her head on her knees. And she'd thought she was so mature, that she could do whatever she wanted just because she was finally a teenager. But it turned out that she was still nothing more than a child, and that frustrated her. She leaned her head back on the wall behind her, and noticed Paul coming down the hall. *Just what I need.*

"Having fun?" he asked. Judging by the stupidity of the question, the slurred manner in which he asked it, and his uncoordinated footsteps, Carolyn guessed he had had a fair amount of punch, too. She stood up cautiously, unsure of how drunk he really was.

"Do I look like it?" she snapped, wanting to leave more and more every second.

"I can help," Paul said, stumbling forward some more. His eyes were anchored on her, yet it seemed that he hardly saw her at all. It was as though he was looking through her to something much farther away.

"Psh, gonna push me off another stool?" she asked defiantly, masking her uneasiness and reluctance to budge from her post outside the bathroom. Paul seemed to find her retort endlessly amusing. *Should I help him? Maybe I should help him find someplace to lie down until he feels more sober? I don't really know what I'm supposed to do… I've never had to deal with a drunken kid before….* Paul reached a comfortable distance for conversation, paused, and continued towards her. At first, Carolyn assumed he was just having trouble standing up or judging the distance between them, but with a sick feeling in the pit of her stomach, she realized what his true intentions were, and by then he was upon her, kissing her hungrily.

In her shock and disgust, she didn't know what to do for a minute. She tried to push him away, but he was too burly. He easily held her against the wall with the weight of his body. Overwhelmed by the stench of alcohol mixed with Hawaiian Punch and far too much Axe, she turned her face to the side and gasped for air. She was too ashamed to call out to Margo, nor did she want to make this anybody else's problem – especially when poor Margo already had to deal with Tori.

Paul continued kissing her neck. Every inch his lips touched seemed to explode into flames. A small cry of protest escaped her lips as his hands began to wander, and Carolyn panicked, wrestling her hands out from between them and clawing weakly at his face and neck with her nails. She wriggled her way to the side and dodged around a door frame into what appeared to be a TV room. Paul followed unsteadily, but at least she had space to back away now.

"Paul, you're drunk," she said rationally. Her hand groped for a light switch, but she couldn't take here eyes off him to search for it, and the room remained half-lit. "You need to lie down."

"No, no, 'm awright," he murmured. Heavy eyelids hid his blue eyes from view. He was far from all right.

"No, you're not. You're drunk," Carolyn iterated. If she could just get him to lie down and sleep it off! "Look, just take a nap on that couch there...." Shaking, she took his arm and did her best to direct him to the sofa. "Almost there," she assured him. He was leaning heavily on her now so that it appeared to be mere accident when, inches from her destination, he put all his weight into it and they tumbled onto the sofa, his body sprawled on top of hers.

She shrieked. So this was her payment for trying to help him? "Leave me alone! *Paul!*" It was all she could do to deter his hands from removing her shirt entirely as he smothered her with acid kisses.

With a sudden crash, he was gone, as though someone had ripped him away.

Carolyn's took a few deep breaths and blinked back tears before looking up at Skitt. *Where did he come from? ...am I ever glad he did. I wish I could be somewhere else right now. I wish I didn't exist right now.* Carolyn watched in amazement and gratitude as her hero dragged Paul, who had rolled off of her and onto the floor with Skitt's first attack, out of the TV room and towards the end of the hall. Paul took a clumsy swing at Skitt's face, catching him off guard. Carolyn gasped. *That's going to leave a mark.*

They were out of her line of vision now, but she could hear Paul slurring, "Hey, come on, man, I saw her first."

From the sound of it, Skitt had responded with a much better placed punch than Paul's. Carolyn righted herself and twisted and tugged her disheveled clothing back into place. Fighting down hysterical tears and nausea, she peered into the hallway in time to see Paul haul himself to his feet, give Skitt one terrified look, and dash for the stairs. She wanted to tackle Skitt with a hug, thank him, and ask if he was all right, but, too ashamed to make an appearance, she shied into the shadows of the TV room. She choked silently, unable to stem the tide of her tears any longer but refusing to allow Skitt to witness her breakdown.

Skitt left her no choice. He stormed into the room, slamming his hand onto the light switch as he did so and suddenly immersing them in much-welcome incandescent light. Then he took her firmly by the shoulders and opened his mouth to lecture her. Carolyn flinched and shrank from his touch. "Are you okay? What were you *doing* up here?" he spluttered. "Do you know what goes *on* up here? Gah, what am I saying? Of course you know *now.*"

She shook her head mutely and, shrugging off his firm hand, tried to imagine something worse than what had just happened to her.

Skitt looked away. "I'm not going to be the one to explain it," he said.

At that moment, the bathroom door swung open. More light pooled into the hallway and a frazzled Margo emerged with her arm around Tori's shoulder. "Carolyn? What's going on? Are you okay?" she asked, blanching at the sight of Carolyn's still-tousled appearance and the livid gleam in Skitt's eye.

"We're going home," Skitt growled, as if they were naughty children who didn't deserve to spend the rest of the day at the zoo, but their relief at finally escaping the zoo showed clearly in their faces. Carolyn, especially, was relieved that Skitt hadn't informed her friends of the situation and speculated on how he had known to come rescue her. She numbly trailed behind her companions, inwardly chanting, *Thank God I've got someone looking out for me* to sidetrack the horrible memories. It was all she could do to pull herself together as they came to the light-bathed staircase. Margo kept casting worried glances backward at her, but Carolyn carefully avoided her gaze.

She and Tori silently waited by the door while Skitt and Margo sought out the others. She popped a pair of tic-tacs in her mouth to get rid of the Paul-ness that was left there, and another pair after that. She offered some to Tori, who took them with gratitude. By the time the others returned, they had devoured the whole pack and had moved on to gum. Skitt stormed out without a word, leaving the door open for them to follow. They all looked at each other wordlessly, afraid to speak aloud in the wake of Skitt's unchecked fury.

Aware that Matt was probably watching, and nervous that Skitt may explode at her if she approached him – but knowing she *had* to say this – Carolyn trotted up to Skitt and murmured, "Thanks for not saying anything to Margo and Tori back there… if you could maybe, not mention it to Matt… or any of the others…." She trailed off.

Skitt looked at her funny. "It's none of my business," he finally said. "Just *take care* of yourself, *would you?*"

Relieved almost to the point of laughing at Skitt's overprotective brotherliness, Carolyn slid into the back seat. Her friends joined her momentarily, and Carolyn tried to look natural. Everyone remained silent as Skitt peeled out.

"Who am I dropping off first?" Skitt asked stiffly. In the rear, the girls exchanged glances.

"I can't go home like this!" Tori said unclearly.

"No, you can't," Margo agreed.

Carolyn realized that she couldn't go home, either. She didn't want to be by herself. She knew that as soon as she closed her eyes, there would be Paul, looming larger than life in front of her face. Just the thought of it made her want to roll down the window and hurl. "I'm not going home either," she said quickly.

"Sleepover at my house!" Anne suggested enthusiastically.

"Yeah," Margo agreed.

"Good idea," Carolyn consented.

"Fine," Skitt sighed. Carolyn felt guilty for invading his living space without exactly being invited, but there was no way she was going to spend the night alone in her room, unable to stay awake because Paul would always invade her thoughts – but unable to fall asleep with him haunting her dreams.

Tori borrowed Carolyn's mom's cell phone and called home, saying clearly enough that she was staying over Anne's for the night. Matt whispered, "Why is Skitt so angry? What happened after I sent him up after you guys?" His breath tickled her ear.

So it was Matt! Carolyn thought. *Matt saved me.* "He was really pissed because none of us were responsible enough to party without supervision, I guess," she replied vaguely. Her lips brushed his ear as she spoke, and she flinched again, drawing back as discreetly as possible and pressing herself to the door to minimize contact. She knew her explanation would not satiate Matt's curiosity, but she stubbornly refused to elaborate.

After dropping off Matt, she and Margo stopped in at their homes to explain where they would be and to pick up a few essentials for the night. Carolyn's parents agreed to let her go, but it worried her how little they seemed to be paying attention. She haphazardly threw toiletries and PJs into a bag. On impulse, she slung her guitar case over her shoulder before departing quickly and silently out the front door. The nuclear fallout of the earlier conflict still blanketed the house, and Carolyn was glad to have an excuse to be sleeping somewhere else for the night.

As it turned out, though, she didn't end up sleeping much at all. Long after Margo, Anne, and Tori had fallen asleep, memories of the evening continued to jolt Carolyn wide awake every time she closed her eyes. Frustrated, she pulled her journal out of her sack of clothes. Hopefully writing about it could lift this burden off her chest.

Jan. 2, 2000 — 1:00 AM

I suppose you could call this the best and the worst birthday of my life. Things started out great at midnight last night, when the clock chimed midnight and Matt FINALLY kissed me! It was wonderful... I felt it all the way down to my toes and back again. I wished it would never end, but it did. I've never been so happy! Just thinking about it helps me forget about the awful events of tonight. But I'm not there yet. I'll focus on the good memories for a little while longer. Jimmie dragged me out of bed this morning so I could open my presents, and my parents got me a GUITAR! I don't really know why, and I'm clueless about how to play it, but I'm sure I'll learn; I can probably find a lot of information online. Now that I think about it, wouldn't it be pretty fun to be a rock star someday? If only I wasn't such a wuss about the strings hurting my fingers and being afraid to break a nail... hahaha. Actually, it really annoys me when girls act all ditzy and wimpy and whine about their nails. Now that I'm THIRTEEN, I hope I'm a little more mature than that.

But maybe I'm not. See, that's what I was

thinking earlier today when Skitt (Anne's older brother) invited us to a party — that is, if I was thinking at all, which I'm pretty sure now that I wasn't. I think for the most part, I was just being hopelessly naïve. The party was terrible, to put it nicely. The music was rather awful, and the dancing was worse. Well... at least it looked that way. It wasn't so bad when you were actually in the middle of it. But the drinks were spiked (which no one ever told US), and Tori got really sick. So me and Margo brought her upstairs to find a bathroom, and Margo went in to help her clean up — but while I was waiting in the hallway, along comes Paul Riley. Grossness of all grossnesses — he was completely trashed and he started kissing me! It was revolting. I STILL feel disgusting from it. God, I hope nobody ever reads this. I couldn't stand it if anyone found out. What if MATT found out? He'd probably try to beat Paul up for me or some silly macho thing like that (not that Paul doesn't deserve whatever he gets). THEN, when I tried to get Paul to lie down and sleep it off, he pushed me onto the couch and tried to take my shirt off! Horror of horrors. Ugh, I feel so dirty! See if I ever try to help HIM out again! Skitt finally came

40

to the rescue and pulled Paul off of me. I think he would have left it at that, but Paul tried to punch him in the face, and that made him mad so Skilt punched him back, and then Paul ran away like a little baby. I was glad to see him running away in terror like that, but.... It wasn't worth what I went through to see it. I can't believe he did that. I'll never forget. I'll never sleep again.

As if that's not bad enough, my parents are fighting about something. I don't know what, but I hate it. They've NEVER fought — at least, not that I've ever known about. Jimmie was wigging out before I left for the party. I don't think he realized that families could fight. I'm hoping it was all just a misunderstanding or stress and the whole thing will blow over.

My parents aren't the only ones acting weird. Matt's grandma has completely lost the few marbles she had left. She's been making Matt and his sister do all sorts of chores, and dragging them off to church anytime she can get them into the car. I honestly don't know where she's getting all this religious stuff from, but it's really weirding Matt out... and me too, for that matter. I hope she doesn't make Matt become some sort of monk or something, or tell him he's not allowed to see me anymore. I think I'd go crazy if I were living there right now — religion is so restrictive. I could never follow all those rules and stuff.

On top of everything, Molly and Chris broke up, and Molly's taking it really hard. It kind of worries me. She doesn't seem to want to do anything or leave her bedroom. I guess she's allowed a few days of the blues, but if she doesn't snap out of this by the end of the week, I may have to take action. What am I supposed to do without my best friend?

Sigh. I can't believe how my whole world is just falling apart around me. In one day, I went from the happiest I've ever been to the most depressed I've ever been. The worst part is that I can't seem to do anything about it. I'm supposed to be the helper, the fixer, the one who solves all the problems; but for once, I can't do anything, and it's kind of getting me down. That was my skill, and without it, I'm nothing. Now I just wish a big hole would open up underneath me and swallow me up into the fiery core of the earth, where I could forget about all of this....

CIB

42

Carolyn closed the notebook with an inward sigh. How could so much have happened in just a day? She felt like she was miles from where she'd been on New Year's Eve, and she had the feeling there was no going back. She could only move into the dark future and hope that somehow she would find herself in there. She put the journal away, completely hidden so nobody could see what was in it. Her personal thoughts, experiences, feelings – nobody in the world could see them. Nobody in the world could understand them. How could someone else understand what she herself couldn't make sense of? And what would they think of *her* after what had happened that night?

Carolyn leaned back and closed her eyes. Moments later, Paul's face swam in front of her once again. Tears of frustration sprang into her eyes. She vowed she would never forgive him for this. She would get even. Somehow.

Carolyn hesitated for a moment before getting up, taking up her guitar, and padding softly out onto the balcony that ran partway around the top floor of Anne's house. The air nipped at her bare arms and face, and she spread her arms to soak it up. A salty aroma drifted in from the ocean a few blocks away, and Carolyn filled her lungs with it. *This is what it feels like to be alive,* she reminded herself.

For a minute, all she could do was gape at the sky's endless host of stars. Hundreds, thousands, millions – who could ever count them? Who could ever know what happened way out there on one of those stars? Who would know if one went out? It would take years and years for scientists to even know it had died. The luminescence that filled her eyes pushed all other thoughts from her mind for one blessed, peaceful moment. Things felt right for just that moment. She was so small, and they were so big. Nobody could stand in their way or change their paths. How could something as infinitesimal as a girl staring in awe at the heavens from her friend's balcony mean anything in such a vast universe? Did the night's events hold any significance at all? Did she truly believe, as she had told Matt earlier, that there was nothing more to life? She listened, but the twinkling stars held no answer.

A siren wailed somewhere far off, cutting through the night and through Carolyn's reverie. Suddenly chilled, Carolyn seated herself on a rocking bench. She moved her hands around the neck of the guitar and strummed almost noiselessly, searching until she found a combination of notes that rang out sad and true and reverberated through the night, echoing her emotions out to sea.

CHAPTER FIVE

The last day of vacation dragged by in an interminable blur of noise and color. Skitt woke the household early by battering away on his drums, a practice which persisted throughout the morning for as long as Carolyn remained at the Donahues'. Carolyn and Margo, their curiosity piqued, visited him in the attic and watched him play for awhile. Anne didn't show much interest at first, but after a few minutes, she came dashing up the stairs with Carolyn's guitar case slung over her shoulder. "Play something!" she insisted, thrusting the instrument at her friend.

"Oh, no... I couldn't," Carolyn countered. "I only know like three chords... and I think I made them up."

Skitt laughed. "Well, I could hook you up to my effects pedal.... Everything sounds better through an effects pedal," he offered.

"I don't want to be a nuisance." Carolyn waved off the suggestion, but the others wouldn't take no for an answer, and moments later she found herself connected to a dauntingly complex pedal and a huge amplifier – only one of several in the room. Carolyn wondered if Skitt was in a band, and if not, what he did up there with all that fancy equipment. While he finished plugging her in, she asked.

"Well, some friends of mine like to mess around up here, but we aren't really a band," he explained distractedly. "Although that could change, since a guy I know says he could get us a gig."

"That's cool! I'd go," Carolyn encouraged him. Anne didn't seem too thrilled about the bonding that was going on between her brother and her friend, and asked him to hurry it up.

"You're good to go," Skitt told her. Carolyn gave a good, hard strum of one of the chords she'd figured out, and, surprised by the sudden explosion of sound, instantly muted the roar of the guitar by slamming her hand onto the strings. Skitt laughed.

"It's not funny!" Carolyn protested, but even she could see that it was, and started laughing along. Skitt gave her a short lesson, for which Carolyn was infinitely grateful, but at last the time had come for her to head home, for fear that she had overstayed her welcome.

The rest of the day was split between the computer room looking up basic guitar-playing tips and her bedroom in a torrent of sore guitar fingers, even sorer flashbacks of the night before, and an icy silence between her parents that the closed door couldn't seem to keep out. In spite of the general chaos and confusion of her life, she slept far more soundly that night than she'd expected to, her mind blissfully void of thoughts and dreams until the alarm jarred her awake at 7:00 Monday morning. The thought of being in the same room – or even the same *building* – as Paul nauseated her.

She still couldn't believe he'd – well, done what he'd done the other night. *Why would he do that?* she pondered as she brushed her teeth rather viciously. Still lost in thought, she flossed and rinsed her mouth with Listerine, as was her new ritual, though it seemed like nothing could absolve her lips of his taste. It seemed to be as permanent as the memory and her hatred for him, which now burned stronger than ever. *It was just because he was drunk,* she assured herself. *If not... Oh, God, no. There's no way in the world that Paul could possibly* like *me...* She shuddered and erased the possibility from her consciousness.

There had always been a corner of her heart that harbored pity for Paul. Granted, it was a remote, cramped corner, but it had always been there. It seemed that his life was a daily battle. His parents fought constantly when they were together – she'd heard them. She knew that they didn't appreciate Paul and made him feel inferior, while he disrespected and defied them. From the brief history Matt had once given her, she had inferred that Mr. Riley had criminal ways and dangerous habits, including alcoholism, that may have rubbed off on his son. Paul had grown selfish and mean-spirited in his own defense – no one else made him a priority, so he put himself first and took out his anger on the people around him. This was the kind of kid she longed to rescue from the pits of his own despair.

But after what he had done, that corner of her heart was all but eradicated.

She applied make-up to disguise her hated, babyish chipmunk cheeks and rimmed her eyes with dark eyeliner borrowed surreptitiously from her mother. That was better; now she could hide. She smoothed her hair and turned sideways to scrutinize her profile. Good enough. At least her chest wasn't as diminutive as it had once been.

Before leaving, Carolyn dug around for her Walkman. She generally didn't use it very often, but for today, if she turned it up loud enough, maybe she could drown out the roaring silence of her home and the incessant drone of her thoughts. She popped in an N*Sync CD, wishing for something with more of an edge, and dashed out the door with her Walkman clutched in one hand and an apple – her breakfast – in the other.

As she rounded the corner, she could see that her posse was already gathered on the front steps, as always; yet though the semblance of normalcy blanketed the scene, Carolyn felt as though nothing could be normal ever again. She slowed her pace, wishing she didn't have to face any of them. As soon as she was within earshot, though, Erin called out to her. Carolyn paused the music and looked up while Erin dashed over.

"Did you hear about the accident?" Erin asked, wide-eyed.

"What accident?" Carolyn asked in surprise and concern.

"On Saturday night, my sister's friend and her boyfriend got in an accident coming home from that party I saw you at," Erin elaborated. Carolyn felt sick, both at the reminder of the party and at the fact that someone may have been seriously hurt.

"Oh my God. Are they all right?" she asked.

Erin nodded nervously, as though still unable to believe it herself. "They drove into a ditch on the side of the road. They're lucky there wasn't a tree or something there or they could have *died*. And…" Erin's lip trembled slightly, but Carolyn pretended not to notice. "And my sister would have been with them if she hadn't been driving me and Shawn and Kate home."

Carolyn was filled with the overwhelming urge to give Erin a comforting hug, so she did. "I'm glad nobody got hurt, especially your sister," she said.

Erin smiled weakly. "Thanks…. Me, too." They ambled in the general direction of the steps, where they joined the rest of their friends. Everyone greeted Carolyn cheerfully and chattered away with as much energy as could be expected from them on a Monday morning, and Matt took her hand in his, but she didn't feel the same connection with them as she had before vacation. She told herself she was being a drama queen and tried to socialize before the bell called them to class, but she kept her headphones playing the whole time – the more distractions, the better. Music temporarily diverted her attention from the crazy circumstances of her life, and for now, to forget was the most she could ask for.

Someone pulled one headphone away from her ear, and Carolyn jumped. "What are you listening to?" Finn asked.

Carolyn relaxed. "N*Sync," she replied. "Why?"

"Gah!" Finn burst out angrily. "You listen to that crap?"

Carolyn shrugged. "It was all I could find this morning." Now that she thought about it, it wasn't so weird for Finn to be asking what she had in her Walkman. Headphones were a constant accessory for him, and she couldn't help but think that his life revolved almost entirely around music.

Finn chuckled and took her CD player, reaching into his ratty messenger bag with his other hand. He came out with a CD, which he switched with the one in Carolyn's Walkman. "Hey! I paid good money for that CD!" Carolyn protested, dropping Matt's hand to reach for her disc.

"And I paid for that one. We'll swap for a day. Let me know what you think." He winked one green eye and grinned lopsidedly.

It turned out that Finn's CD had exactly the edge she'd been wishing for, but even with that and schoolwork to distract her, Carolyn couldn't help but notice Paul's presence in relation to where she sat at every moment of the day, as though she'd suddenly developed super-sensitive Paul radar. It was probably a useful defensive strategy, though she would have preferred not to think about him at all, and it was nerve-wracking to have little sirens screaming in her head every time he came within a ten-foot radius. Whenever he did, she dropped the act that she'd been so determined to keep up in hopes of convincing him that he hadn't hurt her in the least. She couldn't help it. His presence made her mind do strange things.

Thankfully, she didn't have to speak to him at all during the day, and consequently, her spirits had lifted by the time she left school. At home, she refused to pay attention to the situation between her parents. She kept the Blink-182 CD blaring through the headphones all afternoon, and allowed the drum beat to lull her to sleep that night. She determined that the key to making it through the day was simply not to think about The Incident – and that, she was certain, would grow easier with time.

Things are looking a little better today — or maybe I've just tuned out all the bad stuff for the moment. I've been blasting a Blink-182 CD that Finn lent me all day and pretty much just doing my best to ignore things like Paul and my parents. So far it's working, and, well, let's just say that it doesn't hurt that Matt is a way better kisser than Paul. At least he doesn't taste like alcohol meets Hawaiian Punch.

Nothing too exciting happened today, which I guess is a good thing, considering how things have been going lately. It's just, well — it isn't fair? Why did this have to happen to ME? I didn't do anything wrong? Is this some sort of cosmic irony, or what? I get my first kiss, and it's the most amazing, electrifying moment of my life — and then, hours later, along comes a guy whose guts I happen to hate, and.... IT JUST ISN'T FAIR! I WISH HE'D DROP DEAD.°°

I think I may need to invest in a punching bag for moments like this one.

Message from: Leah Sorman <PussyCat240@aol.com>
To: Carolyn Becker <SkiBlink@aol.com>
(no subject)

Hey, Girl! How's the New Year treating you so far? Did you do anything special on New Year's Eve? I, unfortunately, did not. I really wanted to hang out with Jake, but he was hanging out with R-Bi and her friends. They seem to have become his "usual" crowd. Note the total lack of bitterness in that statement (not.) But maybe I'll get over it by the time I graduate. Anyway, enough grumbling from me. On the bright side, things went really well when I talked to my family about feeling neglected since we adopted Née. They felt really bad about making me feel that way and wanted to buy me things to make up for it, but I told them to stop being silly. The important thing is that Née and I are equally loved, and it doesn't look like that is going to be a problem. So overall, in spite of the Jake thing, I'm in a pretty good mood! Looking forward to hearing the exciting stories of your life, since it's always so much more glamorous than mine. Hehe!

Lots of love!

~LBS~

Chapter Six

The week passed without incident, to Carolyn's immense relief; though her Paul radar never really got the message and continued to go crazy every time he came near her. However, she and Matt made plans to go on their first real date that Saturday, and the prospect of a night at the movies with Matt was enough to distract Carolyn from her concerns about her parents' phony, exaggerated hospitality towards each other. It was almost enough to distract her from the memory of Paul. The CDs she kept borrowing from Finn at least helped her to tune out some of the chaos surrounding her and distracted her from her own thoughts, and the black eyeliner she'd bought helped her hide even better.

Saturday rolled around, and Carolyn and Matt met up at the pizza parlor. To anyone else, they seemed to be having the best of times, eating their pizza while attempting (and failing) to master the Dance Dance Revolution game in the arcade and fighting with the claw machine because they couldn't win any stuffed animals. Carolyn kept a cautious watch over her tongue in case she should slip up and mention what had transpired the previous weekend. She jabbered about her latest musical discoveries and the guitar tablature she had been looking up online to teach herself to play, and tried to act interested in what he was saying about the Anaheim Angels and his demon of a science teacher. Overall, she was confident that she had the world fooled into thinking that everything was the same as always.

Of course Matt would be the one to notice that something was off. "You seem quiet tonight," he commented as they entered the theater.

"Do I?" Carolyn stalled. Maybe, all that time, she had only been fooling herself. It had sure felt like she was rambling on and on. But now what? How could she explain away her strange behavior?

Matt nodded. "Is everything all right? Your parents aren't still being weird, are they?"

Perfect. Matt had provided an excuse *for* her. Lying had never been so easy. "Yeah, kind of," she quickly agreed. *It wasn't really a* lie, she told herself. *Just sort of a… an evasive truth.*

"I wish I could help," he offered.

"Don't worry about it," she shrugged. "Is your nutty grandma still being a church freak?"

Matt chuckled. "Yeah. It's pretty crazy. I don't… really… get why she loves it there so much. But I don't really mind going. It's one of those things you just *do* – like school. You don't have to like it; you just have to deal with it." Carolyn laughed. Someone in the row in front of them turned and shushed her.

"Chillax, it's just the previews," she giggled, quietly enough so that only Matt could hear her. She reached up and made bunny ears with her fingers in front of the projector so that the silhouette of her hand appeared huge on the screen. She laughed again, feeling slightly hysterical, and was more relieved that she'd steered the conversation away from herself than actually amused.

"Anyway," Matt continued. "She sent me to youth group last night. That's why we had to make our plans for tonight. I think she wants me to go every week or something...."

"She *is* crazy!" Carolyn commented with dismay. Friday nights should have been *hers* to spend with Matt, not another prison cell for both of them – Matt trapped at his church, and Carolyn shut up at home.

Matt laughed softly. "I guess she is."

The movie started, but Carolyn couldn't pay attention. It wasn't what he'd said – *I guess she is* – it was how he'd said it: as though he didn't completely believe it. She leaned over and whispered, "What do you mean, you 'guess?' You didn't... *like* it there, did you?"

Matt shrugged, still watching the screen. Reflections of the previews danced in the oceans of his eyes. "I dunno," he said uncomfortably. "It was okay. Watch the movie, would you?" So he *did* like it, she inferred.

"Dork," she muttered fondly.

The movie was rather boring, so they amused themselves by pelting the people in the front of the theater with Reese's Pieces until Carolyn munched down the rest of their ammunition. Then Matt put his arm around her, and Carolyn snuggled into his side. The armrest between them dug into her ribs, but she didn't mind that much. This was where she belonged, and this was who she belonged with. She kept the awkward memories at bay by breathing in his scent to remind herself that she was in the right person's arms now. Matt swooped in for a kiss.

Then a strange thing happened. Her guard dropped, and all those memories rushed back at her like a tidal wave. Carolyn reminded herself that this was Matt, her boyfriend, the guy she truly wanted to be with – and yet all she could think of was Paul's despicable kiss last weekend. She waited until she couldn't stand it anymore, and then excused herself with the ostensible purpose of buying more snacks. In the lobby, she caught her breath and choked back tears. The one thing that had made the world so perfect and complete only a week before, and Paul had ruined it for her. *I'll kill him!* she screamed inwardly. *I hate him! I hate him, I hate him, I hate him…* Somehow the mantra was calming and it gave her something to think about while she waited for the popcorn. Hopefully the huge tub would take them the whole movie to finish – so no more kissing.

She toted the bin of popcorn back into the theater, stealing a few of the most buttery pieces off the top on the way. Unfortunately, Matt didn't seem to be as interested in the popcorn as he was in Carolyn. She finally relaxed and allowed herself to melt into his warm arms, letting her emotions override her thoughts. She simply existed, and he existed for her, and that was all she knew or needed to know. Maybe she could be happy now.

10:30. Half an hour past curfew. Carolyn slipped in the side door and removed her shoes so she could mount the stairs as noiselessly as possible.

A shout caused her to jump a foot in the air, and it took her a minute to realize that it wasn't directed at her – her parents were yelling at each other in the kitchen. Her head swam. She hadn't actually witnessed a conflict between them until now – and it was far from pretty. He was angry because his laundry was wrinkled; she retorted that he could do his own laundry if he didn't like the way she did the job. As Carolyn padded up the stairs, she heard him shouting about mismatched socks and discolored shirts. *What a ridiculous thing to fight over,* she thought. She wanted nothing more than to tune them out, but as that was not an option, she couldn't help listening detachedly as if they were characters in a soap opera on television.

There came a scurrying sound from Jimmie's bedroom as she shuffled by, and Carolyn peeked in. Jimmie was pretending to sleep, but she could hear sniveling and knew that he was listening as powerlessly as she. "Jimmie? Are you all right?" Carolyn asked, tiptoeing in and sitting gingerly at the foot of the bed.

"Go away," he said tearfully, pulling the blankets up over his head to block her out.

Carolyn tugged at the quilt but couldn't pry it from his fingers, so she continued talking. "It'll be all right. You know, we're lucky that our parents never fought before this. Some people have it a lot worse than we do." She thought of Paul. "At least they both love us." Jimmie peeped out of the bedcovers, and Carolyn persisted, sensing that his outlook was brightening. But how much was his ten-year-old mind likely to understand? "We fight sometimes, Jimmie. It's just because we live together. When you're with someone that often, you're bound to butt heads sometimes."

"What do you know?" he asked bitterly. "You're never home when they fight. It's always the same when they do. It's always over something stupid, like not having the right kind of cereal in the cabinet. If something that little can make them this mad, then they must really hate each other, Carolyn!" Tears rolled down his cheeks.

Though she couldn't help agreeing with his logic, Carolyn brushed the tears away with her fingers and said, "Mom and Dad got married because they loved each other, and they're going to stay married." *Hopefully. For our sakes,* she added silently. "You don't worry about them, okay? They're grown-ups. They can work it out." *I am such a hypocrite. How can I tell* him *not to worry when worrying is all* I *seem able to do? What if they can't work it out? What if they don't stay married?*

"I hope you're right," he said miserably, sniffling and drawing away from her hand. "I'm fine."

Carolyn smiled ever-so-slightly at his big boy bravado. "I know you are."

Hey! Sorry it took a while for me to get back to you. Hah. My life is hardly glamorous. Eventful, yes, but I'd rather not talk about it. Mom and Dad are in a fight. I don't know what it's about, but if this keeps up, I just know that I'm going to have to play Peacemaker. It really scares me because – well, *you* know they've never fought before. I told my little brother not to worry because they love each other and will stay married, but I feel like such a liar for saying that, because the silliest little details will set them off at each other. It's as if they're just waiting for an opportunity to blow up at each other. If they *really* loved each other, would they start these tirades at the drop of a hat? I just don't think so.

I'm glad things went well with your family. ☺ Sorry to hear about butt-face Jake. He's probably just confused. Boys often are. Oh, wow, they almost always are, let me tell you from experience – though usually they do a pretty good job of confusing the rest of us just as badly. But no grumbling from me, either! I'm lucky to have the one guy in the world that DOESN'T confuse me. OH, that seems like forever ago, but I guess I haven't told you – Matt and I are FINALLY together! So with that said, I have no right to complain about ANYTHING! Right?

Well, I have to go finish some homework now… write back soon and fill me in on the Jake situation!

Lots of love back!
CIB

Happiness evades me. I sit here and watch the days slip by and wait for things to return to normal, but I'm losing count. "Normal" doesn't seem to be a point I can return to. Sometimes I wonder if it ever existed at all, or whether it was simply a figment of my imagination. I cling to the hope that things can and will improve, but I get the impression those hopes are about to cave in. There's no light at the end of this tunnel. Peace only presents itself to me intermittently and only when I'm alone, composing poetry or lost in a song and drifting somewhere far away. Then I can almost imagine that things are all right.... Almost. And I tell people that I am all right, but that is such a lie. Why can't I hold things together???

Me and Matt have made Saturday nights at the movies a tradition. That and my growing collection of CDs burned from Finn's collection are the only things I can count on anymore. Saturdays are a weekend haven from the stress of shunning Paul all week at school, from the pressure of trying so hard to relate to people that suddenly seem to be complete strangers, and from the tense atmosphere

58

at home that occasionally boils over into noisy conflicts. Part of me wishes someone would ask me what was wrong — can't they SEE that everything is upside down? Can't they tell I'm losing it? Do they even care?

Probably not.

CHAPTER SEVEN

When Tori, Anne, and Finn approached her – independently of one another and on completely different occasions – to ask if she was okay, she simply muttered that she was "fine, just kind of stressed out and tired," an excuse that sickened even her, since she remembered Molly using the same one. It hadn't convinced anyone then, and Carolyn wondered if anyone was buying it now that it was coming from her own lips.

"Are you sure that's all?" Tori asked, ignoring the ringing school bell. Carolyn was flattered that Tori was concerned enough about her well-being to risk tardiness to class – not that Tori was a particularly serious student anyway. "You haven't been the same since you and Matt got together... is everything okay between you two?"

"Of course!" Carolyn said quickly. No way was anyone pinning the blame for this on Matt.

"He hasn't... done anything... to you, has he?" Tori persisted, dropping her voice to a whisper and blushing faintly at the awkwardness of the question.

"No!" Carolyn replied in shock. "Matt is as perfect as he ever was. Don't worry about me."

Tori just looked at her skeptically, but said nothing more.

Less than a week later, Anne stopped her when they parted at the corner of their streets. Though it had become habit for them to walk that far together after school, their conversations had dwindled to nothing over the past week or so, and Anne finally spoke up. "Carolyn, what's the matter with you? I feel like you're always sad."

Carolyn reluctantly turned to respond, wearing the inscrutable expression she'd perfected over the month since her incident with Paul. "I guess I'm in a little bit of a rut," she admitted. "I don't really know why. I stressed out so badly over midterms, and then found out that I didn't do as well as I wanted to." Every week brought a new excuse, and now that midterms were over, the excuse was that they had gone badly. It was true that she hadn't aced everything the way she used to, though her marks hadn't been horrible. At least she'd passed everything – though only by a hair. The untruth existed in the fact that she didn't care, which worried her more than anything. She could bring up her grades with some extra credit if she wanted to – but she didn't. She'd always been such a diligent student, but nothing seemed to matter anymore. Her life was coming apart at the seams, and A-pluses couldn't change that.

"Oh. Well, that's okay, if that's all... I mean, knowing you – you'll do fine anyway." Anne left the statement open, waiting for Carolyn to elaborate. She tugged awkwardly at the straps on her backpack.

Carolyn shrugged and pulled her sweatshirt tighter around her against the chill of the February cold spell. Peeking out from under the hood, she said she guessed so and excused herself, dragging her feet in spite of her desire to get in out of the cold.

Later that week, Finn stopped by on his bike to pick up a Green Day CD Carolyn had had for over a week. "Does my music depress you?" he asked, pulling the computer chair out and sitting sideways in it, dangling his feet in their checkered Vans over the side while Carolyn rummaged through the mess on the desk in search of his CD.

"No. I love your music! See, I was looking up the chords for Panic Song," she said, gesturing at the computer screen. "Why?"

She found the CD and spun around to hand it to him, but Finn didn't move. He simply stared at her with the most piercing, searching green eyes Carolyn had ever encountered. "You seem different," he stated. *His eyes are like lasers*, Carolyn thought, and her heart jumped nervously at how exposed her soul felt when he looked at her like that.

"Well… you can't expect me to stay the same forever," Carolyn said, dismissing his comment like she dismissed most everything these days. But Finn persisted.

"I don't see you smile as much as you used to," he said sadly. Carolyn was surprised at the candidness of his statements, and tried to reply in an equally honest manner, but it felt strange to be discussing something so personal with Finn of all people. She would have expected to have this kind of conversation with, say, Leah, or another of her girl friends.

She shrugged and fell silent. "I guess I just don't see as much to smile at anymore," she finally said. Finn nodded as though he understood, and Carolyn had the strangest feeling that maybe he did. "What does Matt say about me?" she asked suddenly.

Finn looked startled, and adjusted his beanie while he thought about it. He combed his fingers through the scraggly mop of red hair, and Carolyn noticed how much he'd let it grow since she'd last paid any attention. "He thinks you've changed, too," he finally said. "He thinks he must have done something wrong, or that you don't like him as much as you pretend to." Carolyn felt her face crumple, and leaned back on the computer table for support. Tears stung her eyes, but she resolutely blinked them back. Finn absolutely could not see her cry.

"Does he really think that?" Her voice trembled. Finn nodded, watching her carefully. Carolyn sighed and put her hand to her head. "It's not true," she told him, as though that alone could change Matt's mind. Finn nodded again, encouraging her to speak. Carolyn sighed again. "A lot has been going on lately.... Stuff I never thought I'd have to deal with," she said, withholding as much information as possible. She realized with confusion that this was the longest conversation she'd held with anyone in a while. Finn remained silent, listening respectfully. He knew there was more she had to say, and was simply waiting for her to say it; but Carolyn didn't think she could.

Finn broke the silence, pushing himself up out of the chair. "Well, if you want to talk about it ever...." He trailed off, and Carolyn nodded.

"Thanks," she said, unexpectedly throwing her arms around him in gratitude. Finn awkwardly hugged her back and retreated out the door with a wave. Carolyn sank into the computer chair, lost in thought.

The sun shone with deceptive brightness as Carolyn biked to Molly's house. After wallowing in self-pity for a while, she had decided that sitting around ruminating on her own problems, which seemed irreparable at the moment, wasn't doing anybody any good – and so, feeling slightly awkward at being the friend taking the initiative instead of the other way around, she was going to straighten things out with Molly. It had been almost a month since she and Chris first split up. Enough was enough. If Carolyn couldn't solve things between her parents, she could at least give Molly the boost she needed.

Now, mounting the staircase, she realized that she had no idea what to say to Molly. What could patch up a broken heart? Words? A hug? Would that be enough?

Molly's closed door was decorated with an enormous stop sign that looked like it may have been real. Daunted, Carolyn knocked.

"What?" Molly replied curtly.

"It's Carolyn."

"Oh – sorry! Come in," Molly corrected herself. Carolyn let herself in. "What's up?" Molly was seated on the drum stool, but her back was to the set; she was typing on a PC that Carolyn was sure used to be in the family room.

"Wow! New computer?"

"Not exactly. My parents were going to throw it away because it wasn't working, but Chris knows some guys who work on computers, so I rescued it from the garbage and brought it to them." Molly's eyes were fixed on the screen as she typed away, and Carolyn marveled at her multitasking abilities. "But my parents didn't think they could fix it and bought a new one last week, so this one's mine now."

"That's cool. Who are you IMing?"

"Chris."

Carolyn furrowed her brow in confusion and sat on the edge of the bed, uninvited. "That's the second time you've mentioned him. I thought you guys broke up."

"Yeah, but then we got back together," Molly announced happily, finally tearing her eyes from the screen. They shone with excitement.

"I didn't know that! Congratulations, I guess."

"Thank you!" Molly trilled. She typed some more, and Carolyn looked around uncomfortably in the quiet. Photographs, posters, programs, and other paraphernalia had overflowed from the bulletin board and now devoured almost two walls worth of space. Jewelry, make-up, and temporary hair dye drowned the top of the wardrobe, and clothing overflowed from the closet. The chaos and clutter were a bit overwhelming.

Molly must have caught sight of Carolyn's scanning eye, because she quickly apologized for the mess. "Things have been too hectic for me to clean up lately," she explained. A long pause ensued. "What's up with you?"

"Huh?"

"How come you came over?" Molly specified.

"Oh. I was worried about you and Chris, but I guess I don't have to be, do I?"

Molly grinned. "Nope!" The clackety-clack of the keyboard resumed, coupled with another lull in dialogue.

"So, what's with the stop sign on your door?" Carolyn asked conversationally.

Molly laughed. Still typing steadily, she explained. "I dunno, one of the computer repair guys had it. I guess someone drove into the post and knocked the sign down, and he just took it. Then Chris bought it off him and gave it to me."

Carolyn laughed too, nervously. "Is that legal?"

"I dunno." Another awkward chunk of silence followed, and at length, Carolyn excused herself, saying she had to be home for dinner. It seemed that Molly had solved her own problems without any help from Carolyn. *That's just fine. Makes my life easier,* she thought to herself, pedaling so slowly that the bike wobbled from side to side. It wasn't that she was upset about Molly being able to take care of herself – that was a good thing. The wound she was nursing now was her hurt over Molly's sudden lack of interest in perpetuating the friendship between herself and Carolyn. *But I guess it's not really* her *fault,* Carolyn rationalized. *I wasn't there for her after they first broke up; I was too wrapped up in my own problems to be a friend. She's probably just upset about that. It's my fault, really.* Relieved that she didn't have to pin any blame on her best friend, Carolyn straightened the wheel and made her way home.

Something must be wrong with me. I think too much. I wish I could be happy.

Whatever happened to the good old days? Geez... I'm not even in high school yet and I already miss my childhood, when it shouldn't even be over yet. I don't know what to do. Nothing seems right anymore. Everything got mixed up after Paul — well, yeah. I'm suddenly not myself. The most terrifying part is that I don't care about ANYTHING anymore. My parents are going to be mad when they see my midterms — C's coming from a straight-A student. They'll start to worry. But just because I know that doesn't mean I care. I guess this is what they call "apathy."

The other scary thing is, I don't know if I can even blame Paul for everything. Sure, he sent me into this downward spiral. I could have enjoyed my "childhood" a little longer if not for him. But how much longer is the question. If not for him, maybe I would still be up on my little cloud nine with Matt — but maybe I wouldn't. And sure, my parents make this house feel less like "home" every day, and it's hard to say whether Molly and I are even friends anymore. But maybe this change was inevitable. Maybe this is who I really am after all.

THIS CAN'T BE ALL THERE IS TO LIFE! There's got to be some way to get back up to where I was! Somehow, I've got to shake this funk I'm in....

I'm concerned for my sanity, above all. Not just sanity as I always saw it before, either — "Wow, you're insane" seemed an appropriate response to someone who was being really hyperactive, but this kind of insanity is different, and a lot less fun. I can't even explain it, that's how far gone I am. All I know is that I probably belong in some sort of facility at this point. But I'm going to bounce back eventually, or I hope I am. I don't want to worry Mom and Dad with my condition. Or my midterms. Maybe I should burn them. (The midterms, I mean — not my parents.) I can't put any more burdens on their shoulders when their marriage may very well be at stake. I mean, I like to think it's not, and I'm pretty sure that for my sake and Jimmie's sake, they're pretending it's not — but I'm not stupid. I know that it is. They think I wouldn't understand, but I've got news for them: being a kid isn't all fun and games. I could handle more than they think I can. But no matter. I don't think I need any extra burdens at the moment, either.

The Jake situation. Yeah. There's nothing to inform. I've all but given up on that boy. In retrospect, I'm glad we never actually got together. Carolyn, you should be glad you never dated him, either. He's just so shallow, he hurts to look at! It's so frustrating to see how the "perfect" guy we'd always considered him to be has degenerated into this self-centered, girl-obsessed, sports-obsessed, study-slacker, just like all the rest. He always stood out. I know you remember, even though you have amazing Matt, who hopefully won't go through the same transformation Jake's gone through. I'd hate to see that happen while you were going out with him. Just be careful, Carolyn! Don't get too attached too fast. Don't let your world revolve around one person. The same Jake that used to treat us to cocoa won't give me the time of day anymore. I just don't know. I'm afraid to put my faith in anyone anymore, when they could so easily turn into the same kind of insensitive clod that Jake has become!

Sorry that I'm ranting. I just had to tell someone how I'm feeling. I hate keeping those things pent up inside, where no one else can see them and sympathize. You've always given good advice. What do you think I should do???

~LBS~

Chapter Eight

Gradually, like the warming of the earth after days of rain, Carolyn began to recover from her Paul-inflicted trauma. She opened her eyes to the world around her again, and saw her friends as though for the first time in years. Her clique had dwindled to Margo, Tori, Anne, Matt, Finn, Nick, and herself. Ashamed at how she'd ignored them recently, Carolyn couldn't bring herself to ask what had happened to the rest of them. She kept her eyes and ears open for clues, turning the headphones down to white noise volume. At lunch, she scanned the cafeteria for her once-best friends.

Kate, Erin, and Shawna seemed to have reverted to their former snootiness (and she'd thought they'd made so much progress). There they sat, the three of them with their sporty, partying, overly-preppy friends, complaining loudly about the lunches their parents had packed them one minute and laughing shrilly at regales of last weekend's party the next. Regardless of the activity, it was always loud, drawing the attention of everyone nearby. Carolyn kicked up the volume on her headphones to drown them out.

One day, she spotted Molly and Chris in a remote corner, seated with a group of kids with what Carolyn had always deemed questionable reputations. She remembered seeing Paul with some of them on certain occasions – not hanging out, necessarily, but discussing something in furtive tones. She also remembered when Matt had bonded with a few of them in the fall, when he'd been wrestling with his mom's tragic illness and had gone through what she referred to as his "dark period." She shuddered at the thought of her good friend under the wing of those kids.

"They didn't leave because of me, did they?" Carolyn asked Margo.

"It's hard to say," Margo began. "Molly and Chris would have left anyway." She rolled her eyes in frustration at her sister's devotion to her junior high sweetheart. "They wanted a little corner to themselves, but it looks like they've made some new friends over there. Kate, Erin, and Shawna were getting on everyone's nerves, so we probably would have booted them before long if they hadn't left of their own free will. They were always talking about stupid things like the latest fashion, and who made out with who and who'd had the most beer at a party. Honestly!" she scoffed.

"Wow," was all Carolyn could say. "Aren't they a little young for all that drama, anyway?"

"One would think," Margo muttered darkly.

"One would also wonder," Tori chimed in, "how they can stand the stuff. Beer, I mean. Remember when I got that spiked punch? Man. That was awful. I'm never getting drunk as long as live." The others laughed and quickly agreed.

"Still, though, I feel like our group is, I don't know, deficient without them," Carolyn mourned.

Margo and Tori shrugged. "You probably couldn't hear them over your music, then, because trust me – they were getting really annoying," Tori assured her. "We'll be better off without them. Let them have their silly popularity." She stuck her nose in the air – a snooty gesture that wasn't too far from how Kate, Erin, and Shawna seemed to be acting.

"Yeah," Margo piped up. "You win some, you lose some. You can't be friends with everybody… although you came pretty close there for a while, Carolyn." Margo prodded her teasingly in the shoulder, and Carolyn smirked a little at the compliment.

"Yeah…. That wasn't really what I meant, though. I was thinking more about Molly and Chris," she said gloomily.

"I know how you feel," Tori and Margo readily concurred.

"But when they were still here, they mostly just paid attention to each other, anyway. It's not that different without them. We just lost the PDA aspect of lunch time, which I can't say is a bad thing," Margo added bitterly.

Carolyn sighed sadly. "I just wish-"

"Hey, Carolyn, are you going to eat those Fritos?" Finn asked from across the table. Carolyn looked up; she had nearly forgotten the boys were there. Matt and Nick were preoccupied with stacks of baseball cards, which they were trading. Finn, she now realized, had been listening intently and unobtrusively to the girls' discussion.

She tossed him the package of chips. "Go for it," she said.

"Thanks!" Finn tore open the bag and started munching. "What do you wish?"

"That Molly and Chris were still here."

"Ah." Finn nodded with that sage comprehension in his eyes. "Me, too. Chris is so whipped. We never see him anymore."

"Tell me about it… and Molly's my sister," Margo interjected. "I wish they could just forget about each other. I mean, I love them both, but come on, now. When they aren't together, all she talks about is wanting to get back with him, and when they are, they disappear into their own little world."

Finn nodded in agreement. "Exactly."

"Do you think it would be worthwhile to invite her to go disco bowling with us or something? I think the alley has discount prices for students...." She trailed off, letting her shoulders slump. "I guess not."

"For now, I don't think there's anything we can do," Tori surrendered.

"You know me. Leaving stuff alone has never been my skill. I always want to fix everything. I'm like the local repair shop or something." Everyone laughed, and Finn told her to lighten up before donning his headphones.

She did the exact opposite, however, when Paul strolled past the table. She tried to mask her reaction and, blushing, inspected her sandwich closely before taking a huge bite. "You know, I heard something about Paul a little while ago," Tori said thoughtfully.

Carolyn's stomach plummeted and she choked on the ham and cheese she'd been halfway through swallowing. Margo thumped her on the back until she stopped coughing. "Thanks, Margo."

"Don't mention it. What were you saying, Tori?"

"Well, I heard that his parents finally split up."

"'Finally?'" Margo repeated. "You say that as if it's a good thing."

"Well, I just mean, everybody saw it coming, the way they fought all the time," Tori elaborated. "Haven't you ever walked past his house and heard them yelling at each other or at him?"

"I have," Carolyn quipped. "I guess it will probably make things a little easier on all of them this way, won't it?"

"That's what I'm thinking," Tori agreed.

"It's a shame, though. You have to wonder how he might have turned out if not for their constant fighting and his dad's alcoholism," Margo pondered.

Carolyn disguised a laugh as another cough, and Margo raised her fist to pound on her back again, but Carolyn stopped her. "Can you seriously imagine Paul having a softer side?"

"*Everybody* has *some* good in them, Carolyn," Margo chastised. "It's all a matter of how they're brought up."

Carolyn merely shrugged. She found it hard to pin the blame for Paul's character on anyone other than Paul himself. But she supposed that anything was possible; maybe he really was just a kid with a messed up life who desperately needed to be loved. *Well, not by me,* she determined, setting her jaw. *Not after…* that.

"What were you saying about disco bowling?" Tori asked. "I think that sounds fun. We should go."

Carolyn drew herself back to the present. "Okay. I think Fridays are disco nights…"

"Great. Let's get everyone to go!" Margo suggested, blue eyes aflame with excitement. "It'll be a party!"

"Hold up," Tori said, her perfect complexion wrinkling with a frown. "I have a paper to write this weekend. And you know I'll put it off until then."

Carolyn joined the pity party. "*Why* did you have to remind me of that?" She had nearly forgotten the assignment.

"Yeah, let's make it next Friday," she consented gloomily. They all turned and started spreading the word around the table, and Carolyn heaved an inward sigh of relief that things were finally returning to normal – just when she'd thought they never could.

Message from: Leah Sorman <PussyCat240@aol.com>
To: Carolyn Becker <SkiBlink@aol.com>
Where are you???

Hey! Where are you? Did you drop off the face of the earth? Did you and Matt run off and get married and forget to tell me?? I hope everything's all right. Miss you and love you!

~LBS~

Life's pretty back and forth this year. But I think I may be bouncing back at last, just like I said I would. Unfortunately, I've missed a lot this past month. I've been hiding behind my music. I know Finn thinks he's helping me by giving it to me, but it might be better if he didn't. I mean, I LOVE listening to this stuff. It's quality music. I think Green Day and Blink are still my favorites, but Five Iron Frenzy is pretty decent, and NOFX is all right if you don't mind a lot of swearing. But the point of this rant isn't "list my favorite bands." The point is that I completely ignored my friends all month, and now half of them are gone. Kate, Erin and Shawna went back to being Queen Bees of the school, while Molly and Chris went off into their own little world. I think Matt thinks I don't like him anymore (at least, Finn says he thinks that, and I wouldn't be surprised if it were true; when I ask him if he's doing anything after school, he usually says he has to study). No one has even told me where Aisling has been lately, and to be honest, I'm afraid to ask. My ignorance is really very embarrassing. It would be different if I'd been out of school for being sick and COULDN'T have known what was going on, but I intentionally CHOSE to block everything out, and there is a huge difference — probably one that is so big that none of them will ever forgive me.

Mom and Dad still haven't resolved whatever it is they've been fighting over. It's not so much that they have screaming matches or anything, though that does happen occasionally. It's mostly that same cold, tense atmosphere that we all know can't be attributed to this ridiculous cold spell. I just can't figure it out, though. Jimmie and I are both good kids. We get good grades. Well, anyway, I always used to, and Jimmie is such a diligent student, probably top of his fifth grade class. He's taking it really hard; he doesn't talk to anyone anymore. I'm sort of starting to worry about him, and I think Mom and Dad are worried about him, too, but he won't say enough to them for them to help him out.

I just don't know what they could possibly be fighting about. Maybe it's the fact that I've got a boyfriend now. But do they even know we're going out? I'm not sure I ever actually told them, though I'm sure they have that parental radar that people seem to get once they're married that allows them to figure out everything about their kids. Or maybe they know about Paul and can't decide how to handle it? Oh, God. How humiliating! *Sigh* I just wish I knew how to fix it. Maybe I'll set up a date for them — make reservations at a nice restaurant, or buy tickets to some show.... Psh, as if I could afford any of that. Maybe I'll just make dinner one night. Yeah, that seems like a good plan. I'll light candles and decorate with flowers for them for Valentine's Day next week! Then they'll remember how much they love each other. They'll realize that they've just been acting dumb by snubbing each other all season. It's the perfect plan.

Chapter Nine

That Friday, things got weird again. Between first and second periods, Carolyn discovered Paul loitering by her locker. She stopped dead in her tracks, disgusted that he would even speak to her after all he'd put her through. She spun around and pushed through the crowd in the other direction, getting elbowed and bumped unintentionally for going against the tide. She'd just have to excuse herself from class to go get her books once he was gone – it wouldn't be that big of a deal. More important was her fragile state of mind, which she was determined to protect against Paul at all costs.

He was there again after period two, during break. Carolyn skirted him by going the long way to the art room. At least she didn't need any books for that class. But he was there again after art, and she needed her math books. She moved in quickly, hoping to escape before he could inflict any harm. He stood in front of her locker like a stone pillar, unmoving. "You're hard to track down," he commented lightly.

"I try," Carolyn replied curtly. Paul's mouth curled into a smile, and his eyes locked on her face, burning through like lasers. Carolyn looked down, wanting to cry. "Think I could get my books? Thanks." She tried to shove past, but Paul would not be moved. "Dude, I'm going to be late for math," she whined.

"I have to tell you something," he finally said, moving ever-so-slightly to the side, but not enough for her to open the locker. He always seemed to begin conversations with these taunting catch-phrases instead of getting straight to the point.

"Yeah, I have something to tell you, too," she said, pulling on the locker handle as hard as she could, but only succeeding in opening it a fraction of an inch.

"Okay. You first," Paul allowed, moving a little more to the side. Carolyn finally wrenched the locker open and retrieved her books. Paul watched her expectantly.

"You suck." She left Paul in shock by her locker, satisfied that she'd stunned him so. Maybe *that* would teach him.

She sat down hard on the bench at the lunch table, squeezing in between Matt and Finn. "How's it going?" Matt asked lightly.

Carolyn breathed out sharply. "Okay, I guess."

"Just okay?"

"Yeah."

"You want to talk about it?"

She felt his ice-blue eyes scanning her like a book that he could read and bristled. "No."

Concerned, Matt persisted. "Did your parents make up yet?"

"That's not the problem," she snapped.

"Matt just wants to look out for you," Finn interjected. Carolyn remembered him telling her that Matt thought she disliked him, and tried to soften her manner.

"They haven't made up," she admitted grudgingly. "But I'm mad right now because Paul's been giving me a hard time today."

Matt half-stood. "Why didn't you say so? I'll take care of him!"

"No, don't! Don't waste your time."

"It's not a waste of time," Matt assured her, scanning the cafeteria for Paul's unkempt, dirty blond surfer boy's hair. She reached up and, grabbing him by the wrist, firmly pulled him back into his seat.

"He's not worth it. Just forget I said anything."

Matt looked at her in confusion but left it at that. Finn returned to his music and lunch. Carolyn swallowed a lump in her throat; her friends were so loyal and protective. She considered telling Matt the whole story but quickly dismissed the idea. If "Paul's been giving me a hard time" was enough to set him off, then she could only imagine what he would do if he learned about New Year's. *It's for Paul's own safety that I'm keeping quiet*, she rationalized. *Not that I wouldn't like to see Matt punch him out; I just don't want Matt in trouble. Besides, I'm finally bouncing back – I don't want to get dragged back down by this.*

Not to mention… I want to be the one to get revenge on him.

On Monday, Valentine's Day, she was fortunate enough to reach her locker before he did. Matt, on the other hand, beat her there, and he'd left a little gift on the shelf for her to discover when she arrived. Carolyn squealed in surprise and delight at the fuzzy pink bunny he'd left, and the sizable heart-shaped box of chocolates. *He's so sweet!* she thought, squeezing the bunny happily. *He always knows just what I need. Maybe Finn was wrong about him not thinking I like him anymore. At any rate, it sure seems like* he *still likes* me.

At break, she repaid him with candy and a card she'd made by hand. "Happy Valentine's Day!" she bubbled, showing her appreciation for his thoughtfulness with a hug and a little kiss on the cheek, which she unexpectedly had to stand on tiptoe to reach. *That's strange. We always used to be the same height. He must have hit a growth spurt recently.* "Thanks for the surprise this morning!"

"Don't mention it," Matt said coolly, returning the hug and kiss. Carolyn gazed up at his sunny countenance with adoration.

"Blehhh!" said Margo to remind them of her presence. She pointed her finger down her throat and mimed gagging. "Valentine's Day is for dorks!"

Carolyn giggled and snuggled into Matt's side, as his arm was still around her. *Now this is what it's all about...* she mused happily. "Well, I guess we must be dorks, then, huh Matt?"

"I guess so," Matt agreed, not sounding particularly upset.

"Good lord..." Margo said in exasperation, swinging her backpack up onto her shoulder and starting off toward her next class. "I'll see you two lovebirds at lunch..."

Lunchtime rolled around, and Carolyn went to retrieve her lunch from her locker. She had temporarily forgotten Paul's stakeout, but thankfully, he wasn't there.

Upon opening the locker, Carolyn became immersed in a deluge of red and white confetti. She looked around frantically – someone must be crouching in a shadow laughing at her somewhere. Blushing furiously, she snatched her lunch and slammed the locker, humiliated at this ridiculous, ankle-deep display of affection from someone who wasn't even her boyfriend. The rattle of the locker reverberated down the hall, mingling with the echoes of her footsteps as she dashed to lunch.

"Okay," she said as she sat down. "Which one of you *dorks* filled my locker with confetti?" She pretended her indignation was merely an act, but in all honesty, she was furious. Nobody had a right to do something like that unless it was Matt, and she knew full well that he was done with his festivities for the day. She looked around the table expectantly, and saw that all of her friends were doing the same. Puzzled faces awaited an admission of guilt from someone.

"Confetti?" Matt repeated, bemused.

"Confetti," Carolyn asserted. Everyone shook their heads "no."

"I don't think any of us did it," Anne said.

"Well then, who did?" They all shook their heads again. No one knew.

There was a time when I would have thought a secret admirer was the best thing that ever happened to me. It's so romantic and mysterious, like something out of a storybook. But I've got Matt now — I don't need any secret admirers. I have all the romance I need. And I'm pretty sure everyone knows that. Besides, I can't imagine why anyone would want to secretly admire ME.

So explain to me why I found my locker full of Valentine's Day confetti this afternoon. I know Matt didn't put it there. That leaves Finn, Nick, and Chris — they're the only other guys I even speak to. Chris is too infatuated with Molly to risk her thinking that he liked me instead. Besides, he's not the confetti type. Nick may have broken up with Margo, but I'm pretty sure his interest is focused on some girl in the seventh grade who has really big boobs. (Gah, boys. They're so dumb. Really.) That leaves Finn. Wow honestly. I know Finn, and even thinking of him filling my locker with confetti makes me laugh out loud! He definitely does NOT like me in THAT way. Hahahaha how ridiculous! Maybe someone was just pulling a prank, or got the wrong locker.... I just don't know....

And speaking of weirdness, Paul is SUCH a creep. He's been stalking me for the past week. I don't know WHY. I wish he'd just buzz off and mind his own business. I didn't want him around before the Incident, and I only hate him more now.

Such fond Valentine's Day sentiments, huh? Well, you can't blame me. Anyway, I'm off to create a lovely, romantic supper for mes parents. And by "lovely" and "romantic," I mean I'll made French toast and light some candles, because I'm sort of a pyro like that.

Carolyn surveyed her handiwork. The candles glowed invitingly and the sleek, white tablecloth cascaded over the rim of the table. Two plates of French toast, served on Mom's fine China, steamed at the ends of the table, and a pair of red roses stood in a skinny vase in the center. The stereo was set up to play a bluesy CD with a lot of saxophones, which had sounded romantic when Carolyn had been sifting through her mother's music earlier. Jimmie and his friend were holed up in the family room playing video games, where they would be out of the way, although it hadn't taken much persuasion to convince them to stay up there when Mom and Dad came home – Jimmie was too afraid of seeing them fight to grace them with his presence unless it was absolutely necessary.

Everything was perfect, absolutely perfect. Even if her own Valentine's Day had been filled with perplexities, at least she could give her parents a nice evening.

Carolyn checked her watch. Dad would be home from work any minute – he usually came home around 7:30. Hopefully Mom would be back from running errands just as quickly, or at least before the meal got cold.

8:00 rolled around, and Carolyn despaired. Her work would be lost. The candles would burn to stubs, and she would have to microwave the French toast, thereby making it soggy and tasteless. *Maybe I should just give it to Jimmie and his friend*, she thought. *At least they would appreciate it. But that might make Jimmie worry more about Mom and Dad…. I don't want to ruin his play-date. I don't see him having fun very often anymore. I'll give it till quarter past.*

Mom finally rushed in the door at 8:10. Carolyn watched surreptitiously from around the corner as her mother entered the kitchen and caught sight of the preparations.

"Jim?" she called out.

Carolyn's heart sank. Her mother thought that her husband had prepared this meal. How disappointed she'd be when she discovered the truth: Jim

Becker was not even home from work yet. Carolyn stepped into the candlelight. "Happy Valentine's Day, Mom," she said softly.

Mom looked bewildered. "Did you do this, Lynnie?"

Carolyn nodded.

"Oh, you're sweet!" She wrapped her daughter in an appreciative hug.

"Yeah, but Dad isn't here," Carolyn muttered into her mother's shoulder.

"Well, I'm sure he'll be home soon," Mom said, hopeful and doubtful at once. "This looks wonderful, honey. Thank you."

"You're welcome." She retreated to her bedroom, listening intently for her father's return from work. A car pulled into the driveway shortly after, and Carolyn leapt to the window, but was disappointed to see that it was only Jimmie's friend's father come to retrieve his son.

I must have missed it, she decided at nine. She passed the kitchen on her way to the shower to make sure they didn't need help with the dishes and was dismayed to find her mother still sitting alone, wilting alongside the roses. "Mom? Dad still isn't home?"

Mom shook her head sadly. "Why don't we microwave this French toast and eat it ourselves so it doesn't go to waste? It looks so delicious." The dejected note in her voice was so obvious that Carolyn could hardly turn down the invitation. They dined in near-silence. Carolyn showered, journaled, and went to bed. She finally heard the garage door go down at a quarter past ten. An explosion of argument followed shortly after. She heard her name and realized that her mom was furious at her father for staying at work so late without even calling, and for leaving all of Carolyn's work unappreciated.

She had heard enough. She reached for her Walkman to help her sleep. As tears streamed from her eyes, she tried to comfort herself by thinking, *at least I tried*, but she couldn't fool herself into thinking that was enough. She'd made things worse instead of better, and the failure left a bitter taste upon her tongue, not unlike the flavor Paul had left there that fateful night.

Haha. Run off with Matt and get married. Don't I wish. I've just been going through a lot lately. Mom and Dad have only gotten worse, and my attempts at playing Peacemaker only aggravated the problem. Jimmie is terrified they'll split up. Meanwhile, my best friend (my best *California* friend, of course; you will always be my best *best* friend) hasn't really been around on account of her boyfriend. But I haven't really been around, either, on account of I can't stand socializing anymore. Like you said: I just don't feel like I can put my faith in anyone anymore. Although I think this madness may be returning to normal soon – I hope, anyway. Sorry again about Jake. Can't come up with any good advice at the moment. Hugs.

I really wish you'd tell me exactly what's going on down there. Do I have to come visit again and patch things up? I don't feel like I'm a part of your life anymore. I'm really sorry your parents are still being dumb. It's so strange to think of them not getting along. But you know, you don't have to be the Peacemaker. I know you think it's your job just because you're good at it, but it's not up to you to make your parents' marriage perfect. There are some things in the world that *you can't fix*, Carolyn. I know you hate to hear that, but it's true, and I wish you wouldn't always blame yourself for other people's shortcomings. Everybody has faults, and you want to fix them, but sometimes you have to learn to leave things alone. At any rate, don't think their fighting is because of you, and don't think that you're making it worse. I know that if nothing else, your parents love you to death. They might be having trouble showing it right now because of how things are between them, but just hold onto that. I *know* it's true, and don't you forget it!

Love always,
~LBS~

Chapter Ten

Carolyn made sure to get to school bright and early the next morning to clean up the mess in her locker. *How inconsiderate of my "admirer" to leave me so much junk to clean up,* she thought bitterly. The residue of last night's disappointment had her in a grouchy mood.

Tori and Finn showed up minutes later and offered to help Carolyn collect every little scrap in a big paper grocery bag she'd brought for that purpose.

"Boy, someone must really like you," Finn mocked, shoving a fistful of the shredded paper into the trash.

"Ah, shut up," Carolyn muttered playfully.

"Carolyn, maybe you should see this," Tori said suddenly. Carolyn whipped her head around. Tori had fished a rose out of the flood. Carolyn stared at it, speechless.

"Better not let Matt see that," Finn said.

"You're not helping!" Carolyn cried. "Who left all this? And what *for?*" An idea dawned on her slowly, and at first she refused to even let it surface in her mind. She felt like breaking something or hurting someone. "Crap..." she muttered, this time, not so playfully.

"What's the matter?" Tori asked.

Carolyn clenched her jaw. "I don't even want to say it, but maybe it was Paul."

"Why would Paul leave all this? He hates you," Finn pointed out.

"Exactly. To embarrass me, to make it look like I was involved with someone else so Matt would break up with me – who knows his motives? To make me miserable. Isn't that enough?"

"I think you're being a little paranoid," Tori ventured, stuffing a fistful of paper into the bag. "Ouch... there's something else here," she said. "Something with a corner."

Carolyn's heart raced as Tori extracted the thing from the bag of trash. It was a little card. All it said was "Happy Valentine's Day!" but the key was the handwriting. "I think Carolyn may be right," Finn said, examining the card as Carolyn tried to keep from crying. "This sure looks like his handwriting." He held it out for her to see, but Carolyn wouldn't take it.

"Get it out of here! Throw it away, burn it, anything!"

Finn's eyes lit up. "Do you want to?"

"Want to *what*?" she demanded testily.

"Burn it?"

Carolyn snorted. "Are you out of your mind?"

Finn shook his head laughingly. "I don't think so. I have a lighter. We can light it up out behind the school. Or wait until after school and do it where no one will notice."

Carolyn laughed again. "You really *are* crazy! What in the world do you have a lighter for? You don't smoke."

"No, that's true. I don't smoke," Finn acknowledged. "I don't know, I guess just to have one. It's good fun to wave it around at concerts. So what do you say?"

"Let's do it."

By lunchtime on Wednesday, Carolyn was famished after a particularly difficult math test, but more than that, she was simply too fed-up with everything to deal with Paul – yet there he stood, at her locker once again. She stopped dead in the middle of the hall and tried to decide what to do, all the while cursing her own stupidity for thinking that maybe he wouldn't come back, that it was safe to store her lunch in her own locker where it wouldn't get crushed by her books. Bodies streamed past her in all directions, but seemed not to touch her at all. Everything had gone numb. Just when she had been ready to move on, he had to come back and torment her some more.

Stomach growling in protest, Carolyn decided to go hungry for the day. She braced herself against the stampede and tried to move in the other direction, but instinctively she realized that Paul had spotted her. She moved with all the more determination. She heard him call her name. Humiliated, she ducked her head and practically ran through the now-thinning masses, jostling people out of her way. She finally broke free of the throng, and looking back, saw that Paul was still following her. She darted into a nearby restroom. Escape!

Carolyn let her backpack drop onto the floor and slumped against the wall in defeat. *This has to qualify as harassment,* she thought. *There must be something someone can do… anyone? Oh, it's hopeless…* Her head snapped up as she became aware of sniffling issuing from one of the stalls. The familiar toes of a ravaged blue pair of Chucks showed under the door: it was Molly.

"Molly?" The sniffling stopped, and a second later, the stall door creaked open. Molly's eyes were rimmed with red. "Molly, what happened?" Carolyn asked. All her worries about Paul flew out of her mind for the moment. She moved forward to offer a hug, and Molly accepted it.

"It's just Chris being a freaking idiot again," she said lightly, running her sweatshirt sleeve under her nose to stop it from running.

"What now?" Carolyn asked. "I thought you guys broke up last week." Not that she could keep up anymore.

"Well, this weekend he said he made a mistake and wanted to get back together. But now he wants to break up again."

"It sounds like he doesn't know what he wants," Carolyn commented. "Maybe you should just forget about him until he figures things out. If he really cared about you, he wouldn't put you through this so often."

"No! No," Molly protested. "I know he loves me. He's just a confused child… but I love him, too. I mean, well…. Maybe, for a little while – no, I couldn't."

"It sounds like you're as confused as he is."

Molly laughed half-heartedly. "I guess so."

"I'm telling you, he's not worth it," Carolyn insisted. "Besides. We're way too young to be in love."

"But how can you be sure? Maybe this is it," Molly argued.

"I dunno…." Carolyn relented doubtfully, not wanting to admit that if true love meant breaking each other's hearts on a weekly basis, she wanted nothing to do with it.

"Well, *I* know. I know how I feel about him. I'm not letting go that easily," she resolved.

Carolyn saw that Molly wouldn't be dissuaded, so she simply urged her to come to lunch, suddenly remembering that she didn't have a lunch. "Okay," Molly said. "I just have to wash up…" She gazed into the grungy mirror and turned the sink on.

"That's okay. I can wait."

Molly splashed cold water on her face. "So," she burbled through the water. "If you're not here to go to the bathroom, then what are you doing in the seventh grade bathroom?"

"Perceptive, aren't we?" Carolyn stalled. "I'm just hiding out from Paul."

Molly looked confused. "Why?" She snatched a scratchy brown paper towel from the dispenser on the wall and dabbed at her face with it.

"Because he keeps trying to talk to me."

"So… why don't you talk to him?"

"I can't talk to him!"

"Why not?"

"Because I hate him!"

"Well, that's nothing new," Molly pointed out, tossing the paper towel towards the trash can and missing.

Carolyn occupied herself with reapplying eyeliner in the mirror, debating whether to tell Molly everything. "I just… can't."

Molly narrowed her eyes and deposited the paper towel in the trash can where it belonged, focusing entirely on Carolyn now. "He's been that bad lately?"

Carolyn nodded hopelessly. "You have no idea." She put the eye liner pencil away and started in on the mascara.

"Why, what's he done now?"

"Oh… lots of stuff…" Carolyn replied vaguely.

"Like what?" Carolyn bit her lip, trying to come up with an answer and stalling further by applying the mascara really thickly. "Ohmygod, did he hurt you?"

Carolyn gave up on the eye make up and shook her head. "That was *last* year," she reminded Molly.

"Then *what*? You can tell me *anything*, you know."

All of a sudden, Carolyn broke down. Molly was her best friend. Wouldn't it feel good to tell just one person? *No! nobody, ever…. But I have to tell Molly something!*

Molly looked like she wanted to reach out and shake Carolyn by the shoulders, shake the answer right out of her. "Oh my God! Carolyn, what did he do? I'll kill him!"

"He – I don't want to talk about it…"

"You have to! I tell you everything!"

"I know! I know... okay..." Carolyn gulped in a lungful of air and let the whole story spill out. It was as though something inside her was saying, *at last! I can breathe again...*

Carolyn finished, and Molly swore. "What a freaking idiot!" she ranted. "Are you sure you don't want me to kick his skull in for you?"

Carolyn managed a wavering smile. "Be my guest," she said. "But wait! Promise you won't say a word! To anybody, not a soul!"

"All right... I won't," Molly promised reluctantly. "Does Matt know?"

"I can't tell him!" Carolyn objected incredulously.

"Don't you think you should?"

"I don't know... maybe, I guess. But I'm not going to."

Molly shrugged in defeat. "Well, that's your choice, I guess. I still think you should... but anyway, let's go to lunch."

"Good idea." Carolyn checked her make-up in the mirror. The waterproof formula had stood up well to her breakdown and masked the resulting redness quite effectively. Molly shouldered her way out into the hallway. "I just have to stop at my locker..." Carolyn was saying. She stopped short, panicked, when she noticed Paul loitering. *He must have heard everything!* she thought dizzily, glowering at him. She moved to brush past him. Paul opened his mouth to speak, but Molly cut him off before he could utter a sound.

"You stay away from Carolyn!" she hollered. "You hear me? Come near her and I'll kick your head so hard it rolls away like a soccer ball!" She was screaming in his face, and looked like she might have kicked him good and hard right then. Paul backed down and held up his hands in front of him as a sign of peace. He addressed Carolyn, though he kept his eye on Molly and made a sort of twitching movement every time she moved.

"I just wanted to say-"

Carolyn exploded. "I don't freaking care! Never speak to me again!" She took off, and Molly followed.

"That seemed kind of harsh," Molly said once they were out of earshot, trotting to keep up with Carolyn's long, angry strides.

"Nothing could be too harsh after what he did. After what he's still doing. I'll never forgive him," she resolved.

Inside the cafeteria, they split up, Molly to go sit with Chris and Carolyn to join her friends. Carolyn squeezed in next to Matt, who was chowing his way through two huge roast beef sandwiches, an apple, a medium sized bag of Doritos, a bottle of Coke, a pack of cookies, and a serving-sized box of cereal. She watched him in fascination until he asked if he had something on his face, and she blushingly looked away, not willing to admit that she had been admiring his perfectly proportioned profile, which looked no less attractive in spite of his ravenous eating. The gentle hands she knew so well reached into the package of chips, and out of the corner of her eye she watched him eat it. She really had scored the cutest boy in Long Beach Middle School. How could she be so cruel as to let him think she was neglecting him?

"Hey Carolyn," Anne called from a few seats down. Carolyn snapped to attention. "Is your mom driving us on Friday? My mom said to ask because she isn't going to be home."

"Oh... I don't know. I didn't think about it."

Margo interjected. "My mom lives for that kind of stuff. She'll drive us."

"Okay, thanks," Anne said.

"What's this about?" Matt asked.

"Oh!" Carolyn had forgotten that Matt wasn't at lunch the day they'd made their plans. "We're going disco bowling on Friday, wanna come?" she proposed. Matt was silent for a minute, and Carolyn looked over to see if his mouth was too full to answer, but it wasn't. "Matt?"

"Uhmmm... well, I have youth group," he reminded her sheepishly, his freckled cheeks growing slightly pink.

"Oh, right," she said, not masking her disappointment. "Can't you skip just one night?" she pleaded. Matt took a tremendous bite of his sandwich to avoid answering. "Come on," she pressed. "What's more fun, a night with your friends or a night cooped up in a silly church? What do you even do, sing 'Kumbaya' for hours on end?"

"Look," Matt snapped, the nostrils of his button nose flaring. "My grandma says I have to go." His ears started reddening too, and Carolyn could see she'd frustrated him, but she persisted.

"You can't play hooky? Just once?"

"*No*, Carolyn, I will not play hooky! What do you have against my youth group?"

Carolyn shrugged. "Nothing, I guess. I don't know. It's just kind of weird."

"Yeah? And how would you know? It's not like you've ever come with me."

"It's not like you've ever invited me!"

"Because you always get like this whenever I talk about my grandma or my church!" Matt burst out. "I'm not going to put myself through your criticism for no good reason." Carolyn reeled as though he'd struck her.

"Am I that terrible?" she asked softly, distressed. He really *did* think she disliked him!

"Sometimes," Matt confessed.

"I – I'm sorry. I thought you felt the same way. You always seemed to think your grandma was nuts for making you go."

"I did. But, I don't know. I guess I see it differently now," he mused. The fuchsia of his cheeks and ears began to fade, and his usual fair golden complexion returned. He continued, "But I'm not the only one who's changed, you know. In fact, I wanted to ask you about that–" The bell sounded, dispersing the students to various classes.

"Maybe we can talk about it after school," Carolyn suggested, dreading the conversation but wanting to appease him after she'd hurt his feelings during lunch. And in the past couple of months, in general.

"Please," Matt consented, dumping his pile of trash into the trashcan. They went their separate ways.

However, Carolyn entirely forgot her arrangement with Matt when Tori and Finn congregated at her locker after the last bell. "Bonfire time!" Tori yelled. Carolyn laughed.

"Shut up, you're going to make people think we're pyromaniacs or something," she giggled. She grabbed the bag of trash from her locker, and they sprinted excitedly down the street to Finn's yard, footfalls echoing in the cold as their breath crystallized the air in front of their faces. The cold spell hadn't ended yet. "You're sure your mom won't mind us setting fire to stuff in your back yard?" Carolyn said worriedly, trying to catch her breath as they veered into the driveway.

"We have a bonfire pit, so, no," Finn replied matter-of-factly.

He unlatched the gate to the back yard, leading them along a brick walkway that disappeared into a huge garden, which Carolyn imagined aloud must have been stunningly beautiful in the summer. A dry fountain hunkered in the center of the garden, coated with ice and filled with dead leaves. At the other end of the path, they came to the edge of the woods, where a bonfire circle was indeed marked out with charred rocks. Carolyn deposited the bag in the ring of stones, and Finn retrieved his lighter from deep in one of the many pockets on his khakis.

"Would you like to do the honors?" he asked, holding the lighter out to her. Carolyn hesitated.

"I've never, uhm, used a lighter before," she confessed.

"It's easy." He thrust it out at her. Carolyn looked it over in confusion, and Finn finally came to her aid, guiding her hand and reassuring her that she wouldn't burn herself. Lambent on their faces, the flame flickered to life. It cast an orange-gold glow over their flesh, and Carolyn fleetingly envisioned them as ethereal beings. "Got it?"

"Yep."

Carolyn upended the bag, and placed the card and rose on top of the pile so she could watch them burn. "Don't put your hand over the part you're lighting, I don't know how fast these things will catch..." Finn warned. Carolyn cautiously ignited the confetti, and it went up startlingly fast. She jumped back, squeaking in surprise. Finn and Tori steadied her, and they all stepped closer to watch the flames eat away at that charade of romance. The odor of singed rose petals filled their noses, and it couldn't have been more satisfying.

February 16, 2000

Molly found out about Paul. From me, that is. I HAD to tell her. She told me everything about her and Chris, so it was only fair. I'm a little worried, though. I don't know how, but I just KNOW it's going to get around to Matt. I guess I'm being paranoid. Even if Molly told Chris, it's not like either of them talks to anyone else.

Well. Paranoid AND judgmental. I guess I win the gold medal tonight.

Matt and I got in a fight at lunch. It really hurts to fight with him. He was supposed to be the thing I could count on to make things BETTER, not WORSE. He thinks I'm too critical of him and his youth group and his grandma and blah blah blah. Well, he used to be critical, too. How was I supposed to know he'd suddenly turned around and decided to LIKE getting dragged to church all the time? Maybe he's just using that as — well, leverage to create space between us. I mean, I guess I can understand not wanting to be with me. First my best friend, now my boyfriend — I must be one really rotten person. That's probably why he wanted to "talk" about me "being different."

Ohhh.... Crap. I just remembered, I was supposed to meet him after school.... I'm such a bad girlfriend! Should I call him and apologize? No, it'll be easier to just deal with it tomorrow. That way, when things get worse, at least I'll have one last night of good sleep under my belt. I think he's so fed up with my bad-girlfriendness that he just may dump me if I call him tonight, and if that happens, it'll be a while before I get a good night's sleep again. Yeah, I'll deal with it tomorrow. That's best.

Okay, so a minute ago, I went downstairs to find a snack, and apparently Mom and Dad had just finished with a great big argument (which I had missed because I was blasting my headphones). Mom was nowhere to be seen, but Dad was crashing around, opening cabinets as though searching for something and then slamming them shut, all the while muttering to himself. I was afraid to get in his way, and he didn't seem to notice me standing there, so I said, "Dad."

He jumped about a foot and tried to cover up his anger by questioning me about school and such. As if things were normal or something. But when I refused to answer him with more than a few words, he returned to his mutterings, this time voicing them for me to hear. I didn't want to hear, and even though I was listening, well, you can't expect me to say anything. Give my dad advice about his failing marriage? Ha! What I got from his rant was that he thought that Mom didn't try hard enough to make him happy. He thought she had stopped caring about their relationship and liked to show it through little things like not buying him the kind of food he liked or moving his stuff around. He seemed to want some sort of reaction to this, so I said I was sure she wasn't malicious when she did these things; she probably just forgot to buy his preferred brand of bologna, and we all know that she likes to keep the house as tidy as possible. As far as I could see, I said, she hadn't done anything wrong. As her husband, he should excuse such small mistakes.

Then he yelled at me for taking sides, and that was about when I gave up on finding a snack and came back up here. Can I help it if I relate better to the woman's point of view? Sorry for trying to help, Dad.

PussyCat240 (8:41PM): CAROLYN!! YOU'RE ONLINE!!!

Away message from SkiBlink: oh, the drama……..

PussyCat240 (8:41PM): Well, sort of, anyway. Maybe I'll just stick around for a few minutes until you come back from snacking or whatever it is you're doing.

PussyCat240 (9:02PM): okay, you must be making a turkey dinner over there or something. Think you could share?

Away message from SkiBlink: oh, the drama……..

PussyCat240 (9:02PM): WHAT DRAMA??!! I have a right to know, you know!!

PussyCat240 (9:05PM): ho hum, so I guess I'll just amuse myself by sending random messages for you to read when you get back.

PussyCat240 (9:07PM): Upsetting conversation I had with Jake online the other night:

> *PussyCat240 (10:14PM)*: haha Nee and I just had a Veggie Tales marathon.
>
> *Itsnotwhatitlookslike514 (10:17PM):* Veggie Tales sucks.
>
> *PussyCat240 (10:17PM):* *is shocked* how can you say that? Singing vegetables don't amuse you?
>
> *Itsnotwhatitlookslike514 (10:22PM):* It's gay.
>
> *PussyCat240 (10:22PM):* it's cute.
>
> *PussyCat240 (10:22PM):* and funny.
>
> *PussyCat240 (10:22PM):* don't be too cool to be a fool!
>
> *Itsnotwhatitlookslike514 (10:29PM):* too many morals for me. Whatever.
>
> *Itsnotwhatitlookslike514 signed off at 10:29PM.*

PussyCat240 (9:08PM): how sad is that? I love Veggie Tales. Takes me straight back to my childhood (or last month.)

PussyCat240 (9:10PM): and you know, that just proves what

I meant about him being so different. "Too many morals?" Where's the Jakie-poo we knew and loved last year before you left??? It's so sad; he obviously dislikes me so much that he couldn't even bear to talk to me online for another second. :'(

Away message from SkiBlink: oh, the drama........

PussyCat240 (9:16PM): Well, you should know that Nee and I really are getting along great now (as you could probably guess from the Veggie Tales marathon thing).

PussyCat240 (9:17PM): it's good to have someone on your side when you're surrounded by people like R-Bi and Jake. Judging by your away message, you probably know what I'm talking about.

Away message from SkiBlink: oh, the drama........

PussyCat240 (9:33PM): I guess you're not coming back. I'm such a reject. ☹ ☹ ☹ Email me or something. Miss you.

PussyCat240 signed off at 9:34PM.

Chapter Eleven

Carolyn reclined against the cold brick wall in the usual meeting place and hugged herself to keep warm. She had asked the others to go ahead without her and Matt so they could talk alone. The final bell had rung five minutes ago – Matt was running late. Of course, she could forgive him since she'd accidentally blown him off the day before. He had grimly reminded her of their arrangement first period that morning.

"Oh! Crap! I'm sorry…. I got tied up doing something else… can we do it today instead?" she had entreated, acting like she hadn't remembered last night and simply decided not to call him about it.

"Just don't forget," Matt had scolded.

Well, here I am. Who forgot now?

"Hey!" someone called from a little ways behind her. Carolyn jumped, and she initially assumed it was Matt, but before she'd even turned around, she recognized the rough voice – and it wasn't Matt's. Her heart sank: it was

Paul, and he was coming her way. She stole one last glance down the hall, but there was no sign of Matt, so she took off down the sidewalk at a fast pace.

"Hey!" Paul called again. He was gaining on her. Carolyn sped up, but she was no track star. "Carolyn!" She gritted her teeth and turned on her heel to face him.

"What?" she spat.

Paul closed the distance between them. "I need to talk to you."

"Seems you already are," Carolyn remarked.

Paul looked around. "Not here," he insisted.

Carolyn stepped back to give herself room to breathe. *What is up with this guy and personal space? God!* "No. Here. Now. Say what you have to say so I can get on with my life." Paul flinched, and Carolyn mentally tallied the score: *Carolyn–three. Paul–gah, I lost count.* She crossed her arms and waited coldly for a response.

Paul spread his hands, his expression supplicating. "I know you hate me," he began.

Carolyn choked back a sarcastic laugh. "You *think?*"

"I *know.* I know, and I don't blame you. I've been a royal jerk to you." *Is this a confession, then? God. I must be dreaming.* "But do you remember when you first moved here?"

"When you pushed me off a stool? Oh, yeah, I remember that. What about it?"

Paul looked pained again. "Before that."

Carolyn didn't bother to stifle her laughter this time. It came out harsh, more like a bark than anything. "'Before that?' What do you mean, 'before that?' There *was* no 'before that!' That was my first day of school, genius!"

"You don't think so?" Unlike Carolyn, Paul remained perfectly calm. "I saw how you were looking at me. You may think I'm stupid, but I'm not *that* stupid, you know."

Carolyn opened her mouth to retort, but no words issued from it. Her heart took off in insane palpitations. *Am I that hopelessly obvious? I only saw him* once *before he pushed me! I have got to stop wearing my heart so plainly on my sleeve!* "Oh, really," she managed to say, feeling the burning fuchsia creeping into her cheeks. "Well, then why did you push me?" the sarcasm drained from her manner.

Paul shrugged hopelessly. "I don't know. It was stupid. I knew what you were thinking." He hesitated, and Carolyn forced herself to look at his face. There was something surprising about his eyes, but Carolyn couldn't hold his gaze. She dropped her eyes and blinked back tears as that January night came rushing back to her. Paul took a deep breath and continued. "And I was thinking the same thing about you."

Carolyn's breath caught. She could only goggle at him as she tried to get some air into her lungs, but her breathing passages seemed to have sealed shut. She searched his face, but for once he actually looked sincere. "I can't talk to you," she finally choked, after staring at him in unbelieving horror for a full minute. She took off towards home, backpack thumping on her back to the rhythm of her frenzied footsteps. *Impossible, impossible, impossible,* they seemed to say.

She dropped the backpack near the verandah without stopping. With the extra weight gone, it was only a matter of seconds before she'd reached her "thinking spot" in the woods. She sank onto the boulder, arching backward until she was spread across the whole thing. She closed her eyes against the illuminated gray backdrop of the sky.

This is not happening. She gulped in a lungful of air, and was startled to hear the brush crackle. She sat bolt upright. Moments later, Paul appeared in the clearing. Carolyn leapt off the rock, beyond annoyed at his insensitive intrusion into her personal space. She glared, but Paul spoke before she could. "But that's only partly true," he continued, as though she hadn't stormed off, and as though what he had to say was so all-important that not even a meteor colliding with the earth could have stopped him from saying it. "I didn't realize until that night last month-"

"Don't!" Carolyn interjected, listening in detached, paralyzed terror. *How dare he bring that up?* Unconsciously, she took a step backward. He was too close. Living in the same state as him was too close.

"-that I still do," he finished. Carolyn gaped, too thunderstruck to gather her thoughts, let alone speak. Her mind whirred around like a gyroscope, spinning faster and faster until everything became a blur, and she had to steady herself on the nearby boulder. Sardonic laughter bubbled up in her throat again.

"Impossible," she finally squawked with a shudder. Paul opened his mouth to speak and reached for her hand. "Don't touch me!" she barked, drawing her fist back to sucker-punch him. "Or I swear I'll..." He backed off a little.

"Don't hate me," he pleaded, his golden-brown eyes peering up at her from beneath those curved eyebrows so that he resembled a repentant puppy. She looked him over, recalling her first impression of his gangly limbs and unkempt, dirty-blond hair. He'd filled out by now, and it appeared that he'd combed his hair within the past week. If she didn't hate him so much, Carolyn knew she easily could have fallen for him all over again. She shook her head to clear it of the unwanted thoughts.

"I do," she insisted. "I never want to see your face again." She pushed past him, tears stinging her eyes as she stole away into the house.

Only in the sanctuary of her bedroom did she finally let herself go, violent sobs wrenching her gut until she ached all over from crying so hard. Buddy trotted in and curled up on the bed to offer comfort, and Carolyn finally dozed off a bit, her head and arm resting on Buddy's golden side.

A while later, she was jolted awake by a knock at her door. "Lynnie? Are you all right in there?" called her mother's voice. Carolyn groggily thought back to the days when her mom had been her best confidante. She had shared all her secrets and feelings with her mom back then, knowing and trusting that not only would her secrets be safe, but also that she could obtain some sound advice. Those days were gone now, she realized with a pang. She couldn't tell her mom any of this, not after the way she'd pushed all her family and friends away lately, and especially not while mom and dad were still fighting. She couldn't possibly burden Mom with all her troubles. She'd lost her favorite listener. Carolyn wanted to cry all over again at the tragedy of the loss. The door swung open, the hinges squeaking softly as her mother's feet padded toward the bed.

"I'm fine," she lied. "I just sort of had a rough day. And I guess I'm sort of PMSing, too. Don't worry about me."

"Are you sure that's all?" Mom asked soothingly, sitting on the bed by Carolyn's head. "You haven't been yourself lately." She put her hand on Carolyn's forehead.

Carolyn squirmed away. "Mom! I'm not sick!" she protested.

"What's bothering you?" Mom pressed. "You don't tell me anything anymore."

Carolyn sighed, scrunching a pillow to her chest. "I don't know. I just had a weird day, that's all," she repeated.

"It seems like every day must be weird, then. You've been so strange lately," Mom commented. "Oh, honey, are you worried about me and Dad?" she asked suddenly. Carolyn nodded. It wasn't the reason she was crying, but the stress of wondering whether her parents could ever get along again had certainly weighed her down for the past few months, especially after her failed attempt at bringing them together with a romantic Valentine's Day supper. Mom looked like she wanted to kick herself. "I'm sorry, Carolyn. I wish we could get along like we used to…. I try, you know. It's your dad who won't put any effort into the relationship. He just hides out from his problems by staying at work all the time…."

"Mom… no offense… but I really don't want to hear about it at the moment." She knew her dad was thinking the same kinds of things about her mom, and they had clearly reached an impasse. Nothing was going to get solved if they both left it up to the other one to put forth more effort. "I kind of need to rest for a little bit, okay?" *I'll play the mediator tomorrow. I promise.*

Mom patted her arm. "Of course. Take a nap, and I'll send Jimmie up to tell you when dinner's ready." Carolyn adjusted her pillows and leaned back on them so Mom could see that she was resting. As soon as the door shut, though, Carolyn yanked her journal out from between the mattress and the box spring and presently found herself composing poetry. She reflected back on the days when she used to write about the simple joys of snow at Christmastime – that was all she'd ever known – and thought how right everyone was about how much she'd changed. Ruefully, she decided the change had been for the worse, but she could never be the same. *Especially now.*

Frustrated, she snatched up her guitar and, plugging her headphones into the output jack, cranked it up loud enough to maybe drown out some of her thoughts. She'd never expected to play so much as a single chord, but after messing around and looking up some information online, she felt she'd graduated from "inexperienced din" to "sophisticated noise." At any rate, she'd discovered the therapeutic value of making really loud noise, and the instrument became an outlet for her emotions, especially when paired with the words she'd scrawled in her notebook – but even then, there was no escape.

Message from: Leah Sorman <PussyCat240@aol.com>
To: Carolyn Becker <SkiBlink@aol.com>
A bit of my life story (can I hear some of yours?)

I'm going on a short-term missions trip to Honduras over April vacation! I guess there's a whole lot of stuff the team from my church will be doing, like constriction and teaching kids about the Gospel. I'm so excited! Plus, there's this guy who goes to my church who is also going on the trip. I don't really know him that well, but he's soooo gorgeous! He's one of those tall dark and handsome types. He seems like a deep and poetic person from the time I shook hands with him during the service the other morning. Hahaha or maybe I just hope he is. He's got to have something going on besides those amazing looks, and I'll scream if it's some sport or other. (Can you tell I'm still bitter over the Jake thing? But I'm trying REALLY HARD not to be, because the Bible says we should forgive those who hurt us. And he didn't even TRY to hurt me, so shouldn't I, like, doubly forgive him or something? I don't know.) Anyway, I'm really looking forward to that! I'll try and send a postcard.

Soooo. What's the latest and greatest in the sunny land of California? Come on, let me hear about your exciting love life, since I don't have one of my own. I can live vicariously through you! I want to know what's going on with your crazy parents, too. Tell me something – anything! Just let me know that you're still alive? That would be grand, thank you, dear.

Lots of love,
~LBS~

Chapter Twelve

At last, Friday had come. This was her night, her chance to go out with her friends and feel like a regular person again, if only for a few short and blissful hours. The anticipation of that night was enough to propel her through the first classes of the day, but as time wore on and her brain got stuffed with useless information, while still trying to cope with the idea of Paul not hating her – and not only that, but actually *liking* her – she grew tired, and consequently jumpier than ever. It was break, and Carolyn had tunnel vision: get to art as fast as humanly possible, and sneak in a few winks before class started.

When a hand suddenly closed on her wrist, Carolyn jumped a mile and spun around furiously, "Leave me alone!" already halfway out her mouth. She'd had just about enough of Paul and his stupid game, and she planned to tell him so – when she realized that it was just Matt.

Taken aback, he dropped her hand like it was a flaming coal. "Whoa. Are you okay?" he asked, eyeing her like she might bite his head off at any second.

Carolyn mentally kicked herself. "Oh... yeah, sorry..."

"Look, this just proves what I wanted to talk to you about." *Talk? Is he breaking up with me already? Gah, but I probably deserve it.* He scuffed the polished tile with his sandaled foot, not making eye contact. "Lately... you've been different," he began, trying to be gentle about it. Carolyn wanted to explode. *Yeah, I was the one who flipped the whole world on its head.* "You've been really high strung and unreliable. You realize you've blown me off twice in two days? I'm not saying this to make you feel bad," he assured her, noting the glassiness of her eyes. "I'm saying this because I'm worried about you."

At least he isn't breaking up with me. Yet. "Don't be!" she told him, the phony cheeriness of her voice grating against her conscience like fingernails on a blackboard. "I'm fine. Better than ever."

Matt didn't fall for it, nor did he even pretend to. "I know you too well. Something's off, and I wish you would tell me. I wish you knew that you can tell me anything. I wish you would still treat me like a friend instead of a stranger." Carolyn was silent. "Don't you care about me at all?" Matt's voice rose. "For crying out loud, I can't understand you, Carolyn! You say you want to be my girlfriend, but you won't tell me anything!"

Carolyn could barely hear her own voice as she responded. "I love you."

Matt exhaled loudly. "That isn't the point. It's like I don't even know you anymore. We call ourselves boyfriend and girlfriend the same way we call ourselves kids. Maybe that's what we are, but we aren't acting like it."

Carolyn stared at him hopelessly, wishing he knew but afraid to tell him. "What do you want me to do, Matt?"

Matt ruffled his already-tousled hair, and Carolyn noticed how truly concerned he appeared. He must have been worrying about her day and night. *I'm sorry,* she wanted to say. She wanted to throw her arms around his neck, to feel his strong baseball player's arms around her forever and ever. "I don't know," he admitted in exasperation. "What can I tell you? Would it be useless to ask you to change back into the Carolyn I kissed on New Year's? You're obviously a completely different person."

"Yeah…. It would be," she affirmed tonelessly. "I don't know what else to say besides 'I'm sorry.'"

His voice rose in volume and pitch. "Um, maybe an explanation for this sudden change?"

He needed to hear something – something that sounded genuine, and held at least a grain of truth. "I feel so hopeless," she confessed. "I keep watching things fall apart, and I can't do anything about it."

"You mean your parents."

Carolyn nodded. "And your family, now that your mom is gone. It's like you're missing a piece. And Molly doesn't speak to us anymore, even though she was supposed to be my best friend, and she and Chris are always off and on…. And even Paul's parents split up. It just seems like no one can hold anything together." *Okay, that was more honesty than I was aiming for. That's it exactly; why couldn't I explain it to myself before? Everybody and everything is falling apart, and I, the Fixer, can't do squat about it.*

"Carolyn, those aren't your problems. I know they affect you, but that doesn't mean you have to solve them." He took her hand lightly in his own, as though afraid she might slap him if he touched her. "Let's focus on keeping ourselves together and just hope that the rest of them will catch up, okay?"

She gently squeezed his hand. "Okay."

The bell sounded, and she dodged into the art room. She would try.

Disco bowling didn't appeal as much that evening as it had in the morning, but Carolyn hopped into the Gilman family car when it pulled up, and made an effort to laugh louder than all the rest of them so they would see how perfectly all right she was. At the alley, she danced enthusiastically in the black lights and disco ball glimmer, imagining this was another universe where nothing else she'd known before mattered. She may not have been as coordinated as Tori, but she discovered that she was actually enjoying herself, and that was the most important thing. Finn started break-dancing in the middle of the alley, and they all cheered him on until one of the staff said they'd have to ask him to leave if he didn't get off the alley.

"Spoil-sports," he muttered under his breath, still grinning. "Arcade games, anyone?"

Carolyn was in last place, and she quickly jumped up to join him, along with Nick. "Look!" Nick shouted over the music. "They've got DDR!"

Carolyn laughed and recalled the last time she'd attempted to play this game. "No way are you getting me to play that. I'm the worst dancer ever."

"It's not even real dancing," Nick snorted.

"I still suck at it."

"You seemed fine back there," Finn pointed out.

"Well…"

"Just do it," Nick insisted, and refused to play until Carolyn had given it a fair try.

"Okay," she said breathlessly once she'd finished (and had her butt kicked by Finn four times in a row). "That was actually pretty fun."

"See?" Finn teased.

"Now watch a pro…" Nick bragged, taking Carolyn's place by Finn. "What's the hardest one on there?" He and Finn agreed on a song, and Carolyn watched them with amusement, their feet moving faster than she could think. *I'm going to have to get better at this game*, she thought.

"Just you wait," she told them when they were done. "I'll be that good someday and I'll whoop your butts." The guys just laughed at her as they wandered back out towards the alley, where the rest of the group seemed to be getting ready to go.

"You think so, eh? Not a chance!" Nick jeered.

"You're on," Finn said. "I'll take you on again next week."

"Next week?" Carolyn asked. "Are we coming back next week?"

"Yeah, Tori decided to make this a tradition," Nick explained.

"Oh. Sweet. Then yeah, I'll take you on again next week," Carolyn accepted. She grabbed her purse from the bench, and everyone piled back into the Gilmans' car. "Guys, I don't want to go home yet. It's only 9:30. Anyone want to do something else?" she asked as they rode home, not wanting the night to end so soon. Not wanting to be alone again.

"Like what?" Tori asked. "How much later were you planning on staying out?"

"Oh, I don't know. I just don't want to go home yet, that's all."

"My parents would probably let you guys hang out at my place for another hour or so," Finn proposed.

"My mom's expecting me home about now," Anne said sadly.

"Yours is, too, Margo," said Mrs. Gilman.

"Aw, mom!" Margo protested. "I want to go!" Mrs. Gilman, however, was adamant. "There will be plenty of time for late nights when you get older. You're still in middle school, so your curfew is still ten," she said. Margo pouted.

"I can go," Tori announced, pocketing her cell phone. Mrs. Gilman stopped at Finn's house and dropped them off. Nick joined them, saying that his parents probably wouldn't care since he was over there most nights anyway. Instead of taking them into the house, though, Finn led them up a flight of stairs on the outside of the garage to a cozy little room that he'd illuminated with rope lights and decorated with posters of obscure bands and different music festivals. He flipped a switch, and a light bulb blinked on over their heads, revealing a mess of sound equipment, a drum set, and three guitars, one of them a bass, along with a TV set, which appeared to be held together by duct tape, and a huge box overflowing with video games.

"Geez! You've got even more crap up here than I remembered!" Tori commented.

Finn grinned. "I've added to my collection of random musical equipment since then," he said, taking a seat on a big amplifier. "Sit wherever," he invited them. "Amps make good chairs." Carolyn moved a fiery red electric guitar off the top of a second amp, and leaned it carefully against the wall.

"Why do you have so much equipment?" she asked. "You can't possibly play enough instruments to need all this."

"It's not *all* mine," Finn admitted. "A lot of it belongs to the other guys in my band. Not that I don't mess around with it when they aren't here..." he smirked mischievously, and Carolyn was caught off-guard at how charming it was. She ignored the odd feeling she'd just experienced and asked which guitar was his. "That red one you just moved. You play, don't you? Play us something."

"Oh, I don't know..." Carolyn blushed. "I just sort of mess around, I write a lot of my own stuff but it's mostly crap."

"I'll play if you do," Finn encouraged.

"Come on," Tori chimed in. "I want to hear, too. The only impression I have of you playing that thing is from the first day you had it and you whined about breaking a nail."

"Oh, is *that* the kind of guitarist you are? Then never mind," Finn dismissed the idea.

"Hey! I'll play," Carolyn caved in, already snatching the guitar up from where she'd left it against the wall.

Finn laughed. "Reverse psychology... works every time." He reached over the side of the amp he was sitting on to turn it on, and then looked at Carolyn expectantly.

"Oh, get out of here..." Carolyn muttered, starting to strum furiously. It was one of her favorite "angry" pieces, and always helped her let out a lot of pent up energy. Finn's face registered surprise at how wild the song was, and looking at the others, she saw that they were shocked, too. As she played, she watched smiles spread across their faces, and felt one growing on her own. *This* felt good, even if everything else had fallen apart. Her friends cheered when she'd finished, and Carolyn let her first real grin in months take over her face.

"Dude! That was *awesome!*" Tori exclaimed. "How come you never play for anyone?"

Carolyn shrugged. "I don't know. I never really thought I was that good."

"But you are!" Finn countered. "You could practically play guitar in any of the bands I listen to."

Nick nodded in agreement. "Yeah. And trust me, Finn would know. You should hear the music he's comparing you to…"

"Well, he can't be talking about the CDs he's been lending *me*," Carolyn said. "Come on, now. I'm just messing around."

"But that's why it's so impressive!" Tori remarked. "This is you 'just messing around.' Imagine what you could do if you really worked at it!"

Carolyn thought. "I don't know, I guess." She passed the guitar off to Finn. "Your turn, play us something good."

"I don't know if I can follow that act…" he teased, but he took the instrument anyway and launched into a complicated solo.

"Yeah," Carolyn said sarcastically when he was done, "you couldn't follow that act." Finn snickered as they all applauded him, reddening bashfully at the praise. "Do you and your band ever play any shows? I'd go."

"Me too!" Tori agreed.

"Aw, well, we've tried a few gigs, but the other guys have social lives, so there aren't a lot of days when we're all free…" Finn said disappointedly. "It's looking like we might break up any day now." He dropped his eyes dejectedly.

"You guys played that one party," Nick reminded him. "In January." Carolyn thought she remembered someone mentioning that, and she'd meant to go, but things had gotten so crazy....

Finn laughed. "Yeah, but everyone was too drunk to pay attention. Man, I hate gigs like that. Can't people just have a good time rocking out, without getting hammered?"

"That would be nice," Carolyn agreed. "I'm glad I've got friends like you guys who don't *need* alcohol to be absolutely nuts...."

"Hey!" Nick objected. "We aren't crazy!"

"Yeah, yeah, tell that to the DDR machine," she teased.

"Well, all right... maybe a little."

"It's stuffy up here," Tori said suddenly. "Can we go outside?"

Out in the dark of the night, the stars twinkled coldly overhead. Carolyn shivered in her hoodie, saying, "I think I heard it's finally supposed to thaw out a little next week." *It's funny how I complained so badly about the heat when I first moved here, and now I can't get used to the cold again...* She pulled the hood up over her head.

"It's about time," Tori said with relief. "I could use a little sunshine. So... what are we going to do now?"

Nick looked at his watch. "Probably head home," he said. "If you're walking, that is."

Tori shuddered. "Ugh. I didn't really think about having to walk home in the cold dark," she said nervously. "Hey, Finn, can I borrow a flashlight or something?"

"Maybe I should walk you home," Nick said to Tori. "You're just around the corner from me; it won't be too far out of the way."

"All right, thanks! Mr. Gentleman, aren't we?" Tori teased. Carolyn shook her head in amusement. Something about Tori's manner made it seem that she was always flirting, even if she didn't have any interest in the guy.

"Um... Maybe *I* could borrow a flashlight?" she asked hopefully. She lived farther away than Tori, and Nick lived just a couple houses down from Finn, while Carolyn had a few blocks to go, and she definitely didn't want to cut through the woods at night.

"I'll walk you home," Finn volunteered.

"Oh, I don't want to make you come all that way!" Carolyn objected. "I'll be fine. I mean, unless you *want* to come.... I don't mind or anything."

"I'll come."

Everyone said good night, and at the end of the driveway, they split up. Finn jammed his hands into his pockets and seemed to be at a loss for words. Carolyn, too, felt a bit awkward walking home at night with a boy who wasn't Matt. *Actually, it probably would have been awkward even if it was Matt, especially after today...* "Matt talked to me today," she said suddenly. "About me being different, I mean. I wish he wouldn't worry so much about me..."

She had expected Finn to be surprised at this statement, but if he was, he didn't show it. He jumped right into the conversation as though they had these kinds of talks every day. "Maybe he's right, you know."

"About what? Me being different? Yeah, I already knew that."

"No." Finn sounded exasperated. "You know that's not what I meant. I mean maybe he's right to be worried about you."

"Not you, too!"

"I didn't say *I* was worried – well, I mean, I am, a little bit. But if you were him, wouldn't you be worried about you?"

"Yeah, I guess," Carolyn agreed slowly. "But still. He goes on like I've changed on purpose, just to get to him."

"I don't think that's the way he intends it to sound."

"Maybe not. I don't know. What was it he said.... Oh, right: 'We call ourselves boyfriend and girlfriend, but we don't act like it.'"

Finn hesitated. "I'm not either of you, so it's hard for me to say what a boyfriend and girlfriend *should* act like. I think it's different for everybody."

Carolyn pondered that for a minute, and asked, "Do *you* think we act like boyfriend and girlfriend?"

Finn laughed. "Whoa, I am *not* getting involved! This is between the two of you."

Carolyn sighed. "Everything has to be so *difficult*," she complained.

"Only if you make it that way."

"What's that supposed to mean?"

"Secrets complicate things. I don't know what you're keeping to yourself, or what you might have told him that you haven't told me, but anytime someone in that kind of relationship tries to hide something, things get complicated."

"I—" Carolyn stopped short. It *was* her fault, really, no matter how hard she tried to pin the blame on anyone else. "Something happened," she began slowly, barely above a whisper. Finn slowed his pace so that his footsteps wouldn't drown out her voice, and Carolyn could tell he was listening – not just hearing, but understanding; not prying, but caring.

"It wasn't my fault, but I'm afraid that Matt would resent me for it, or break up with me for it, or... I don't know what." *What* would *Matt do? What am I so afraid of? God, it's not like I asked* him *to go as far as he did. ...Why in the world am I telling Finn all this?* Under the cover of night, it was easier to reveal the things inside of her that normally didn't see the light of day, and she continued with her story. "It was back in January..."

For the second time, she let it all spill out, but this time she didn't break down. She felt a tear roll down her cheek, but she brushed it away without letting Finn see. Their walk had slowed to a mere shuffle, and they had only just reached her block by the time she finished.

Finn kept silent until he was sure she was done. "That's what all this is about?" he finally asked.

"Look, it was a bigger deal to me than it would have been to most people, okay?" Carolyn snapped. She didn't want to say what she was thinking: *I'd only gotten my first kiss the night before.* She also couldn't bring herself to add what Paul had told her only yesterday. She would do her best to forget that had ever happened.

"No, I understand that. Completely. I just mean, you might be taking things too seriously, or worrying when you don't have to. ...Maybe I should shut up."

Carolyn managed a small laugh. "It's all right. You're one of the only people I can talk to like this. You're a good listener, you know that?"

"Oh... uh, thanks," Finn said uncomfortably. Carolyn laughed again at his shyness.

They made it to the end of her driveway. "Thanks for walking me home," Carolyn told him. "See you Monday."

"See you Monday," Finn repeated, locking his green eyes on hers for an instant. Carolyn couldn't be sure, but it looked like those eyes were sharing in her pain. "Take care."

I don't know why I did it. I went and told Finn everything. I mean, it was one thing to tell Molly. She's supposedly my best friend, even if neither of us is acting like it right now. She's not going to talk to Matt, and neither is Chris if she tells him — no matter how paranoid I get, I know it just isn't going to happen. But Finn — God, he and Matt are, like, best friends. If Chris had told me something like this and asked me not to say anything to Molly, do you think I'd be able to keep quiet about it? Psh, heck no! It's as good as over. I'm such a freaking idiot. WHY did I have to go and blab about it?

It's just that, I've always felt like I could trust Finn. I don't know. He's the kind of guy who understands everything, and always has some grain of wisdom to offer once I'm done ranting. I should be grateful I can talk to ANYONE these days, I guess, even if that someone is likely to reveal all to his buddy.

But what do I know? Maybe Finn will keep my secrets to himself. Maybe everything will be okay. As if that could ever happen, right?

122

February 28, 2000

Well, I was feeling inspired after talking to Finn (he tends to have that effect), so today, I was in such a generous mood that I spent all afternoon playing video games with Jimmie, and I even made him dinner. I was sort of hoping he'd open up and talk about his thoughts on Mom and Dad — I keep forgetting that boys don't do that kind of thing. But in spite of all my own problems, I've still found time to worry about that kid. I always used to be annoyed by him; it was a love-hate sort of relationship and for the most part, things worked out best when we left each other alone. But I can't leave him alone now, not when Mom and Dad are so absorbed in their conflict that they aren't putting enough effort into making sure he's all right. Someone's got to look out for him, and right now, I think it's going to have to be me. It's always me, isn't it?

CHAPTER THIRTEEN

The phone jangled in the next room, and Carolyn dove for it. "Hello?"

"Carolyn! Where are you?" asked a cheery Matt at the other end of the line. Since their dispute a few weeks ago, he'd seemed to forgive her odd behavior, though for a little while they'd been giving one another the cold shoulder. Carolyn, in turn, had made her best effort to clean up her act. Matt was right: she needed to focus on the two of them staying together, not everybody else's issues – and certainly not Paul. Carolyn learned to take every opportunity to let loose and enjoy herself, dropping in on parties every so often just to dance, and wandering the streets at night or skipping rocks across the ocean in the moonlight with her friends. Unfortunately, this behavior had prompted her parents to enforce her 10:00 curfew, which Carolyn resented, and she broke it by a good half an hour more than once. At least they hadn't grounded her for it, though they seemed to be losing patience with her rebelliousness (or maybe just with each other).

"Well, silly," Carolyn replied happily, retreating into her bedroom with the phone, "I'm obviously at home, since I'm talking to you."

Matt chuckled. "Well, talking's more fun face to face. Do you want to meet up?" Carolyn looked at the clock, but the reply was already on her lips.

"Absolutely. See you at the corner in five?"

"Sure thing." Waves of excitement zipped through the wires between them. She could practically hear him grinning, and realized that she already was. *I hope he kisses me...* she thought as she skipped down the stairs, out of the house, and along the sidewalk. *It's been too long since last time.*

Moments later, her wish came true. *Now* this *is how things were meant to be.... I can always count on Matt to make everything okay,* she mused happily. Ecstasy bubbled up inside of her like soda pop, fizzling over the top of her mind and covering both of them in bliss. *He never has to know about Paul. You* don't *even have to think about Paul. Forget he ever happened – that will be better revenge than any attention you could pay him.*

It was nearly an hour later when they found themselves sprawled on the beach, fingers entwined, Carolyn's head nestled into the nook between Matt's head and shoulder. She closed her eyes and breathed in the refreshing aroma of cologne and shampoo, a smile playing across her lips. His messy, strawberry toned hair tickled her forehead when the ocean breeze passed over them. Carolyn snuggled closer, wishing the tranquility and security of that moment could last forever. No more Paul, no more Mom and Dad, no more Molly and Chris, no more divas – just her and Matt, forever.

"What are you thinking about?" she breathed into his ear.

"That your hair smells like fruit," Matt replied, fingering a strand.

Carolyn giggled. "That's a funny thing to be thinking."

"Well, I didn't want to lie to you."

After another spell of silence, Matt said, "What are *you* thinking about?"

Carolyn sighed softly. "I'm thinking about how perfect this is right now, and how I wish it would never end, because I don't want to go back to school drama and my parents fighting."

Matt made a sympathetic noise. "They're still fighting?"

"Yeah, but I didn't really want to talk about it. I just didn't want to lie to you."

Matt chuckled. "Sometimes it's good to talk about those kinds of things."

She could tell he was fishing. He wanted her to say something so he could give her advice and be the supportive boyfriend. Not wanting to disappoint, she said, "I just don't understand what went wrong. They were always the perfect parents before, and now all of a sudden they just can't stand each other. How can two people who are in love make a one-eighty degree turn and suddenly hate each other's guts? It makes me feel like *I* must have done something to upset them, but I can't figure out what."

Matt didn't say anything at first. If he had been anyone else, Carolyn would have been offended, but Matt always took his time to formulate just the right response, so she waited patiently. Finally, he said slowly, "I can't say for sure what happened to make them change like this, but I can guarantee that it was nothing you did. Not everything is your fault. Not everything has to do with you. The world doesn't revolve around you."

"Everyone keeps telling me that!" Carolyn burst out, sitting up angrily. "It's just because they feel bad for me. *You* feel bad for me, I know you do."

"Carolyn!" Matt interjected, so reassuringly that Carolyn cut her rant short. Sitting up, he took both her hands in his. The sand grated between their palms. Carolyn held on tightly, fighting back tears, and forced herself to meet Matt's eyes. It was as though she was looking through them to the sky beyond, and that comforted her. Cautiously, almost imperceptibly, Matt leaned in. Their lips met, and Carolyn settled back into peacefulness.

Avoiding Paul that last week before spring break was easier than Carolyn had anticipated. Avoiding the divas was not. Carolyn had almost forgotten about Kate, Erin, and Shawna since they'd abandoned the group to return to popularity, but the three of them had apparently noticed the difference in Carolyn, and they latched onto her struggles like parasites, making her life more miserable every time she failed to evade them. The beginning of the week was bad, but Thursday was the killer.

Kate and Shawna approached her, with Erin tagging along behind them like a parasite on a parasite. Carolyn narrowed her eyes. Enough was enough. She determined to keep her mouth shut. "Hey, emo girl," Kate sneered. The other two laughed, and Carolyn's lip curled in disgust. She retorted in her head. *Having problems doesn't make me emo. In fact, I think I'm better off than the people who drink until they can't remember their names — let alone their problems. I think we can all guess who I'm talking about, here.* "Where do you get those nice outfits you always wear?" Kate feigned actual interest, but Carolyn continued to ignore them. Lately she *had* been wearing darker colors — black Converse sneakers, dark jeans, black and white checkered belts — the darker the color, the better. She figured that people were more likely to leave her alone when she dressed edgy. She knew for a fact that the divas would not be caught dead in an outfit like that, especially not with spring in the air — they were all about the pastels and flouncy skirts. There had been a time *she* would not have been caught dead in an outfit like that, either.

Times had changed — *but some people never do.*

"Because, you know," Kate continued in her most superior tone, "Erin is having a costume party, and Shawn and I thought it might be fun to dress up like *boys.*"

Carolyn and Erin opened their mouths to protest simultaneously, but Carolyn checked herself, and Shawna jabbed Erin in the ribs to keep her from saying anything. Carolyn surmised there *was* no costume party, and Kate had merely invented it as an excuse to pick on *her.*

127

"Emo girl, how come you don't talk to us anymore?" Shawna asked, pouting insincerely. "Do you hate us all of a sudden?"

"Well, why shouldn't I?" Carolyn burst out. "I'm not the one who abandoned the people who were supposed to be my friends. I'm not the one who goes out drinking every weekend! I'm not the one who can't keep a boyfriend longer than a week, and I'm not the one who traded the friends who actually cared about her for ones that just pretend to – and only for as long as you play along with their games! No, that was *you*, and I'm sick of putting up with all your bull. Just get lost and leave me alone, okay?"

"O-kay," Kate said, widening her make-up rimmed eyes and acting frightened of Carolyn's tough front. She tugged at a red curl, winding it around her finger over and over. Carolyn mentally fingered her own limp, mahogany hair. She hadn't had the energy to blow dry it in a while, and the lack of effort showed. "Well, you know, I think you *are* the one who's abandoned her friends. I mean, look at us, look at Molly, look at Chris." Kate counted them off on her fingers. "Look at how you didn't speak to any of *them* for a month, and look at where that's gotten you. No friends." She smiled in satisfaction.

Carolyn snorted. "I do, too, have friends. Margo and Tori and Anne and Aisling and Matt and Finn and Nick are *all* my friends."

Kate rolled her eyes. "Okay," she said again, implying that she knew something Carolyn didn't.

"And another thing," Shawna piped up, not wanting to let Kate get all the attention. "If you think *we* can't choose a boyfriend, look at yourself. I haven't had a boyfriend since the beginning of seventh grade."

Carolyn laughed bitterly. "Really. Then what was Paul?"

"Oh, just a fling. Flings are my specialty." She flipped her perfectly groomed, waist-length mane of artificial gold as if to say, 'and rightfully so. Who wouldn't want *this?*' Carolyn remembered the days Shawna's hair had been as dark as her deep black eyes, and resented her for dyeing it. Black was

128

so much more attractive than that silly, fake platinum blonde. At least she had ditched the phony blue contact lenses, which in Carolyn's opinion had always clashed with her olive complexion. "You, on the other hand, can't seem to make up your mind. First Matt, then Paul and Finn. You can't have them all, you know."

Carolyn felt like she'd been punched in the stomach, and gaped speechlessly before retorting. The girls had already turned to go, reveling in the success of the hunt, when she snapped, "I can't believe you would even think any of this! I have never *once* been disloyal to Matt! I hate Paul's guts, and Finn happens to be a *friend*. Yeah, have you ever heard of the concept of boys as *friends?* Sometimes they make a whole lot more sense than *girls.*"

Shawna laughed, turning back to face Carolyn and doing her best to appear magnanimous. "Carolyn, Carolyn," she chided. "Everybody knows that Finn likes you, and everybody can see that you like him back. And don't think Paul hasn't told us about the two of you." She winked. "Better pick and choose. You can't have every boy in the school, now. It isn't fair."

Carolyn gaped and tried to force her fisted hands to loosen as she searched for a response. Paul had told *them?* "Are you fricken kidding me?" she burst out. The other girls' chins dropped, and Carolyn actually felt pleased at drawing out such a dramatic reaction.

"Somebody's a potty mouth," Shawna trilled. "Watch it there, Mrs. Trucker-Smith-Riley-McGregor," she simpered, prancing away with her obnoxious cronies. She glanced back to smirk, and Carolyn flipped her off. She kicked the nearest locker in frustration as soon as they'd rounded the corner. *I hate them, I hate them!* She kicked the locker again and stormed off down the hall. One more class to go, but she wouldn't be there. She wished she never had to be there again. She checked the hall furtively, but most people had already made it to their next class, and the ones who hadn't were rushing to beat the bell and didn't spare her so much as a passing glance. Even as she made for the door, she told herself this was crazy. *Just let it go. They aren't worth it, and they're only spewing lies anyway.*

Gah, but I just can't take it! I'm gonna explode if I have to stay here forty more minutes. Carolyn took off out the side door. *God, what do you think they're going to do to you for skipping out?* she wondered.

After wandering aimlessly for a time, she wound up at the beach, where she took off her new sneakers, rolled up her pants, and ran into the ocean, desperately wishing she could just let the tide carry her away somewhere. *Why did we ever have to leave Alaska?* She hadn't missed home so much once she'd adjusted to California, but now the same old feelings of resentment toward her new home came rushing back at her. Nothing had *really* gone right since she'd arrived. She'd just convinced herself things had been great.

Carolyn waded out as deep as the waistline of her pants, wishing for a swimsuit. Goose flesh appeared all over her body, and Carolyn relished the cold. All of a sudden, she dove under and made for the deeper water. She stayed under the surface, swimming away from the beach with all her might and keeping close to the bottom of the sea, for as long as she could hold her breath. The frigid temperature of the water, the weight of her clothing and the water pressing down on her somehow comforted her, in a twisted way, and she never wanted to surface. She waited, waited, until her lungs burned and cried out for oxygen. Finally, when she couldn't take it anymore, she pushed off the bottom and rocketed toward the surface. *This isn't right!* She thought in panic. *It's too far up!* Miles and miles up, so far up she couldn't see the sky from where she was. *I wonder if anyone would miss me if I drowned,* she pondered. As an automatic reflex, her lungs inhaled – hard – and she swallowed salt water. *I hope not, cause this is it – I'm dead.*

Suddenly, a set of arms wrapped around her and pulled her upward. Carolyn felt the body warmth of her rescuer and realized how cold she had become. In her delirium, she was certain she was in the arms of an angel. She snaked her arms around his neck and held on for dear life. They broke the surface, and Carolyn sputtered, coughed, and wheezed as her able hero transported her somewhat awkwardly to safety. She gasped for breath and tried to clear her vision of the little black dots swimming around in front of her eyes. When her thoughts straightened themselves out, she realized she hadn't seen a lifeguard when she arrived at the beach. No one had been around – it was only the middle of March, and for the most part, people still had school and work to keep them away from the beach during the day. The tourists weren't around since spring vacation hadn't yet begun. *Who, then...?*

They reached the shoreline, and as the angel deposited her on the shore, Carolyn was finally able to catch a glimpse of her rescuer. The reality startled her beyond speech. *"Finn?"* she finally blurted. "How the heck did you find me?" She clambered away from the water and sat cross-legged in the sand, unable to forget what Shawna had said earlier about Finn liking her. *It's ridiculous, of course. Can you imagine...?*

"I have a better question," he said grimly, shaking the water out of his hair, which, in seeming defiance of gravity, returned to its original mussed appearance. "What the heck were you doing?"

Carolyn nodded slowly. "That's fair. I don't really know. I had a run in with Kate, Erin, and Shawna after lunch–"

"I already know that. Kate was going on about it in science. She said she'd make sure you got suspended – not that I'd believe *her*," he quickly reassured Carolyn as she stared at him in horror. "But I can't figure what you were thinking."

"You should have heard the things she was saying. She said I cheated on Matt–"

"And did you?"

"NO!"

"Then why let it upset you?"

Carolyn shook her head. "They've been at it all week. I can't take it anymore. I hate it here. I want to go back to Alaska."

"That's not an option," Finn said sternly, sitting in the sand nearby. "You have to stop running away from your problems, Caro. They can run faster than you. They'll catch up to you every time."

Carolyn groaned and hugged her knees close, digging her cold toes into the rough sand for warmth and finding none. "I still don't get how you found me," she said, changing the subject.

Finn smiled and decided to humor her. "Nick said he looked out the window and saw you booking it down the sidewalk. As soon as I got out of class, I took off in the direction he said you went, but I never expected to find you. But of course, I showed up at the beach just in time to see you disappear underwater, and when you didn't come back up for a long time, I started to worry that you were trying to drown yourself."

"Why did you come after me?" Carolyn asked bemusedly.

"So you wouldn't drown yourself!" he said, exasperated.

"No, I mean, why did you come in the first place?"

Finn seemed unable to give a coherent answer. "I don't know, I guess to tell you you were stupid."

"Gee, thanks."

"Well, you're lucky I did," he pointed out. "And now I think you're doubly stupid. *Were* you trying to drown yourself?"

"No. I was just... I don't know. Thanks, I guess."

"No problem."

They sat quietly for a little bit, and Carolyn's thoughts raced. *'To tell you you were stupid' isn't really an answer. Who does that? Why would Finn really track me down? Geez. What a weird kid.*

A second voice in her head joined the argument. *Because he's your friend and he actually gives a crap about what happens to you. Is this a new concept to you? Caring about other people? I thought that was what you did best.*

The first voice counterattacked. *But why Finn? How come Matt didn't show up? Where are the rest of your "friends?"*

Oh, come on now. How could they have known?

How could they not *have known? If Finn could figure out you were in trouble, how come no one else could?*

Finn's very perceptive like that. If the others had known, they would have come. You're just overanalyzing because of what Shawna said. She envisioned things getting really awkward between them now that that little seed of question had been planted in her mind.

Oh, my God, I'm arguing with myself. I must be insane. Carolyn groaned out loud.

"What's the matter?" Finn asked.

"Everything about me is such a mess."

"No! No, you're not a mess!" Finn objected gently. Carolyn closed her eyes to hide the tears and lay back on the sand.

"I'm not?"

"No!" She could hear a laugh in his voice, and couldn't decide whether to be upset or thankful that he could laugh at a time like this. "Carolyn, we've all got issues. If we were all normal – well, how weird would that be?"

Carolyn found herself laughing along. "Yeah, I guess that *would* be pretty boring," she agreed. "I don't know. I just feel like something is so wrong with me...."

"Do you remember when I told you that you were taking life too seriously?"

"Yeah. After that I tried to lighten up. I was doing a good job, too, until Kate and Shawna ganged up on me."

Finn shook his head. "But then you weren't doing a good job. If you're not taking life seriously because there's nothing there to take seriously, then it doesn't count. It only counts if something *could* be taken seriously but *you* are able to rise above it."

"Geez, where do you get all this stuff?"

Finn chuckled. "Honestly? I B.S. about half of it." Carolyn opened an eye and glanced up at him incredulously. "But does it make you feel better?" She nodded. "Then it's worth it."

"But Finn," Carolyn said after a pause, following the path of a meandering seagull across the overcast sky. "Do you want to know what they said about me? Or about *you?*"

"Not really," he admitted. She could feel his eyes on her, and continued staring fixedly at the sky to avoid making eye contact.

"Well…. Can I tell you anyway?"

"Sure," Finn chuckled.

"They thought that there was something between you and me. They said I was cheating on Matt with you."

For the second time that day, Finn seemed to be at a loss for words. "That's ridiculous," he told her. "Like I said: Don't listen to them."

"If only I could be that confident…."

I just about got in a fist fight with Kate, Erin and Shawna today. Yeah, three on one — the odds were hardly fair, even in a catty verbal fight. I'd almost rather they punched me out. It would be better than listening to the kinds of things they say to me, and it would have felt a lot better to just hit them back. I'm going to feel really awkward around Finn because Shawna's got this idea that he likes me, but I mean — it's Finn, for God's sake. We're like, best friends. But now that the idea is there — well, I can't help but wonder if she's right, especially after he pretty much saved my life today, and let me tell you, wondering if she's right EVERY TIME I see him is going to complicate things once again. Even worse, I went and told him what they said about us, so now the idea is there in HIS head, too. But then again, guys probably don't let that kind of thing faze them the way girls do.

    I do find it rather funny the way that Erin tends to mess up their schemes to torment me. She doesn't mean to; she just isn't very bright, and I don't think she's as catty as the other two — she's just permanently latched onto Shawna and can't escape the expectations those two have for her. Anyway, it sort of reminds me to take whatever crap they give me from the source, even if it makes me spitting mad — chances are, they just made something up because they knew it would make me spitting mad. I'll have to think of that next time they say anything.

I miss preschool, back when me and Leah and the neighborhood boys would finger paint together at a low wooden table, all one big happy family.

One big happy family. It's like the epitome of the American Dream. Everyone wants to know what the American Dream is, but it's not hard to figure out. Get rich, and live in a freaking huge mansion with your family while other people do all the hard work like cooking and cleaning. A mom and a dad, raising their two or three kids in Clonesville, Suburbia, where teachers will one day pressure them to be successful and live out the American Dream, while peers pressure them to look, act, and talk just like everyone else. Looks like the Dream got twisted into a nightmare. How far has it actually gotten me, huh? That's right. It's all bunk.

I don't even think I'm making sense anymore. Well screw that, anyway. I'm off to bed. At least when I'm asleep I can pretend like things won't always be like this.

I feel like a skipping record. I'm just stuck like this. Someone help me.... Please.

Message from: Carolyn Becker <SkiBlink@aol.com>
To: Leah Sorman <PussyCat240@aol.com>
Re: A bit of my life story (can I hear some of yours?)

I'm with you on the Veggie Tales thing. Take me back to kindergarten. No more drama, please. Hope you have fun on your missions trip. Good luck with church boy. At any rate your luck will probably be better than mine. Please don't ask about my love life anymore.

CIB

YOU'RE ALIVE!!! I'm so happy! Aww, but I want to send you a zillion hugs in an envelope, too. What's wrong with your love life? Don't tell me you and Matt broke up already? Just when mine was starting to look up (and by that, I mean I got to shake church boy's hand during greeting at the Sunday service again. I don't even know his name.) So you're probably still better off than me. Sigh. My life could use a little more drama. No fair that you get it all. Just because you live in Soap Opera Central. Haha just kidding, just kidding. Praying for ya!

~LBS~

CHAPTER FOURTEEN

Spring break finally rolled around to bring respite from the constant torment of the terrible trio. Carolyn spent every possible moment with Matt and avoided contact with Finn, just to prove that there was absolutely nothing between them. She also dedicated another afternoon to hanging out with Jimmie. They walked to the nearby ice cream parlor and Carolyn treated him to a huge sundae, even though the expense meant forgoing her own snack.

"Why are you being so nice to me?" Jimmie asked. His wide hazel eyes, matching his sister's and their father's in shade, narrowed. Carolyn automatically reached over with a napkin to wipe fudge off his innocently rounded chin, but he snatched it away, insisting that he could wipe his own face.

Carolyn merely shrugged in response to his question. "Are you having fun?"

Jimmie nodded. "Then that's why," she said by way of explanation. Jimmie's smooth, broad brow furrowed. Carolyn could tell that he was more bewildered than ever and smiled to herself as he slurped down chocolate and melting ice cream. She still had it in her. If nothing else, at least she could help her little brother.

The phone rang Wednesday afternoon. Carolyn lunged for it, expecting to hear Matt's smooth and eager tone, but it was Margo's voice that reached her. "Where have you been all week?"

"With Matt," Carolyn said dreamily, remembering the way she sparkled every time he kissed her.

She heard Margo sigh somewhere down the line. "Snap out of it, Carolyn! We're Millennium Girls, not Millennium Girlfriends: for Boys Only. What about your *friends*?"

"I – I guess I've been neglecting you a little lately, huh?"

"A little might be an understatement." Margo sounded hurt. Carolyn knew how sensitive she could be, and hurried to solve the problem.

"We can hang out today if you want. Call the girls up, and we'll have an old fashioned Millennium Girl Party," she suggested.

"It's not 'old fashioned,' Carolyn," Margo corrected harshly. "You just haven't been around enough lately."

"Oh. Well… I'm sorry, I guess. I didn't realize. Can I make it up to you?"

"Why don't you?" Margo said icily. "Come on over and we'll chillax. See you in a few." Margo hung up. Carolyn winced and placed the phone in its cradle. *Yes, I screwed this one up pretty nicely. Once again. Bravo. This seems to be my new trademark.* With a sigh, she laced her Chucks and wheeled her bike out of the garage. *When will I get something right?* Pedaling seemed to take far more effort than it should have, yet she arrived at the Gilmans' sooner than she would have liked. Margo opened the door before Carolyn even had to knock, and led her upstairs in silence.

The walls of her room were pale yellow and reflected the sunlight streaming in through the open window. "Did you paint your room?" Carolyn asked by way of small talk.

Margo glowered. "Yes, in *January*, which you would have known if you'd been around like a friend is supposed to."

Carolyn winced. "I didn't mean to-"

"Of course. I *know* you didn't mean to. Molly didn't mean to, either. But you know what, Carolyn? I'm not going to watch everyone I care about leave me behind because they've found *boys* they happen to like better than me." Margo paced to the window and yanked the curtains shut, throwing the bright room into shadow. "That's not what Millennium Girls were supposed to be, Carolyn," she whispered tearfully. "We were *never* supposed to let boys come between us."

Carolyn felt tears welling up in her own eyes. "Margo, I'm so sorry..." she muttered. "It's not what you think, either. It's not Matt's fault. Please don't blame him for this."

"I know. It's *not* Matt's fault. It's *your* fault for ditching *us* for *him*," Margo accused.

"No! You don't understand." *I can't tell her about Paul... I can't, but I might have to. God. What will she think of me?*

"Yeah? I think I'm seeing a lot more clearly than you."

"Maybe that's true. Look, Margo, I realize I've been a bad friend. Everything else you're saying is completely true, but I never ditched you for Matt. I didn't mean to *ditch* anyone." She stopped, hoping she wouldn't have to go further, but Margo didn't speak. She sat delicately on the spring green bedspread and awaited an explanation. Carolyn sighed in frustration. "I *really* don't want to talk about this."

"Well, you're going to have to, Carolyn. I'm not convinced yet." Margo's face was stony, her features carved in granite like an emotionless statue, so unlike her usual concerned self.

Carolyn groaned and sank down beside Margo on the bed. If she wanted to keep Margo as a friend, she was going to have to spill, but the more people who knew, the more likely it was that Matt would find out. *Matt or Margo?*

"Margo… you have to swear never to tell anyone about this, okay? Molly found out, and I'm not really worried about her talking since she only talks to Chris and he only talks to her. But you and me, we're friends with the same people, and I don't know what I'd do if they heard this. They'd think I was terrible."

"God, Carolyn, what did you do?"

"It wasn't my fault!" Once again, she told her story.

"You're right, Carolyn, *you* didn't do anything! It was all Paul's fault, *not* yours!" Margo wrapped Carolyn in a hug and stroked her friend's hair soothingly. "Why do you blame yourself for everybody else's mistakes?"

"I'm not blaming myself, I'm just… embarrassed. And scared. Of what people will think of me, I mean."

"But you are! I know you, Carolyn, you're blaming yourself for what *Paul* did, and I know you blame yourself for your parents' fighting, too."

Carolyn threw herself backwards onto the bed, letting the poufy comforter console her. Margo was right again. Carolyn had never figured out what exactly the two of them were fighting over, but she couldn't fix it, and it suddenly became her fault. She'd become so used to their alternating bickering and cold silence that she'd almost forgotten they were fighting. "Right again," she admitted.

"But *why*, Carolyn? It's between the two of them and has nothing to do with you!"

"But it has *everything* to do with me. I have to live there. I have to go to sleep wondering if they'll get a divorce. I have to act like everything's perfect so they don't have any extra burdens on their backs, and so Jimmie will believe me when I say they'll stay married. God, I miss talking to my mom. She would know what to do," Carolyn mourned. "But I can't make her worry about her marriage *and* all *my* issues."

"Oh, *you* don't have issues. You have to deal with other people's issues. Namely, Paul's," Margo reassured her.

Carolyn smiled weakly. "I just wish everything could be the way it used to be."

"I know what you mean," Margo concurred. "I wish that every day, but I don't think we're ever going back. Just do me a favor, okay? Don't carry all this stuff by yourself. If you *must* take everything so seriously, tell someone about it. I hope you know you can tell me anything, Carolyn. I'm here for you. I'm still your friend, okay?"

Carolyn sniffled, nodded, and hugged her friend again. "Thanks, Margo."

"Don't mention it." Margo pushed the shades back and let the room fill with sunlight again, her countenance mirroring its brightness. "So what should we do today?"

"Let's get the girls together and just hang out," Carolyn suggested. They trotted down the stairs and out into the rapidly warming springtime afternoon. "Where to first?"

"Let's go around the block and get Tori, then barge in on Anne and make her bake us something," Margo proposed.

"Excellent."

Tori made them wait on the doorstep while she styled her hair and put on make-up. Carolyn found a piece of chalk and decorated the front stoop while they waited. "Why does she need eye-liner to go to Anne's house?" she whined.

"Because she thinks she can get a date with Skitt," Margo said seriously. Carolyn laughed, but she quickly realized that Margo wasn't kidding.

"That's ridiculous! Skitt's a senior!" She pressed down too hard and snapped the chalk in half by accident, scraping her knuckles in the process.

"I know." Margo bent over and traced her name in the dirt by the steps. "But try telling her that. You know Tori."

"That's true. She loves her older boys. And boys in general." Carolyn chucked the broken chalk out into the street and watched a passing car crush it into purple dust. "Well, the good news is she'll probably be over him by this time next week."

"I don't know, I think she's got her heart set on this one."

"She'd better be careful or she'll get it broken," Carolyn commented.

"She's had enough broken hearts by now. She can handle it," Margo said spitefully.

"Margo Riley! Are you jealous?"

"Hah! As if!" Margo barked. "Well… maybe a little. It's just, how is it that she can have a new boy every week, and I've only ever had one, and I mean… well, look at him." She wrinkled her nose to express just what she thought of Nick now that they were no longer dating.

"Nick isn't so bad," Carolyn countered. "Well, I mean, it's not like I've ever gone out with him. But he's pretty good at Dance Dance Revolution."

"Great, that helps a lot."

"Well… DDR is the bomb, what can I say?"

Margo laughed. "I suppose the boys you want are the ones you can have a good time with. The ones you feel comfortable around. The ones you can be yourself in front of and not worry about being uncoordinated on the dance floor. Or pad, in this case." Carolyn laughed too.

The door opened behind them, and both girls leapt to their feet. Tori emerged wearing a miniskirt and a short-sleeved v-neck, plus about ten pounds of make-up. "How do I look?" she asked excitedly.

"…Too old to be Tori," Carolyn said candidly.

"Wash off some of the make-up," Margo suggested, squinting in the sunlight.

Tori gave them both a look. "You guys are just jealous that Skitt's going to like me better," she pouted.

"Oh, yeah, that's it, all right," Carolyn said sarcastically. "Because I would sooo much rather have Skitt than *Matt*."

Unable to come up with a clever response, Tori stuck her nose in the air, pushed past them and led the way to the sidewalk. "Well? Is anyone else coming?"

Carolyn and Margo leapt to their feet, exchanging a helpless glance as they pattered down the concrete walkway. "There's nothing we can do to stop her," Margo mouthed, shrugging in defeat.

"I'm not sure I want to be associated with her," Carolyn mouthed back. Margo rolled her eyes as if to say, 'me, either.' Tori walked briskly, and even Carolyn with her long legs was struggling to keep up. The green trees had begun to show their flowers, and the palm trees were looking perkier now that the warmer weather had moved in. It had taken them longer than last year because of the cold spell, but the hibiscus were in bloom, lending cheery colors to the scene and failing to indicate the ridiculous drama they were all caught up in. Carolyn sighed and wished her life could be as serene as the California coastline.

They followed Tori up Anne's driveway and saw that Skitt was shooting hoops out beside the house.

"Good luck even getting *that* one inside," Margo muttered in Carolyn's ear, gesturing at Tori, who was too blinded to pay any attention to them anymore. "God, see what I mean? Everyone I love is too in love with someone else to pay any attention to me anymore." She snorted in disgust. "I thought we all decided to put each other first, and look how far *that's* gotten us."

Carolyn put her arm around Margo's shoulders sympathetically. "Let's get Anne to whip up some cookies, okay?" Margo nodded, and they veered toward the door. Margo let them into the Salt and Pepper Shaker Room and shouted for Anne. Anne appeared at the top of the staircase in the living room.

"Oh, God," she moaned, and turned and ran back up.

Carolyn and Margo looked at each other in confusion. "What?"

"Is she mad about me and Matt, too?"

"Not that I ever knew about."

"I suppose we should go find out what's wrong then." They treaded cautiously through the Shaker Room and the living room, up the stairs, down the hall and up to Anne's closed door.

"Anne?" Carolyn said to the oak.

"Go away." Anne's voice was muffled, hardly audible through the thick wood between them.

Instead, Margo barged into the room. "Dude, what's going on? Why are you so upset?" Anne was lying in a heap on her bed. The covers were all over the place, and pillows and stuffed animals were strewn across the floor. The blinds were shut over the sliding door that led out to the porch. Anne rolled over and it became clear that she'd been crying.

Margo rushed over to give her a hug. Carolyn hovered awkwardly and took a seat on the vanity chair. Margo murmured comforting things to Anne, and Carolyn waited expectantly for an explanation.

"Well, you might remember… a while ago, my parents made me take those entrance exams for Santa Catalina."

Carolyn didn't remember, but it was probably her fault for not listening rather than Anne's for not telling her, so she nodded.

"Well…. I got in."

"Congratulations! Why are you crying about that?" Carolyn squealed.

"Because it's a *boarding* school," Anne said, as though instructing a particularly stupid pre-school student. "A *Catholic, all-girls* boarding school in *Monterey*."

"Are they making you go?" Carolyn asked indignantly, standing up and knocking the chair over in her anger. "They can't *make* you go, can they?"

"They're my parents. They can make me do whatever they want." Anne laughed grimly. "They wanted Skitt to go to private school, too. Apparently he bombed the entrance exams on purpose." She laughed again, a bitter, painful, choking sound. "I was smart enough to get in, but not smart enough to figure out how to stay out."

"God, this sucks," Carolyn said, collapsing on the bed beside her.

"What will we do without each other?" Margo asked tearfully, stroking Anne's peeled-banana colored hair. Anne could only shake her head.

After a nice long pity party, which involved chocolate ice cream, hot fudge, whipped cream and every other topping they could find in the cabinets, Anne seemed a little less blue. "At least we've got e-mail now," she said. "Imagine if I'd had to go ten years ago before the Internet was invented."

"How can you always see the bright side of things?" Carolyn asked in wonder. "All *I* can see is no more disco bowling Fridays, no more ice cream fests – like the one we just had – no more sleep-overs-"

"Carolyn, don't be such a doom-spewer. God. Let me have my little moment of happiness," Anne said. "I can't have an ice cream sundae every time you get me down."

"Well, you *could*," Margo said pensively. "But you might get a little fat."

Anne laughed. "And then get expelled right out of Santa Clause School or whatever it's called because I can't play sports anymore. Right, good plan."

"Hey, if it'll get you expelled..."

They drifted outside, where Tori was taking Skitt on in HORSE, and apparently losing. "I've got H," Skitt announced. "Tori has, like, Horse running and jumping over the fence in the pasture."

"Shut up, Mr. Six-foot-five basketball star." Tori faked throwing the ball at him, and Skitt flinched. "Can you get an 'O' for that?"

"Sure, if it makes you feel better. But I still won."

"Hey Tori, if you could stop, uh, *socializing* for a minute here, Anne has some news for you," Margo said.

"What's up?" Tori turned and gave them her attention, beads of sweat standing out on her face and a flush, which could have been caused by the heat, the exertion, or the presence of Skitt, turning her face and neck pink as the blooming hibiscus.

"Can we... not here?"

"I don't think that's a verb, but sure," Tori agreed. She waved over her shoulder at Skitt and flipped her hair as the girls ran inside.

"Oh. My. God," Tori said as soon as Anne told her the news. "We're never gonna see you again! Omigod! I can't believe this is happening! This is the worst thing ever! How far away is Monterey, even? It's got to be like a day's drive! I can't *believe* your parents are making you-"

"Tori, could you like, *try* not to make her feel worse?" Margo suggested coldly. "We've already been through this once. No more ice cream, okay?"

"Oh, it's okay, I don't need any ice cream," Tori declined quickly. "I'm on a health kick. See, I've lost weight already!"

"Tori, this isn't about you!" Carolyn snapped. "You've got to stop with the crazy diets!"

Tears welled up in Tori's eyes, and Carolyn knew she'd done it now. Tori had a sensitive (or just histrionic) soul, and she'd upset the balance. "I thought you were my friend. You're supposed to be supportive of me!"

"Yeah, and know what? If you were *fat* and trying to lose weight, I would be!"

"You're just jealous I have a better body! It's not like you ever let anybody see yours, anyway, though, with your stupid jeans in the 80-degree weather. Punk!"

Carolyn reeled. "Anorexic!" she shot back. Margo and Anne backed away nervously, sensing a catfight.

"Goth!"

"Slut!"

Tori gasped. "I hate you!" She ran out the door, slamming it behind her. Carolyn winced. Oak is heavy. She got déjà vu as another shaker crashed to the floor.

"That's it!" Anne growled, practically in tears. "Everybody get out! I'll wallow in my misery by myself." She stormed up the stairs without another word, leaving the remnants of a ceramic rooster for someone else to sweep up.

Skitt appeared in the doorway moments later. "I guess she took the news a little hard?"

"I wouldn't talk if I were you," Margo warned. "You might set off the bomb." She glared pointedly at Carolyn as she said this, and didn't quit glaring until she'd made it out the door.

"Why? What did you do?" Skitt asked.

"She put me up to it!" Carolyn defended herself.

"Who, Tori?" Carolyn nodded. "Well, Tori's very competitive," he granted, digging through the fridge for a drink. He emerged with a red Gatorade and downed half of it in seconds. "*Very* competitive," he repeated.

"And sensitive," Carolyn added. "And she can be *nasty*. You should have heard the things she was saying to me! I was only retaliating for what she did first."

"What did she say?" Skitt asked, almost with amusement. Carolyn, realizing she could turn Skitt against Tori by revealing what she'd said, gladly shared.

"She told me I was a bad friend because I didn't support her trying to lose weight," Carolyn began, leaning against the marble countertop.

"*She's* trying to lose weight?" Skitt interrupted, incredulous. "Is she anorexic?"

"I don't know. So far I think she's just insecure, but I guess she could be." Carolyn pondered for a minute, figuring she probably should be worried but too angry to let herself care. "But *then*," she continued, dismissing the problem as though it didn't exist. "*Then* she told me I was *jealous* of her 'figure,' which really won't be much for long if she stays on her so-called 'health kick,' which is Tori-code for 'diet.'"

"If it makes you feel better, the anorexic thing kind of scares me. I think you have a better figure than Tori."

"And *then* she – wait, *what?*" Carolyn stopped short. *Did he really just say I had a good figure? I think* I'm *a little scared, myself.* She looked at Skitt, who had a silly grin stretching from ear to perfect ear. "You're not helping!" Carolyn exploded, and she took off too. Skitt seemed absolutely mystified at her response, and Carolyn nearly laughed at the look on his face, but in all truth, she felt more like crying. Tori hated her, Margo and Anne were mad at her for being a jerk to Tori (who *totally* deserved it!), and even if she could convince them to be her friends again, it wouldn't change the fact that Anne was leaving at the end of the summer.

When Carolyn came to the corner of the street, she turned back down Margo's road, but not to visit with Margo. No, right then, what she really needed – even more than an ice cream sundae, though that had been good – was a nice, big dose of Matt. She composed herself and approached his front door, which opened before Carolyn even reached it.

"Carolyn! How good to see you!" Mrs. MacMillan cried, throwing her arms around Carolyn's waist, which was about as high as she could reach.

"Good to see you, too, ma'am." Carolyn returned the hug and scanned the downstairs for signs of Matt. "Is Matt home?"

"Oh, don't be in such a hurry!" Mrs. MacMillan chided. "Come have some cookies!" She took Carolyn by the hand and dragged her over to the kitchen, where the scent of *something* filled Carolyn's nostrils, but it was hard to tell exactly what. "I'm afraid they might have gotten a little burnt...." Mrs.

MacMillan chattered away, presenting Carolyn with a tray of charred circles, which vaguely resembled chocolate chip cookies. To be polite, Carolyn took the least black one she could find. "Have some milk! If you dip the cookies in it, they'll soften right up!" She busied herself finding a glass and a carton of milk.

"Oh, don't worry about it," Carolyn said. "I just need to talk to Matt for a little bit... had a rough day."

"Well, then you'd *better* take another cookie!" Mrs. Macmillan insisted, offering her the tray again. Carolyn smiled shakily and helped herself to another. "What happened?"

Carolyn dunked the cookie in the glass of milk Mrs. MacMillan had placed in front of her. "I don't know exactly. Anne's going to private school next year in Monterey. Tori was too busy flirting with Anne's way older brother to pay attention, and then she started complaining about how we aren't supportive friends, and she called me stuff, and I called her stuff, and now I think most of my friends hate me." She didn't mention Anne's way older brother hitting on her, though. Carolyn's voice broke and she let her head fall onto the table.

"Aww, sweetie, I'm sorry," Mrs. MacMillan said comfortingly. "Friends can be difficult, especially at your age. There's so much drama in high school. You've just got to learn to rise above it, dear. I'll be praying for you, all right?"

Carolyn nodded, wishing that was as reassuring as the poor old lady had meant it to be. "I'm not even *in* high school yet," she reminded Matt's grandma.

"Well, I should warn you that it doesn't get much better, so learn to handle it delicately now," she said sagely. "Don't let it get you down. By the end of the week, you'll all be friends again."

"I hope so."

Footsteps sounded on the stairway, and Carolyn lifted her head off the table. Matt came into view, peering curiously into the kitchen. "Carolyn? I thought I heard your voice! What are you doing here?" He sniffed and wrinkled his nose. "And what burnt?"

"Just the cookies, dear," Mrs. MacMillan explained. "Have one! They're quite good when dunked in milk, right Carolyn?" She winked conspiratorially, and Carolyn nodded energetically, dunking the cookie and taking a big bite to prove it, and doing her best not to grimace.

"No thanks, Grandma. I need to talk to Carolyn."

Talk? Talking can be bad. I hope he didn't overhear everything and decide to break up with me for being a jerk...no, that's ridiculous! You didn't say enough to make him want to break up with you. Of course, you haven't exactly been a little ray of sunshine lately. Maybe you depress him. Like Anne said. Doom-Spewer. She followed Matt downstairs, where the TV and other electronics were kept. They sat on the ugly green couch, the one that looked like it must have seen better days when the family bought it, let alone *now.* "What do you want to talk about?" Carolyn asked nervously.

"We don't have to talk," he said with a sly smile. "I just said that to give Grandma peace of mind. She doesn't think we should kiss."

"...Oh."

"But that's not stopping me," he whispered, leaning in. Carolyn leaned too, and moments later she was right back on Cloud Nine where she belonged. *Matt can make everything right,* she thought. *Always. I can always count on him to make me feel like I'm flying, like I'm sparkling with magic, like I'm more alive than ever before. Maybe Molly was right. Maybe we* can *figure out what love is this soon, if only we find the right person.*

I love how I have these little internal monologues while I'm kissing...

"Carolyn," Matt said suddenly, pulling back. "This doesn't seem... right."

"What do you mean?" Carolyn asked, offended. "Not because of your grandma?"

Matt shook his head. "Only partly." *Oh, God. What did I do wrong? He must have found out about Paul!* Her thoughts and heart raced. *And I thought today couldn't possibly get any worse.* "I'm different, I guess," Matt began. *Oh, I'm getting the 'it's not you, it's me' speech. How touching.* "No, I *know* I'm different." He got up and began pacing. Carolyn watched his feet, worried he might trip over the game system cords before he could explain this madness. "I'm not the Matt you were at the movies with two weeks ago."

"Don't be silly! Of course you're the same Matt." She brushed the comment aside. *Unless… unless he's been cheating on me with someone! Maybe he had a Paul incident! Uh… with a girl, I mean.* But she had to make sure: "You still like me, right?"

"Don't you dare think for one second that I don't like you!" Matt said sharply. "In fact, we are only having this conversation because I care about you… a *lot*. And because I've completely changed." There he went again, talking about how different he was as if it should be obvious! Carolyn scrutinized him. She knew him so well! Why couldn't she see this change he was talking about? Had he trimmed his hair? How was that "completely changed?" It must be something else.

"What are you talking about?" she finally asked. "You seem the same to me." *Except you're spewing nonsense, but aside from that.*

"Here's the thing," Matt began earnestly. "You know how Grandma moved in when Mom got sick." Surprised at the randomness and unnecessary nature of the comment, Carolyn furrowed her eyebrows.

"Of course. She started in with all that crazy religious brainwashing of hers, and she burnt all the cookies. So it *is* about her, after all!"

"That isn't it!" Matt objected. "This is me. A gut feeling. Or a God feeling." *Okay, he's starting to scare me now.* "Carolyn." As if he had to say her name to get her attention. "After she started dragging us to church, something…

well, something finally *clicked*, you know?" Carolyn shook her head. No, she *didn't* know. "Maybe it's one of those things you have to experience to get. But that isn't the point. I was all over the place for a while there, after Mom...." He cleared his throat, incapable of completing the thought, and not seeing any need to do so. "Last winter. I wanted to believe that she wasn't just *gone*, but how could I convince myself of that when I knew that I only *wanted* it to be true? I was looking for answers about what happens next, about what our purpose is in life, and now I've finally–"

"*Wait.*" Matt paused to let her speak. Carolyn stood up and got in his face. "I *knew* this was coming! You're saying you're one of them now, aren't you? You're a church guy. A *Jesus freak.*" Carolyn grew distressed and began wringing her hands, desperate for some distraction.

"If that's how you'll say it... then yes." Matt didn't appear to be in the least bit ashamed. Nor did he seem proud of his decision. He just wanted to share it with her. Carolyn found it hard to be mad at a guy whose lightning blue eyes sparked with such sincere conviction. Looking back at the past week they'd been in school, she realized she should have seen the change in him – and might have, had she been less concerned with Kate, Erin, and Shawna. Something seemed almost radiant about him. He didn't just smile; he *beamed*. Until now she'd assumed her growing fondness of Matt had only made him seem to glow, but now she could see quite clearly that this wasn't about her.

Oh, that's preposterous! You didn't really *notice a difference until he pointed it out. Nothing is* really *different; he just thinks it is. It's only a phase.* She sank back down on the couch, which veritably swallowed her up. "When did you decide all this?"

"Well, like I said, I was struggling with this for a long time. I resisted the truth at first because I thought I would only use it as a crutch – that I needed to believe in something, and anything would do. But I finally realized how far off that theory was, and gave my life to Christ at youth group the other week."

He explained all this quite matter-of-factly for someone who was, in Carolyn's opinion, rambling on about something so completely *not* factual.

Carolyn parroted those last words, hoping he'd hear the absurdity of the statement and retract everything he'd just told her. No such luck. "That's… grand." She aimed for an encouraging tone, but she only achieved sarcastic. Hurt and anger boiled up inside of her. *How completely unfair is all of this? If the God Matt believes in so fanatically really exists, he must be one sadistic character.*

"Look," Matt said in exasperation. "I knew how you'd react to this. I just wanted you to know where I stand. As for me, I don't think making out is really what God wants from us, especially when we disagree about whether He even exists."

"But I like it!" Carolyn told him, feeling like the whining child who wanted another cookie, regardless of how badly Grandma had burnt them.

"I do too, Carolyn! Who wouldn't? You're amazing." The way he said it made her feel like he'd never met anyone as wonderful as her, and she felt her heart swell up like a balloon and drift away into an endless sky. "Please try to understand that I'm not doing this because I want to. If I could have it my way, we'd never be apart." He sat down beside her, and the couch gave way a little more, thrusting them together closer than Matt had anticipated. Carolyn basked in his proximity. It might not come again for a while. "I'm trying to do what *God* wants me to do, and believe me, I never thought this would be easy. I just don't think making out is His will for us."

Fuming, she checked her tongue and spat, "Baloney!"

Matt laughed sardonically. "There's a lot more to a relationship than what you've seen," he told her.

"And when did you become an expert?"

Matt groaned. "I'm not an expert. Believe me. I'm only doing what I feel is right. I wish you could try to understand. The old Carolyn would have." *That's right, lay on the guilt.* "I'm not changing my mind."

It was true: the old her *would* have tried to understand. But the new Carolyn had all but given up hope that sense could be made of her life. Also abandoned was the belief she had once held that she could fix everyone and everything; the one thing she now understood was that she couldn't fix herself, and she couldn't control anybody else, either. "Fine," she retorted.

"I can see you're mad at me," Matt said calmly and rationally. "I'm sorry you're mad, but I'm not sorry about my choice. If you want a couple days to sort things out...."

"Maybe that's best," Carolyn said quickly, taking the initiative of getting up and seeing herself out the door. *So much for always being able to count on Matt.* This changed everything.

Well, this is it. Now I've lost everything. My home, my best friend, all my other friends, my boyfriend.... My sanity. It can't get any worse. What did I do to deserve this? WHY ME?????

What does Matt think he's doing, going all Jesus freak on me?

And what does Paul think he's doing, getting all sentimental? Wow that was weird. Doesn't he know I already have a boyfriend? (Or, at any rate, had.) Ugh. Maybe I should have agreed to go out with him that time he said he liked me. At least he wouldn't be repulsed by the idea of kissing me. Clearly.

WHAT AM **I** THINKING??? Paul? How low can you stoop? Matt will snap out of this and things will go back to normal. Just give it time.

And if it doesn't, at least you know Skitt thinks you have a nice figure.

Ugh. Everything is such a mess. I wish I could fall asleep tonight knowing I would never wake up, and if I did, it would be because none of this ever happened or could happen. Everything would be normal and make sense, and the world wouldn't hate me and I wouldn't have to hate them back.

The more I think about it, the more I think I should go hang out with Skitt a little. Which sickens me a bit, seeing as I was just in a catfight with Tori, and I'm pretty sure it ended with me calling her a slut for flirting with guys that much older than her. But, you know. He likes my figure.

Message from: Carolyn Becker <SkiBlink@aol.com>
To: Leah Sorman <PussyCat240@aol.com>
Re: Re: Re: A bit of my life story (can I hear some of yours?)

Oh my God. I am such a pretender. I am such a liar. I am such a fake. You should see the way I can go about any ordinary day, and act like everything's all right. I should be nominated for a frickin Grammy.

I'm sorry I've been neglecting you. Margo just informed me that I suck at being a friend. Trust me, you don't want this drama. I've got this whole wacky triangle lined up quite nicely. The guy I love, the guy people think I like, and the guy I hate are all getting mixed up. I wish this would all just end. I want to come back to Alaska... if you'd even still be my friend, after all this time that I haven't been paying attention. All right, if you really want my advice on church boy, you need to at least find out his name. Other than that, I need more info. What kind of music does he listen to? That's always an important factor for me. I say "always" as if I have all this experience, but I'm just making suggestions and wasting words because I just don't know what to do with myself anymore. More importantly than GIVING advice, I think I could use some advice, myself. Gahhhh.

Haha you're so silly, Carolyn. Music isn't at all important when you're choosing yourself a boy. But that isn't so important right now. Church boy can wait. I really want to help you and give you the advice you need, but I don't know enough about the situation. Please let me back in the loop!

Lots of love,
~LBS~

Chapter Fifteen

Upon arriving home after a day on the rocks, Carolyn was shocked to find her mother crying at the kitchen table. "Mom? Is everything all right?"

"Carolyn, honey, sit down, okay?" Mom said, rather indistinctly. She reached for a napkin to blow her nose.

Carolyn obeyed. "What's going on? Is Dad hurt? Is Jimmie all right?"

"No, no, nothing like that!" Mom reassured her, forcing a wan smile. "Everybody is safe and healthy. Now, Lynnie, I know this might come as a shock to you, but Dad and I agreed this is for the best right now." Without realizing it, Carolyn started jouncing her leg out of nervousness. What *did they decide? And how come I get the feeling it might not really be for the best?*

Mom continued, "Dad and I are going to… take a little break. It's not a divorce, so don't you worry," she said quickly, when Carolyn's head snapped up in surprise. "But you know how tough it's been, lately. We both think the separation will do us good. It's only on a trial basis, honey, and Dad will probably move back in by summertime."

"Oh," was all Carolyn could think of to say. She wanted to ask, *Will we still see him? What's going to happen if you* do *get a divorce?*

Mom sniffled. "I know this will be hard on you, Lynnie. I can tell you take our fighting personally. But it's not your fault. Mom and Dad have been together a long time—" *Did she really just refer to herself in the third person? This is worse than I thought.* "—and sometimes, when people live together for that long, they can get on each others nerves. It happens to *all* families, Lynnie. Some just cover it up better."

"But, Mom…. Well… You're right that I hate it when you guys fight, but can't you just, I don't know, talk about it or something?" Carolyn pleaded desperately. "Anything but…. *Splitting up.*"

"We can't just *talk*, Carolyn. Every time I try, your father turns it into a fight. The farthest we could talk it out was to agree to this trial separation."

"I wish you wouldn't always blame him!" Carolyn shouted, standing up so violently that she nearly knocked down her chair. "It's your fault, too, you know! Don't pretend like you're the victim, here! If you would just *try*, I *know* you guys could work things out, but you both just blame each other!"

Fresh tears stood out in her mother's eyes, but in her confusion and fury, Carolyn didn't see. "Don't speak to me that way," Mom ordered, pulling herself together enough to discipline her daughter. "I don't know what's gotten into you. You used to be so sensitive and compassionate, always putting other people first, always caring about their feelings, and now all you think of is yourself!"

Carolyn clenched her jaw and stalked out of the room. She'd been *trying* to put her parents first. She'd been *trying* to stop them from separating by telling her mother to talk things out. Bitter tears of frustration flowed from her eyes. Not even Mom could understand her anymore.

That night, she played and played her guitar, unplugging it at bedtime but continuing to play. She relished the way the steel strings cut into her fingers even through her calluses, and the parched way her throat began to stick shut after she'd been singing for so long. The discomfort distracted her from the real problem, which was more than her parents splitting up – it was everything inside of her, everything she'd never wanted to have anything to do with and had somehow, effortlessly, become.

Carolyn left the house almost immediately after waking up. It had been a few days since Matt had ruined everything, and Carolyn had certainly "thought about it," but not, she knew, in the way Matt had meant. She simply couldn't *stop* thinking about it, but the more she did, the more she wanted to go hang out with different guys – ones who would appreciate her for the reasons Matt wouldn't let himself. There had been a time when she felt guilty about leaving Jimmie at home with their parents, but that time had passed. Dad was gone now. Carolyn had to keep reminding herself of that. At least Jimmie wasn't being exposed to their fighting anymore. With that in mind, Carolyn took off for Anne's house, only halfway intending to spend time with Anne.

Unlike Margo, Carolyn wasn't quite comfortable letting herself in at her friends' houses, so she rang the bell and waited. Anne answered the door rather sullenly.

Anne leaned on the doorframe. Next to the dark wood, she and her blonde, blonde hair looked paler than ever. "Hey."

"Hi. Can I... come in?" Carolyn asked.

"Sure." Anne moved to let her enter.

"I'm sorry about your mom's salt shaker," she said conversationally. "I guess that was kind of my fault."

"Mmm."

"Are you mad at me?"

"Just kind of disgusted at the way you acted towards Tori," Anne said. It was the longest phrase she'd said all day.

"Me too," Carolyn confessed. "I was also a little disgusted at how she acted towards me, you know."

"That much was obvious."

"What, you don't agree?"

"Well, I do, but it's Tori," Anne rationalized. "She's such a drama queen. You know she didn't mean any of it. You, on the other hand…"

"Aw, you know I didn't mean it either! It was all said in the heat of the moment!" Carolyn protested.

"Yeah, I guess you're right," Anne yielded, perking up considerably. "Well, on that note, want some brownies? I put peanut butter chips in them."

"Oh, what the fudge? It's not like I haven't had enough sweets this vacation, another brownie won't hurt," Carolyn said with a grin.

When they'd finished snacking, Carolyn asked casually if Skitt was home.

"Why do you care?" Anne asked suspiciously.

Carolyn had anticipated that kind of question from Anne and created a story ahead of time. "I wanted to mess around with his effects pedal. I was hoping he'd let me borrow it," she said smoothly.

"Oh." Anne looked relieved, and Carolyn felt guilty. "Well, he isn't home, but you could probably just take it."

Carolyn's heart sank, but she wore her game face. "Oh, I wouldn't do that. He might need it or something…. I'd rather ask him first. Next time I'm over, I guess."

"Yeah, sure." Anne seemed to be drifting away.

"Still thinking about Santa Catalina?"

"Yeah. I can't believe it. I guess I just never really thought I'd get in. Aisling got in too, you know," she said suddenly.

"*What?*" Anne nodded. "Are her parents making her go, too?" Anne nodded again. Carolyn put her hand to her head. "Well.... At least you'll have each other while you're there," she said, trying to look on the bright side, like Anne usually could. "God, I'm going to miss you guys though."

"I'll miss you more," Anne said. "At least you have a whole posse to keep you company."

"Maybe not anymore. After me and Tori. And me and Matt. I guess you'll want to hear about that."

"What *about* you and Matt?" Anne pressed.

Carolyn told her how Matt had gone church-happy on her and refused to kiss her anymore.

"Well, it could be worse," Anne pointed out. "At least he still likes you. Come on, the kid's got your best interests at heart, and you haven't spoken to him in three days?"

"Uh... yeah."

"Carolyn, it's not fair to hold something like that against him!" *If I don't want him to hold what happened to me against me, I suppose I should probably forgive him... But that's not even it. If we're not kissing, what's the point of "going out?" We might as well just be friends. Maybe... maybe we should just take a break from this whole going-out thing. If Mom and Dad can do it....*

"I just thought of something!" Carolyn exclaimed. "I'm sorry; I've got to go talk to him!" She got up quickly and rushed out the door.

"To tell him you forgive him?" Anne called hopefully after her.

"Something like that!" Carolyn called back, careful not to slam the door.

The run to Matt's house seemed to take an hour or more, and Carolyn was completely out of breath by the time she reached the door. When Matt came to the door (thankfully it was him, and not his Grandma offering more burnt cookies), she couldn't figure out what had made her want to get there so badly, because she couldn't decide what to say. She remembered something about following her parents' example.

"Can I help you?" Matt asked jauntily, inviting her in with a wave of his hand. Carolyn stayed on the doorstep.

"Matt... Do you think it might be a good idea to... No." *Starting over.* "Do you think we should maybe– well, because of what you said the other day, I was thinking...."

Matt raised an eyebrow in amusement. "Do you need one of Grandma's cookies? Brain food, you know."

"No! I just.... Think... well, maybe since we don't agree on things, we should.... I don't know... God, I feel like a nutcase now. Do you think we should take a break?"

"From talking? It's that bad?"

Carolyn wanted to scream in frustration. "Nnnooo! From – you know. Going out."

Matt didn't have a quick response for that. "I don't know if that's a good reason to break up or not," he said quietly.

"Not break up! Just... temporarily separate?" *Okay, this feels like the chicken's way out, but if it works for mom and dad, maybe it can work for me.* "Come on, admit it – I know your church doesn't approve of people like me. The heathen. Or whatever."

"Carolyn, this is crazy talk!" Since she wouldn't come in, Matt shut the door behind him and joined her on the stoop. Carolyn backed up to allow him space, but not as much, she knew, as he would have liked – and not as little as *she* would have liked. "My church doesn't decide who I date and don't date. *I* decide that." Matt sighed. "They would let you in, you know. If you ever wanted to go. They wouldn't kick you out. The Church welcomes everyone. It's welcomed worse sinners than you in the past, believe me."

"Well, I don't want to go. I don't know why they'd want me around. I'd probably do something horribly wrong like eat holy bread with my peanut butter and jelly or something."

Matt just shook his head hopelessly. "Maybe you're right. Maybe we should try… just for a little while… just to see what it's like.…"

Carolyn recalled how this conversation had started, and for a moment she seriously regretted even showing up in the first place. *No,* she told herself. *This will be better. You won't be tied down to someone who doesn't even want to kiss you. You won't have to feel bad about liking other guys. Do it.* "Yeah. Okay. Right. Let's try it. All right. Cool."

"Well, I can see *this* experiment is turning out well," Matt joked, forcing a grin for her benefit and letting himself back inside. A rush of cool air passed over her from within the house, and Carolyn realized how hot and sticky she was.

"So how will we know when we get back together?" she called after him, before he could shut the door.

Matt shrugged. "When we can't take it any longer? I don't know. This was all your idea. Come up with something." He closed the door abruptly, and Carolyn got the distinct impression that he was more irked than he'd tried to let on at first. *Well, I thought I was making something better, but it appears I've only made it worse. Again. I should go live in a hole somewhere where I can't cause any trouble.… Do you think there is such a place, Toto? …And now I've cracked.*

Carolyn joined her friends at the beach, where they perched on the rocks along the edge of the public area, just past the Jumping Point. She'd convinced her parents that she was mature enough to go to the beach with just her friends, and even hang out on the Boardwalk. Since then, the boulders had become her favorite place to sit with her friends and listen to them talk. The sky and the water faded into one another until it was impossible to discern which was which. Like snow drifts, the sand dunes rippled smoothly and whitely across the beach, dotted with tropical-colored, Christmas-light umbrellas. Surreal, that was the word for it – it was too bright, too perfect, too – everything. Carolyn couldn't have made it better if she'd tried. *So why do I feel so rotten?*

The guys were surfing, weaving across the water and miraculously managing not to collide with one another. Carolyn sat in silence on a towel she'd spread across the boulder, hugging her knees in spite of the heat generated by the jeans she was wearing, sharing her friends' company but not their conversation. She knew what would come out if she opened her mouth, even if it wasn't what she wanted or meant to say. It was the same thing that was still plaguing her mind, a week after it had happened.

She and Matt were broken up.

Yeah, we called it 'taking a break.' But regardless of what we call it, we aren't together anymore. I ruined it, just like I ruin everything else.

"Carolyn, are you with us or what?" Tori asked, snapping her fingers close to Carolyn's ear.

"Yeah, yeah, I'm good," Carolyn replied distractedly.

"You don't seem it," Anne commented. Even she, the pale, easily-sun-burned beauty, was wearing a swimsuit. "You're way quieter than usual. Remember when we used to do stuff like have pillow fights in the furniture store?"

Carolyn mustered up a smile for her. "Yeah." *That was a long time ago, though. I haven't been much more talkative than this for a while now. Well, okay, I used to string together complete sentences. I just don't feel like it anymore.*

Anne continued disappointedly. "I just don't see you doing that now."

"No, me either."

"But *why?*" Tori wanted to know. Margo kept tactfully quiet.

"Stuff," Carolyn replied, skirting around the specifics.

"It's just," Tori said carefully (though not carefully enough, as far as Carolyn was concerned), "it's sort of…. Gloomy, having you around but never hearing you say anything."

"Gloomy," Carolyn repeated tonelessly. "Well, if that's how you feel… I wouldn't want to rain on *this* parade." She indicated the idyllic scene with the wave of a hand as she got to her feet, gathered her towel and SPF 30 sun block, and made her way back to the sandy part of the beach, where she practically collided with a tall, tan surfer just coming out of the water, who was too busy shaking the water from his blond, sun-streaked hair to notice her until the last second.

"Hey!" he cried, stumbling backwards to stop them from bumping into each other. Then he realized who it was. "Watch yourself, Alaska," he growled, almost coming across as defensive, as though he had reason to be afraid of her. Carolyn would have found this strange if it wasn't how Mark and his buddy Jason always treated her. So instead of responding verbally, she flipped him off and walked around him.

"Hey, what was that for?" Mark asked in outrage, spinning on his heel to follow her. Carolyn exhaled gustily.

"I am *not* in the mood, Mark."

"The mood for what, explaining why you just flipped me off?"

"Think about it, Mark," Carolyn instructed acidly. "I'm sure a boy with your mental abilities-" (none, so far as she was concerned) "-can figure out just why I might be upset with you."

Mark seemed puzzled, and paused in the sand, scratching his wet, blond head. *Really, why does it always have to be the hott ones that set themselves against me? And is there some law I don't know about that the best-looking ones have the least going on underneath their pretty hair?* She took advantage of Mark's perplexity and dashed off (as well as one can dash in dry sand, anyway) toward the parking lot, where her bike was padlocked to the bike rack. She unlocked it with lightning fingers and took off down the winding seaside road.

Anything was better than being around people these days, a fact that Carolyn was loath to accept because of her previous status as a social butterfly – pre-Paul, pre-Molly, pre-mom-and-dad. *And I'd thought things may have been going back to normal, but I get it now. Someone out there is ROTFL making my life miserable. Well, don't stop on my account, whoever you are.* Carolyn felt a shudder of disgust go down her spine, and the bike wobbled a little. She steadied herself.

Get a grip. God. You're as bad a drama queen as Tori sometimes, I swear it.

But is it really exaggerating to say my life is ruined?

I'm pretty sure I can get away with that one.

I've really done it now. I ruined things between me and Matt for good, and Finn didn't even have to help me. I did it all by myself, just the way I do everything these days: alone. Nobody wants me. Pity party. I'll provide the food (chocolate ice cream) and entertainment (me, slamming on my guitar because nothing else feels as good as steel strings digging into my fingers and steel notes cutting into my eardrums.)

Chapter Sixteen

Vacation was over. Back to school. Back to interaction with other people…
one of Carolyn's least favorite things these days. Kate, Erin, and Shawna
were going to be all over her, especially if they'd heard about her and Matt;
but that, Carolyn assured herself, was highly unlikely, as she hadn't yet told
anyone they were "taking a break." *And why should I be expected to share
that little tidbit with anyone? It's my personal business. My personal life isn't
something to be scrutinized by the entire school.*

Even worse than the Terrible Trio, as Carolyn secretly referred to them,
would undoubtedly be Paul. He'd given her so little grief that last week of
school, he must have something really bad in store.

Not to mention, seeing Matt regularly was not going to do wonders
for her mood, and considering how they would most likely behave towards
each other, people were probably going to figure out they'd split up really
quickly.

Carolyn sighed. It was a black eyeliner day, from the looks of it. She knew her mom hated to see her leaving the house with her eyes rimmed in ebony, though, so Carolyn put the pencil in the front pocket of her backpack next to a bunch of Number Twos and hoped it would blend in.

First thing upon arriving at school, she ducked into a bathroom to put on the make-up. As soon as she opened the door, she heard voices talking around the bend – about her! She stopped short. The bathroom made a turn almost immediately after the door, probably so no guys would be able to sneak a peek into the room, and Carolyn waited motionlessly, soundlessly, in the little alcove by the door and listened to the girls by the sink discuss her.

"She's gotten so weird lately." With a pang, Carolyn recognized Tori's voice. "I don't understand it. She finally scored Matt. Wasn't that what she wanted?"

"I thought so. We all thought so," said the other voice, which Carolyn couldn't pin down to any individual yet.

"I mean, you know, I *want* to be there for her. That's what friends do, right?" Tori said. "But she kind of scares me. I mean, she's turned into one of those… one of those…" Tori's voice filled with disgust, and Carolyn wasn't sure she wanted to hear the sentence completed. "*Punks.*"

"Yeah, but a punk who happens to want to go out with every datable boy in the school – and some others besides – *at the same time,*" the other voice added irritatedly, and Carolyn finally nailed it: Tori was talking to Kate. *Kate? What on earth is Tori talking to Kate for? About* me, *no less – and not nice things about me, either. Some friend.*

"I don't really think there are many datable boys in this school," Tori said thoughtfully. "Let her have them, for all we care. We can do so much better. Now if she starts moving in on the local high school boys, then we've got trouble."

Kate snorted. "I don't know why you're even worried, Vic." *Vic? Tori's letting Kate call her* Vic? *How long has this been going on??* "It's not like any of them would want to date *her*." Carolyn felt the contempt in the word 'her' like poison shooting through her veins. *I can not believe what I'm hearing.* "I mean, *look* at her, for God's sakes. If you were a boy, wouldn't you be scared of her?" Kate paused, and Carolyn could only presume Tori must have nodded, because Kate continued. "Besides, any boy who *isn't* afraid of her probably isn't our type anyway."

Carolyn staggered back towards the door. She'd heard enough. Unfortunately, she hadn't paid attention to the metal trashcan by the door, which she crashed into. Aside from making a horrible racket that even the deafest custodian probably heard from the other side of the building, Carolyn also managed to lose her balance and fall on her knees. Kate and Tori's faces immediately appeared around the bend.

Kate's eyes widened in glee when she realized who was staring up at her from that grimy tile floor. Tori, on the other hand, looked about ready for someone to flush her down one of those toilets into some alternate universe. She swore.

Carolyn got gingerly to her feet.

"Glad I've got so many loyal friends," she spat, before turning on her heel and leaving Tori to figure out how to get herself out of *this* mess.

Things cannot possibly get any worse, Carolyn thought Tuesday morning. Fortunately, things didn't get any worse that day, but they certainly didn't improve, either. Tori was too ashamed to sit at their table at lunch, and she'd convinced Anne to join her elsewhere so she wouldn't have to be alone. Carolyn didn't want to hold anything against Anne, who was so sweet and really only wanted to make sure that everybody had a friend. If only everybody could, but Carolyn could feel hers slipping through her fingers, one by one.

That left Margo, Finn, Nick, and Matt at Carolyn's table, which, as she had anticipated, was highly awkward, since Nick and Margo wouldn't speak to each other, and she and Matt weren't exactly on friendly terms at the moment. Finn, for his part, tried desperately to initiate conversation, but his efforts, however valiant, always seemed to fail miserably.

After a few days of this, Matt made sure to get himself a seat next to Carolyn. "Look," he said. "I know we're… doing that whole trial separation thing. But as I recall, there was nothing in there about not speaking to each other."

"Mmhmm" was all Carolyn said.

"I don't want to be enemies with you, Carolyn!" Matt calmed himself, and Carolyn waited expectantly for him to speak, encouraging him only with her silence. "Do you want to come to youth group tonight?" Matt laughed bitterly. "What am I asking? Of course you don't want to go. I know, you think it's gay. But I wish you'd come, just once…"

"We're going disco bowling," Carolyn told him. "You know, *normal people* fun." Only a partial truth, of course – because of her recent aversion to people, Carolyn had decided she probably wouldn't go. So many had let her down lately that it hardly seemed worthwhile to bother with them anymore. She gave a phony smile, one so huge and cheesy that anyone could have guessed it was not as innocent as she intended for it to appear. "We'll miss you."

Matt had picked up on her half-truth, of course. "You're burning bridges, Carolyn," he warned. "I know you're not thrilled with my decision – you know, to put my faith in Jesus – but I think you're being – well, I wish you wouldn't shut yourself off from everybody."

Of course, he was blaming himself for her attitude, without realizing he was only part of the problem. "Don't blame yourself," Carolyn pleaded.

"Why not? It's clear that I'm the cause for all this." Carolyn couldn't tell if he really believed himself to be guilty, or if he only wanted to extract the truth from her in as non-confrontational a manner as possible, so she simply objected. "Then why are you acting like this?" Carolyn dropped her eyes. She couldn't look him in the face, not while lying outright like she was about to.

"I just – my parents," she said sadly, and, she thought, convincingly. "And Molly. And now Tori. Everything's just happening at once."

Matt's expression softened faster than a Popsicle dropped on the sidewalk on a hot summer's day like that one. "There's nothing you can do about any of that. Carolyn, please listen to me. None of that is your fault. I wish I could make it stop, but I can't. All I can tell you is that somehow, it's part of God's plan, and I'm praying He'll help you out of this."

Carolyn groaned and rolled her eyes. He'd only made matters worse. "Please, just, don't talk to me. Go have fun at your Jesus party."

"You don't even know what you're talking about!" Matt said incredulously. "I've never seen you like this!"

"*You* don't know what *you're* talking about, either. You think *I'm* crazy, but at least I'm not turning into your grandmother!" Carolyn inwardly kicked herself as soon as the words came out. Lately, she'd been treating everyone the way she treated Paul, which was not so far off from how Paul had always treated her.

Matt was dumbfounded. He simply picked up his lunch, got up, and moved to the other table with Anne and Tori. Carolyn only watched, letting him do as he pleased. She deserved it.

Paul was quick to corner her at her locker after school. "Trouble in paradise?" he smirked. *Is this kid spying on me? What a creep.* Carolyn simply did not have the energy to flee, so she stood her ground.

"Shut your face or I'll do it for you," she threatened, looking anything but vicious as she slouched against the locker in defeat. Even the metal couldn't stay cool in the sort of weather that had become increasingly frequent with the onset of spring, and instead of sending chills down her spine, the locker just stuck to her back, bare in the cranberry halter top she'd worn that day. Paul, she noticed, sidled closer – almost imperceptibly so, but enough to make her breath catch nervously and her heart rate pick up.

Paul's smirk grew even more complacent. "I'm sorry to hear that." He didn't sound it, and Carolyn said so. "Well, you'll have to forgive me, then," Paul said casually, though his intense gaze was anything but nonchalant, "because I can't help but think that now, maybe, I stand a chance…" Carolyn chose not to grace this comment with a response. They were back to square one, and she just didn't feel like wasting her energy on him.

Paul, however, seemed to interpret the silence a little differently. He suddenly leaned in, and for the second time, began kissing her. But this time he knew what he was doing. This time he didn't taste of alcohol. And this time, Carolyn didn't object. At least somebody wanted her.

In an effort to keep up a semblance of normalcy, Carolyn reluctantly showed face at disco bowling that night, but company was the last thing she wanted. She bowled her usual low score, and lost to Finn and Nick at Dance, Dance Revolution – all things that had become routine, and even enjoyable, over the past month or so, in spite of the fact that she kept losing. But she couldn't enjoy herself, not with the lead weight of guilt in her heart.

Matt may be crazy, but he's never done anything to hurt me, she kept thinking. *And then along comes Paul and kisses me, and I let him, and not only that – I liked it! That is sick. Even I know that. But then why am I so desperate for it to happen again?* The same sequence of thoughts ran through her mind in dizzying circles. *What have I done?*

Margo finally found the opportunity to talk to Carolyn. "Are you upset about what happened at lunch today?" she said in a low voice, allowing the music to mostly obscure what she was saying so no one would overhear. Carolyn nodded mutely. *She only knows the half of it.* "I would be, too," Margo said sympathetically. "I wish you two were still as cute as you were when you first got together." She smiled dreamily as she remembered. "God, you two were *perfect* for each other… and then… all that crap with Paul happened."

A shadow crossed her face. "I can't believe how badly he screwed everything up for you," Margo said vehemently.

Carolyn, entranced by the colored lights dancing on the floor and caught up in the beat of whatever song was blaring, nodded again to show her agreement.

"I mean," Margo continued, "Matt was the best thing that ever happened to you. We all knew it. And then along comes Paul, and-"

"Margo," Carolyn interrupted. "You're not helping."

Margo bit her lip. "Right. Sorry." After a minute, she continued again. "It's just, I don't think you should let that stand in the way of you and Matt."

"That isn't the only problem."

"Oh." For a while, Margo seemed stumped. "Well, what else is wrong?"

It's not necessarily between me and Matt, Carolyn wanted to say. *It's a combination of everything that's turned me into something he'd rather not be around. And I don't blame him. I wouldn't blame you, either, if you didn't want to be around me.* Instead, she pointed to the TV screen hanging from the ceiling, which displayed the scores for their lane, and said, "It's your turn."

Fought with Matt again. Ditched my friends again. Cheated on my boyfriend again. Not much else to say. I've whined and ranted enough to bore anyone who might bother to read this crap to death a thousand times over.

The missions trip was great! I made so many new friends that I never even realized went to my church! And I learned that Church Boy's name is Ian, and for your benefit, asked him what music he listened to. He just said "everything. Hardcore." Don't really know what he means by that. But I also found out that he writes his own music, and happened to come across his notebook and catch a glimpse of one of the songs he'd written, and – it was beautiful. See, I told you he must be deep. Then I felt bad about reading it without asking and told him what I did, and he just gave me this knowing smile. He doesn't say much. For some reason, that is really attractive. Why is that so attractive??!!! Anyway, wow, I definitely just had my first good boy spiel in a long time. And it felt really good! I'm so happy since we came home from this trip, and not just because of Ian. I feel like I helped make the world a better place, and seeing the way some people live gave me a new perspective. I'm counting my blessings – and there sure are a lot of them!

How is your love quadrilateral going? I hope things have settled down a little. How about your parents? Is Jimmie doing okay? Have you and Molly made up? Fill me in!

Lots of love,
~LBS~

Chapter Seventeen

It was Friday afternoon again. Another week of waiting for the weekend, finished. At least this weekend couldn't be like the rest of them. Usually, Carolyn would hope for something to change, and return to school on Monday to find that nothing had. But that was all right, she was used to it by now. She was used to the absence of Matt and the fruitless anticipation of his phone call, the one in which he broke down and admitted that he *needed* her, and couldn't she come back? Because everything he'd said before, it was just silliness, and he was back to normal and now they could be together forever. And things would be perfect. Forever.

By now she'd learned there was no such thing as forever, and if there was, then she wished there wasn't, because it was going to be miserable living alone in a galaxy of faces, familiar ones that should have been reassuring but really only sickened her.

But this weekend was different because school was out. It sure didn't feel like it. Carolyn had never felt more imprisoned in her life. But summer had indeed arrived, and Carolyn tried to be happy, though she couldn't help thinking that more free time meant nothing but more time for her to wallow in her misery.

The hand appeared out of nowhere. Carolyn just suddenly found it on her arm – not in an aggressive way or anything. It was just there. Someone wanted her attention. Carolyn turned and came face to face with Paul. She didn't bother to greet him, but she didn't bother taking off either. Both options took too much effort.

"What's going on with you?" Paul asked in the most concerned voice Carolyn had ever heard him use. She snuck a glance at his face, avoiding eye contact, to see if he was trying to pull one over on her, but it didn't seem that way. "You seem like something's wrong." *How can you be so obvious? This is all your fault!*

"I'm fine." She started on her way again, watching the sidewalk beneath her feet with rapt attention and subconsciously counting the cracks. The grey cement reflected the overcast sky and mirrored her hopeless emotions.

"No, really," Paul pressed, keeping pace.

"Kate, Erin and Shawna are driving me crazy." It was the longest sentence she'd said all day, and Paul seemed acutely aware that *he* had been the one to draw it out of her. She could feel smugness emanating from his form as they walked, and wanted to punch him out for it. Carolyn barely glanced up to check for cars before crossing the street to the corner near her house.

Paul moved on, and Carolyn could tell this was the real reason he'd stopped her. "Have you and Matt made up?"

I can't believe he just asked me that! Carolyn turned slowly and fixed him with a stare of disgust, hatred, and disbelief all rolled into one acid glare. Paul grew even smugger as the answer became clear: no, they hadn't made up yet. "Well, then, you don't think he'd mind..." And with that unfinished question, he pressed his mouth to hers again.

Carolyn backed up a little, breaking the connection. She wasn't surprised he'd tried something like this, but that didn't change the fact that it was just *wrong.* "Probably," she said, eyes darting around the street nervously to see who could bear witness. An old man was disappearing into a driveway with his dog. Other than that, the heat had kept everyone inside. "But he's not here," she said quickly. Paul's crestfallen expression vanished, and he moved back in.

A tiny voice in her head screamed, *this isn't right!*

But it feels so good… She pressed herself closer to Paul. He seemed surprised, but he placed one hand on the small of her back, sending chills up her spine, and pulled her still closer. *You can't do this to Matt!* the first voice complained, but Carolyn silenced it. She could do whatever she wanted.

"We should probably stop," Paul mumbled after a time, his lips tickling hers as he spoke.

"Probably," Carolyn agreed, trying to catch her breath. All the same, their lips met again.

"If Matt sees us…" she muttered after another minute had gone by, but she still didn't want to stop. *It's so wrong, but it feels so right.*

"If Erin sees us…" Paul agreed.

Carolyn leapt back in horror. "Erin?" she practically shrieked. The pitch of her voice was several octaves higher than usual. *"Erin?"*

Paul shrugged indifferently. "We're going out, I guess."

"You *guess*? You *guess?!* You say that like it doesn't even matter!" Her voice grew higher and higher with agitation.

"Well, right now, it doesn't," Paul said with cold apathy. "She's not here. Besides," he added, and Carolyn braced herself for the real stinger. *"You're* going behind Matt's back. Doesn't *that* matter?"

Hearing it in words made the situation sound that much more twisted, and Carolyn despised herself. "God… look what I've become…" she murmured hopelessly. "Look what *you* did!" She was screaming again, and no matter how different the shrieking voice she heard sounded from hers, Carolyn couldn't stop it from spewing out of her mouth. "None of this would have happened if not for you!" She flung an accusatory finger in his direction.

Paul spread his hands out. "I'm sorry," he said.

"*Sorry?*" Granted, she hadn't expected to hear that word from Paul Riley, but "sorry" couldn't cover everything he'd put her through. Carolyn felt sick to her stomach. It was going to take a lot more than "sorry" to fix all the problems he'd caused.

"If it helps at all… I didn't come after you today intending… well, to do what I did," he said sheepishly. "I mean, what I really wanted to say all along was that I was sorry for everything. For pushing you last year, for being a moron since then, for making you cheat on your boyfriend. God. I can understand why you hate me. And look, I've gone and screwed up again."

"*Sorry?*" she repeated incredulously, only halfway hearing his confession. "You'll have to do better than that." She stormed off down the sidewalk.

Things only got worse.

She was greeted by a stern-faced mother, who had seen enough of the scene outside to ground Carolyn for the next week. *A week. So much can happen in a week.* That much she'd learned. A week was like a mini-lifetime – or maybe it only felt that way because she'd never been grounded before. At any rate, she'd lost her one, weekly opportunity to get out and, if not enjoy herself, at least not sit around playing her guitar and thinking about how much life sucked.

"I thought you didn't even like that boy," Mom said in confusion.

"It's complicated," was all Carolyn said before stomping up the stairs to her bedroom, where she played her guitar and composed in her journal until her fingers hurt too badly to even make a fist, but even that couldn't assuage the emotions boiling inside of her.

Welcome to Rock Bottom. Population: me. I've stooped as low as I can go. But I'm only stating this as a fact. By now I've pretty much reached a point of total indifference towards everything. I can watch things go by, and I've given up on feeling them. Screw everything. It's better this way.

PART TWO

"THERE IS A TIME FOR EVERYTHING,
AND A SEASON FOR EVERY ACTIVITY UNDER HEAVEN:
A TIME TO BE BORN AND A TIME TO DIE,
A TIME TO PLANT AND A TIME TO UPROOT,
A TIME TO KILL AND A TIME TO HEAL,
A TIME TO TEAR DOWN AND A TIME TO BUILD,
A TIME TO WEEP AND A TIME TO LAUGH,
A TIME TO MOURN AND A TIME TO DANCE,
A TIME TO SCATTER STONES AND A TIME TO GATHER THEM,
A TIME TO EMBRACE AND A TIME TO REFRAIN,
A TIME TO SEARCH AND A TIME TO GIVE UP,
A TIME TO KEEP AND A TIME TO THROW AWAY,
A TIME TO TEAR AND A TIME TO MEND,
A TIME TO BE SILENT AND A TIME TO SPEAK,
A TIME TO LOVE AND A TIME TO HATE,
A TIME FOR WAR AND A TIME FOR PEACE."

ECCLESIASTES 3:1-8

Chapter Eighteen

The clock said 6:00. Maybe she could still make it to bowling. Sneaking out the window wouldn't be that hard. After all, what right did mom *really* have to ground her for kissing a boy? Granted, it had been a boy she was supposed to hate. And granted, she didn't usually kiss Matt as passionately as she'd just kissed Paul, and *he* was supposed to be her boyfriend. *But it's my life, not my mother's. I can make my own decisions. Who's she to take away my one chance to get away from all the crap that's been weighing me down all week? That's it, I'm going.*

Carolyn started throwing things into a backpack, calling Anne as she haphazardly yanked clean clothes out of her dresser. Anne seemed most likely to cave in and let her stay, even though Carolyn hadn't exactly been the best friend lately. "Not to invite myself over or anything, but can I spend the night at your house after bowling tonight?" she asked, trying to be quiet so Mom wouldn't guess anything was going on.

"Oh… is something wrong?" Anne asked, her voice instantly filling with worry. Tears sprung to Carolyn's eyes. How could Anne still care so much about her after Carolyn had been such a horrible friend? She hadn't spoken to anyone in ages, especially Anne and Tori, since they'd left her lunch table almost two months earlier, and yet Anne was so ready and willing to help.

"Can I tell you later?" Carolyn didn't want her mom to hear her talking.

"Sure, yeah, but I'm not going to-"

Carolyn interrupted. "I'll be over in like two secs. Talk to you then." She hung up and hurried out the window, sticking a clipboard in it to keep it open just the tiniest crack, in case she needed to come back in the same way she went out. She prowled along the rooftop, cat-like, her heart thudding louder than her footsteps as she dropped down to the next level of roof. She left her guilt atop the verandah and faded noiselessly into the woods.

Once she reached a safe distance from the house, Carolyn began to run, blinded by anger and hardly noticing the damage the brambles were doing to her legs. She could have avoided it if only she'd worn jeans like she usually did, but it had been so hot and sticky lately that she'd caved and thrown on capris that morning. She arrived at Anne's bloody and breathless, not to mention unpleasantly damp from the drizzle that had picked up as she ran.

Anne stared. "What the heck happened to you?" she asked, reluctantly letting Carolyn in but not letting her step off the mat just inside the door.

"I took the woods route," Carolyn said briefly, taking her shoes off and finally noticing the condition of her shins and ankles.

"Okay… and why are you here?"

"Because I hate my life." Carolyn balked at the honesty of the statement and quickly moved to cover it up. "Well, actually, mostly just my mom. She grounded me for a week." Carolyn wanted to smack herself, because, of course, the next question was, "why did she ground you?"

"I dunno, something stupid…. You don't mind that I'm here, do you?"

"Well, no, but I'm not going bowling tonight," Anne explained apologetically. "Skitt's taking me to a party."

Carolyn's heart sank. "Oh, God, I can't take another party," she moaned. "And I especially can't go in *this* condition. Have you got some Neosporin?"

Anne opened a small medicine cabinet over the stove and started rummaging for ointment and bandages. "You don't *have* to come. That's just where I'll be. You can…. I dunno. Stay here, I guess."

"That seems a little awkward," Carolyn noted. "Don't you think your parents would mind? Or even if they didn't, they couldn't help but notice me, and when my mom calls around looking for me, they won't hesitate to say I'm here."

"Good point." Anne handed Carolyn a tube of Neosporin and a box of Band-aids, and Carolyn started to tidy herself up. "Well, I don't know what to say, Caro. I'm definitely going with Skitt…"

"It's okay," Carolyn quickly reassured her. "As long as I can spend the night. I'll find something to do until… whenever you get back."

"You know, won't whoever drives you to the alley tell your mom where you are if she asks?" Anne mentioned.

Carolyn stopped short and groaned. "I didn't think of that."

Skitt swept into the room at that moment, the aroma of cologne trailing behind him. He looked at Carolyn as though thinking, 'how could this girl possibly want to go to a party again?'

"Hey," Carolyn said with a weak smile. He was so handsome. Maybe she could go to the party and just stick close to him. *Maybe* very *close,* she hoped. *I don't have a lot of options. If I go bowling, Anne's right – someone is bound to tell Mom where I am.*

"Hey," Skitt replied. "Are you coming?"

"Yeah, I guess so," Carolyn said, surprising even herself with her spontaneity. "Well, where else am I going to go?" she asked in response to Anne's shocked expression. Anne shrugged.

"Do you need help with those Band-aids?" Skitt asked. Carolyn couldn't help but think that he was looking for an excuse to touch her leg, and she couldn't help saying "yes." Anne seemed a little bewildered, but she jumped on the chance to be helpful and started sponging the scratches with damp paper towels.

"So, uh, what did you do to yourself?" Skitt asked, mildly amused.

"I ran through the woods," Carolyn admitted, feeling foolish.

"I see." Skitt dabbed Neosporin on one of the worse cuts and gently smoothed a bandage over it. Carolyn suppressed what she suspected would have been a silly, fatuous grin. Finally, when she was all cleaned up, Anne collected the trash and shoved it in the bin in the pantry closet. Meanwhile, Skitt helped Carolyn to her feet. She pretended to be unsteady for a second so she could hold his hand longer, but finally, she reluctantly let go. "Let's head out," Skitt said, already halfway out the door.

He made Anne sacrifice shotgun for Carolyn, a move that Anne seemed to deeply resent. "She's wounded," Skitt said by way of excuse, but Carolyn hoped that wasn't the real reason he let her sit there. She rolled down the window and discreetly gulped fresh air. *I'm going to a party with Skitt!* She exulted inwardly.

Carolyn realized too late that they were passing the Smith residence, and that Matt was just coming out the door, apparently on his way to youth group. Carolyn instinctively ducked back, but the car was going so slow, and her reaction was so delayed, that they made eye contact anyway. Something stirred in Carolyn's heart, and tears stung her eyes. God, how she missed him.

Before she knew what she was doing, Carolyn demanded, "Stop the car!"

"What?" Skitt asked in alarm.

"I… I have to… go somewhere," Carolyn explained feebly, unfastening her seat belt with a click that seemed to echo through the car.

Skitt slowed down. "Where could you possibly have to go?" Anne asked from the back seat.

"I'll see you tonight," Carolyn said. It wasn't much of an answer, but it would have to do. She leapt out of the still-rolling car and stumbled, feeling the awkward sensation of going from a moving surface to solid, motionless ground.

"Are you crazy?" Skitt yelled from the car.

"Probably!" Carolyn called back. Once she'd found her legs, she dashed back the half-block to Matt's house just as his grandma was backing out of the driveway in her steel blue Oldsmobile. Matt had already jumped out of the car and was running across the lawn towards her.

"Are you all right?" he asked. "Better yet, are you *sane?*"

"Yes to the first, not sure to the second," Carolyn replied.

"What do you think you're doing?" Matt asked, concern and anger vying for dominance in his voice. The last thirty seconds caught up with her, and Carolyn blushed, feeling utterly foolish.

"It was only going like ten miles per hour," she muttered.

"Why aren't you bowling?" Carolyn couldn't tell if the edge in his voice was caused by their ongoing dispute, or his opinion that she was crazy for jumping out of a car.

"I want to come with you," she said simply. The surprise registered on Matt's face was nothing next to the surprise she felt. *What am I doing? Maybe I really* am *crazy. Well, it's not like I can back out now.*

Matt blinked. "Well... get in!" he stammered. He hurried to open the front door for her, and then, once she was securely in, settled himself into the backseat. Carolyn buckled herself in and pushed the lock down so she couldn't do something stupid again if she changed her mind. Matt's grandma welcomed Carolyn warmly, and if she was surprised, she hid it well, appearing completely unfazed as she continued pulling out.

"I haven't seen you in months!" she gushed. "How have you been, dear?"

Carolyn couldn't help but smile at the heartfelt greeting. "Things have been crazy lately," she said by way of apology and explanation. At any rate, she was ashamed to let Mrs. MacMillan see her in this state. If she knew, who knew what she would do? *Drag me through confession, probably, or something equally painful and humiliating.*

Mrs. MacMillan made a sympathetic sound as though she already knew everything Carolyn hadn't told her, and Carolyn wondered how much she'd pried out of Matt. She instantly berated herself for thinking like that. It was so hard to think badly of people like Mrs. MacMillan, especially once you got within a ten-foot radius of them. They were just so hard to hate. "Well, I'm praying for you, honey," she assured Carolyn. Carolyn smiled and thanked her, restricting her groan to the confines of her mind.

She rested her head against the cool glass of the window and watched the world pass in glum silence. Hopefully she'd chosen the lesser of three evils that night, but she had yet to find out.

Fifteen minutes later, Carolyn had just started to fidget and wish that she'd just stayed at home like a good little girl when they pulled up at a huge building that Carolyn had been in once before, for Mrs. Smith's funeral. It was bigger than she recalled, and looked less like a church than she'd pictured. "It used to be a department store," Matt said at Carolyn's astonished look.

"You go to church at an ex-Bradley's?" Carolyn asked in shock. "That's got to be sacrilegious or something." Mrs. MacMillan waved and drove away, and Carolyn despaired as her only hope of salvation from this ordeal vanished down the street.

Matt laughed. "There aren't as many rules as you seem to think," he said. "It's not about traditions and rituals and such. The important thing is a relationship." They walked straight past what Carolyn had assumed was the entrance, and Matt seemed to be aiming for a dumpster out behind the building. Carolyn followed bemusedly.

"Hold on," she interjected. "What about like, First Communion and Confirmation and all that – stuff?" She'd been about to say 'crap,' but she figured it was better to avoid calling religious traditions 'crap' in the parking lot of a church and refrained.

"You're thinking about Catholicism," Matt explained. "That's not what we practice here. This is a non-denominational church." At her confused look, he added, "That just means we aren't Catholic or Baptist or anything, really. We don't want to discourage anyone from coming by putting a restrictive label on the church." Carolyn nodded like this was a perfectly normal conversation to be having, but she was waiting to be introduced to someone she could talk about Sugarcult or that new band, Fall Out Boy, with.

They reached the Dumpster, and Carolyn realized that that hadn't been their destination. The hulking green piece of rusted metal was blocking a basketball court from view, and past the court was a grassy area where kids were already gathered and chatting away. Half of the court was being taken up by a game of knockout. On the other side of the court, someone had set up a wooden hexagon and kids were playing a version of dodge ball that Carolyn wasn't familiar with. There were no teams. It was a free-for-all within the wooden hexagon, and Carolyn heard the other kids calling it "Ga-Ga," which she thought was a ridiculous name for a sport – but then, it was a ridiculous sport, so she supposed it evened out. "You have youth group outside?" Carolyn asked in surprise. "You don't, like, sit in pews and listen to some guy talk?"

Matt laughed again. "Is that where you thought I was going on Friday nights all this time?"

Yes. Carolyn shook her head 'no.' "Of course not!" she lied.

Matt just laughed and set about introducing Carolyn to his friends, most of which happened to be guys. *Typical. I guess I should be glad he's not hanging around the girls trying to find a replacement for me.* Some kids on skateboards whisked past them and right through the heart of the game of knockout as she watched. *How come Matt can't introduce me to those kids?* She wondered. *At least they're likely to know who No Use for a Name is.* She put up with Matt's introductions until he was done, and then, as soon as she saw the opportunity, she slipped off and introduced herself to some of the skateboarders.

"Carolyn?" said a familiar voice behind her. "What are you doing here?"

Carolyn spun and found herself face-to-face with Finn. They weren't necessarily face-to-face, since he was standing on a skateboard and happened to be a good deal taller than her anyway, but the fact that he was there at all startled her beyond all speech. *How does he always appear at the most random times?* "Holy sh-nikeys," she caught herself. "What are *you* doing here?"

Finn grinned. "I asked first."

"Well…. I jumped out of a car and told Matt to bring me."

"Oh. Well that's not as exciting as my story, I guess." Finn stepped hard on the end of his skateboard to make it fly up into his hand, and tucked the board under his arm as they talked. "I came here a few times with Matt before we all started going disco bowling on Fridays. But uh, the past few weeks have been really awkward at the alley. I mean, well – you know what I mean. You and Tori, and just – yeah." Finn adjusted his beanie uncomfortably. "I've been coming here instead."

"You don't have to feel bad about saying it," Carolyn said softly, focusing on a point just to the left of his head instead of meeting his eyes. "I know I'm a little black rain cloud over everybody's parties."

Finn shifted his weight from foot to foot and searched for a response to that. "You just have to let loose and have some fun," he advised. "You used to do it all the time. Now you only think about all the things that have gone wrong and how much your life sucks, which gets old really fast."

"But my life *does* suck," she reminded him.

"Maybe it wouldn't seem so bad if you didn't make it that way."

196

"Are you saying it's *my* fault?"

Finn shrugged. "You could stop yourself if you wanted."

Carolyn snorted. "No I couldn't!"

Finn stepped sideways into the range of her vision and stared into her eyes, a knowing smile still pulling the corner of his mouth upward. "That's where you're wrong." Carolyn found it extremely hard to break the connection once their eyes met. Finn had that sort of intensity about him. She wrenched her gaze away and looked to the parking lot behind him.

"Look," she said distractedly. "There's a Papa Gino's delivery car here! Boy, I could go for some pizza."

"You're in luck then," Finn told her. He and the rest of the kids gravitated toward the car, and Matt fell into step beside them.

"Finn! You made it! We could have given you a ride, you know," he said.

"You mean they're bringing pizza for *us?*" Carolyn asked, ignoring Matt. "Do we have to pay for it?"

Finn and Matt both laughed until they realized she was serious. "Of course not," Matt said.

"Good, because I don't have any money." Carolyn watched a tall guy with tidily cropped sandy blond hair exchange some bills for a stack of pizza boxes. "Who's that dude?"

"That's Jiles, the new youth pastor. He's just out of college," Matt explained. "He's great. He really, you know, *gets* it." Carolyn wanted to ask *what* he "got," but she was more concerned with getting some food into her hungry stomach.

"Whoa, tiger," Finn said, grabbing her arm and pulling her back.

"We have to pray first," Matt said. Looking around, Carolyn saw that the rest of the kids were forming a circle and holding hands.

"Okay, this is weird." Ignoring the strangeness of the situation, Carolyn eagerly crossed her arms in front of her and took Matt's and Finn's hands.

Matt's hand was warm, soft, and familiar. Finn's was big and kind of rough. She could feel calluses even bigger than her own on his fingertips. Everyone bowed their heads, and Carolyn followed suit, feeling like a poser for joining in where she so clearly did not belong but preferring to blend seamlessly into the situation.

Finally, she was allowed to delve into the cheesy mess and satiate her hunger. She sat with Matt, Finn, some of the skaters, a few of the kids she'd been introduced to earlier, and a couple girls who Carolyn thought looked like they could relate to her life story. The crowd sat around the edges of the Ga-Ga pit and talked and laughed joyfully. Carolyn made the acquaintance of two girls, Raven and Juliet, whom the boys referred to as "Rae and J." One had short, funky hair with a faded magenta tinge, while the other had sleek, stick-straight black hair that Carolyn totally envied, and both appeared to be of Asian descent.

"Have you been coming to this church long?" Carolyn asked.

"I've been coming since I was in like third grade," Raven (pink-hair) said. "I started dragging J to youth group two years ago."

"So what's it like here? I mean, this is so not what I expected was going on when Matt kept saying he was going to youth group."

"It's great!" J piped up. "We do all sorts of great youth events. There are these weekend retreats, and they take us to summer camp, and sometimes they take us on all-nighters or bring us to concerts!"

Carolyn perked up. "What kind of concerts?" she asked.

"Christian concerts," Raven said quickly. "Five Iron Frenzy, Audio Adrenaline, Relient K, those kinds of bands."

Carolyn shook her head. "I don't know them. I guess they wouldn't take you to, like, Dropkick Murphys?" Raven and J just laughed, and Carolyn sighed. "It figures."

"Hey, the ones we've been to have all been really good!" J said. "I never expected Christian music to be any good, but you'd be surprised. Jiles will lend you CDs if you want a listen."

"I'll ask him," Carolyn said agreeably, not really intending to do so. "So you guys really do have fun around here." She was still amazed by the amount of cool things that went on at this church. Raven and J nodded vigorously.

"Sorry to interrupt..." A stocky Latino guy who Carolyn thought was named Drew tapped Raven on the shoulder. "But Rae, we've got to sound check real quick..."

Raven shoved the crust of her pizza in her mouth and got up to follow Drew. "Sound check? What do they have to sound check for?" Carolyn asked J.

"Oh, Rae and Drew are on the praise team," J said, as though that should explain it all.

"Which means what?"

J elaborated. "They lead us in worship. Rae plays the bass. Drew plays drums. And there are a couple girls who play guitar and sing."

"Are you telling me you guys get a free concert every week?"

J laughed. "Not exactly. It's not a concert, silly. They're just leading us. We're supposed to sing, too."

Carolyn blanched. "I never let anyone hear me sing."

"That's okay," J said nonchalantly, reaching for another slice. "No one will be listening to *you*, personally. It's not about how good we are. It's about worship."

"Right." *Okay, now I'm totally confused.*

"Hey, everyone, let's head up!" Jiles shouted over their heads. Carolyn followed the horde of people into the church and up a flight of stairs to a room furnished with a scratchy red carpet and several couches that had seen better days and, Carolyn could only guess, had probably been donated by church-goers who had been sensible enough to want to buy new ones. The lights were dim, and an overhead projector shone on the one wall that wasn't covered with pictures of kids on the retreats J and Raven had mentioned. Raven, Drew, and a few others stood off to the side, clutching instruments that Carolyn could tell were just itching to be played.

Matt directed Carolyn to a couch towards the front of the room, where she was less likely to get distracted by her new skater friends, who'd crashed on the couches in the back. "I didn't know this was going to be, like, a church service," Carolyn whined, even though she'd been expecting the whole thing to be one big, long lecture.

"You can't expect us to completely ignore God at *youth group*," Matt said, somewhat irritably. "Try and pay attention, okay?"

"Sure." *Yeah, right. I still can't believe I wound up* here *on a Friday night. This is so awkward.* Jiles stood up front and leaned into a microphone. "Let's pray," he said. Carolyn rolled her eyes as the kids around her obediently bowed their heads. Carolyn half-listened. *Encountering God? What* is *he going on about? Gah. How can all these people be so sure He's really there? I've never seen any proof. What's God ever done for me?*

Jiles finally said "amen," and a chorus of mumbled "amens" from the kids signaled the end of his prayer. *Still, this beats disco bowling with traitor Tori and the others. I'm having more fun now than I have since... since New Year's, when Matt kissed me.*

Everyone stood up, and Raven and the others started playing. Carolyn found her toes tapping to the beat a little, and forced her foot to stay still. *I always blamed Paul, but I don't know. Maybe Finn was right when he said I could have stopped myself. Maybe I couldn't change what happened, but I could have used an attitude adjustment. Only I could ruin a perfectly enjoyable night like this one by thinking about...* him.

Carolyn finally gave up on sitting still. Maybe religion wasn't as miserable as she'd always thought. She followed the example of the kids around her, who were jumping around, waving their arms, and singing at the top of their lungs.

It was like being at some sort of exclusive concert. She couldn't help trying to sing along, even though she didn't know any of the songs.

After the praise team had finished a few songs, Carolyn leaned over and muttered breathlessly in Matt's ear, "Who would have guessed you can worship with electric guitars, bass, and drums? It's not all boring hymns with thee's and thou's and other weird words."

Matt laughed at her again. "You really had no idea where I was all this time, did you?" Carolyn glowered at the fact that he was so amused by her incredulity. "It's not a matter of *how* you worship. The important thing is your attitude. If you're playing guitar with a worshipful heart, then it counts."

"No kidding?"

When the praise team was done, Carolyn made room for Raven on their couch. "Hey, Pink! You guys are awesome!" she commented. Everyone else seemed to have calmed down quite a bit, but Carolyn was totally energized, and wished she could run over, snatch up one of those shiny guitars, and start rocking out.

Raven laughed softly and tugged at the elastic in her long, dark, smooth hair. "We're pretty terrible, really, but thanks."

"At least you've got a band to play with," Carolyn pointed out, thinking of the solitary hours she spent jamming her cares away.

"Only on Fridays," Raven corrected. "Other than that, I pretty much play alone, which is a little weird. A bass line doesn't sound like much by itself."

"You seem like you know what you're talking about."

Raven smiled. "I try."

"Maybe we can-"

Matt flicked her on the arm and hissed, "be quiet and listen to Jiles." Carolyn made a face for only Raven to see. Raven giggled, but a glare from Matt quickly silenced her. When he'd turned his attention back to Jiles, Raven discreetly pulled a little memo pad from her purse and started scrawling on the first free page with a fine-point Sharpie.

'Maybe we can what?'

Carolyn took the pad and scribbled, 'Rock out sometime.' Raven's face lit up, though she tried to hide it. Her writing became more frenzied.

'You play an instrument?'

'Guitar.'

'Sweet! Yeah, we should get together.' She wrote her phone number and address on another free page and tore it out. Carolyn took it and put it in her purse. Raven shoved the memo pad at her, mouthing "yours?" Carolyn printed her info on the page and gave it back.

'Yay! I'm so stoked. Are you out of school? We could get together this week or something.'

'Yeah! Def-'

Matt reached across and snagged the memo pad and marker, reading what they'd written and holding it just far enough away so Raven couldn't reach over to get it back. Carolyn tried to snatch it, but Matt just held it farther away. Then he started writing with the Sharpie: 'Would you two <u>Pay Attention!</u>'

Carolyn and Raven pouted at him. Raven took her pad back and scrawled in huge letters, 'SPOIL SPORT.' Matt just shook his head and tried to focus on what Jiles was saying. Carolyn shook her head for a different reason and slouched back into the cushion, exasperated at what a bore her boyfriend could be.

Jiles seemed to be sharing an abridged version of Jesus' life story, or maybe even the entire history of Christianity. Carolyn wasn't sure. She was paying more attention to how familiar he looked than what he was saying. *Where have I seen that face before?* She racked her memory, but it just wasn't coming to her. *I must be imagining things. I wonder how much longer he's gonna drag out this history lesson.* Jiles talked about the Creation of the world, and the way that the first people, Adam and Eve, had turned away from God by eating forbidden fruit in the Garden of Eden. Carolyn took Raven's Sharpie and started coloring her nails. Matt gently plucked it from her hand.

"Hey! I still have four nails left!" she objected. "Look. Doesn't this look silly? Let me finish."

"Of course it looks silly. You just colored your nails black with a marker," Matt said pointedly. "Listen, would you?" Carolyn pouted. Jiles was now talking about the consequences of human rebellion: eternity in hell. *Are they allowed to say that? I thought hell was a swear word. What are they doing using it in a church?* As she listened, though, Carolyn realized Jiles was talking about what sounded like an actual place. Not a place on *this* Earth, certainly, but a real place that people could go to when they died – and *would* go to, if they didn't accept Jesus as their Savior.

"Isn't that kind of closed-minded?" Carolyn whispered to Matt.

"Closed-minded doesn't matter if it's true," Matt responded. "If everyone else thought the sky was green, but you knew it was blue, would it make the sky any less blue because everyone thought it was green?"

Carolyn looked at him like he was crazy. "No," she said, just to appease him. Mostly what he'd just said was as jumbled a mess as everything else in her mind. "What time is this over?"

Matt sighed. "Eight forty." Carolyn looked at the clock. Ten more minutes. She could stand that – maybe.

Jiles was still going on about Jesus being Savior and keeping people from going to hell. "'If you confess with your mouth that Jesus is Lord, and believe in your heart that God raised him from the dead, then you will be saved,'" he quoted. "All you have to do is believe. That's all it takes. If you ask God to save you and trust that He will, then He will." Carolyn thought about that. Jiles seemed awfully confident for someone who had no power to make sure what he'd just said actually happened.

Jiles prayed and dismissed them. Carolyn was taciturn as everyone fought to be first out the door, and as Finn and Matt jabbered on about some baseball game that Finn's family apparently had tickets for, but Finn didn't want to go to. Outside, the rain had picked up. Matt offered Finn a ride, and the three of them made a run for Mrs. MacMillan's car, parked halfway across the parking lot. Their clothes were damp and clingy by the time they clambered in, and Carolyn picked uncomfortably at her shirt, which had been tight to begin with and would only shrink now that it was wet.

The ride home was almost painfully silent. After they'd dropped Finn off, Matt leaned forward in his seat and asked Carolyn what she'd thought. "It was… good," she said uncertainly. The thing was, she *had* enjoyed herself, and for some reason she really wanted to go back. "Maybe I could, y'know, tag along next week?"

Matt's whole countenance lit up. "Are you serious?" Carolyn nodded. "Of course you can come!" He gave her that winning smile of his, the genuine one she hadn't had directed at her in months, and to her own surprise, she genuinely smiled back.

"Could you drop me at Anne's? I'm spending the night," she said as they entered the neighborhood.

"Of course, dear. I'm glad you had fun!" Mrs. MacMillan chirruped, pulling up alongside Anne's house when Carolyn pointed it out.

"Thanks for the ride, Mrs. MacMillan!" Carolyn called, splashing up the walkway and letting herself in without knocking. Skitt happened to be in the kitchen, digging through the medicine cabinet. He spun around in surprise at her sudden entrance.

"Where have *you* been?" he asked. "God, you're soaked. Hold on, I'll get you a towel." He sounded more like an older brother than ever. He left the room with a bottle of aspirin and a glass of water, and Carolyn was struck by the strangeness of the situation. It was barely past nine. He should have still been at his party.

When Skitt returned, without the aspirin and water but with a fluffy blue towel, she asked why he was home so early.

"Anne wasn't feeling well." He shook his head. "I keep telling her never to drink anything at those parties, because you never know what the older kids might put in it, but I think she got thirsty and had some punch, and of course they'd spiked it as always… Load of irresponsible dunderheads," he added scathingly. Carolyn wrapped the towel around her shoulders and used the corner of it to dry her face.

"Oh. That sucks. Are you going back?"

"I don't think so. Why, did you want to go?"

"Oh, no. I was just wondering."

After a rather awkward silence, Skitt asked if he could get her anything else. Carolyn shook her head 'no.' "All right. Well. If you want, you can come up and watch me practice… my band has a gig tomorrow night."

"Sounds good." She was still wet, but at least she wasn't dripping anymore. She followed Skitt up to the attic and made herself comfortable on the ratty couch he had up there. Skitt positioned himself behind the drum set, but he didn't play. Carolyn hugged her knees. "Well?" she asked expectantly.

Skitt shrugged. "I'm not really in a drum mood," he said. "Are you?"

"Uh… I didn't know there was such a thing," Carolyn said, getting up to look more closely at the drum set. "I don't know anything about drums," she continued. "Can you teach me?"

"What, to *play?*" Skitt asked. Carolyn nodded. "I guess I could show you some basics…" He got up, stepped backwards, and gestured for Carolyn to take a seat on the stool. He handed her a pair of drumsticks, which Carolyn took dubiously and held in her fists. Skitt laughed. "No… like this," he corrected, reaching around from behind her and moving her fingers to grip the sticks properly. Carolyn felt her heart rate pick up. He was leaning so close that she could feel his breath on the back of her neck. Just that afternoon, she would have done anything to be in a position like this, but things were turning around. Matt wasn't as crazy as she'd thought. Things might just work out between them after all. That smile he'd given her when she said she wanted to go back to church…. but Carolyn couldn't focus with Skitt so close.

"Skitt," she interrupted, twisting in the stool to face him. It was an automatic action, turning to face the person she was speaking to, but in this instance, it was a mistake. His face was so close that her nose almost collided with his. Skitt leapt back in surprise, and Carolyn jumped to her feet.

"I'm supposed to be grounded," she said quickly, blushing, and trying to pretend nothing odd had just happened. "My mom's going to worry about me. I thought it would be a good idea to spend the night here, but if I don't go home, she's going to kill me." Carolyn started for the door. "She's probably already a basket case, trying to figure out where I could be." *Stop babbling*, she ordered herself. "But, you know, maybe you can teach me the drums some other time." Words just kept spilling out of her mouth, and Carolyn didn't know where they were coming from. She hadn't said this much in ages. "See you later, thanks for the towel and all…"

She shut the door behind her and took a deep breath before descending the dimly lit stairs. That was close. She snatched up her bag from the corner where she'd left it earlier and stalked out the door. The rain had let up a little, but twilight had set in, and with it came a slight chill. Carolyn shivered while she walked.

The lights were on in the kitchen at home. Carolyn crept around back and tried to choose the best place to climb. The screened-in verandah had a board that ran all around the enclosure at what, for someone inside, would have been waist-height. Carolyn threw her bag up onto the roof and scrabbled for leverage, wishing for Molly's strong softball arms. Finally, she managed to straighten her arms and swing her leg around. With a great effort, she pushed and pulled herself up onto the board until she was balancing on the narrow bit of wood. Once she'd gained her confidence, Carolyn reached for the edge of the roof. *Almost… just a little bit further…*

Suddenly, Carolyn found that the board simply was not under her feet any longer.

She let out an involuntary cry of surprise, which was cut short when she landed on her back, narrowly missing a rose bush. The breath rushed from her lungs, and Carolyn choked and struggled to breathe in. A light came on in the verandah, and Carolyn tried to call out to whoever was inside, but all she could do was cough.

"Is someone there?" Mrs. Becker's voice called out nervously. *I'm here!* Carolyn wanted to shout. She coughed again. Carolyn heard her mom's footsteps cross the room. *Faster, mom! I'm going to die out here at the rate you're moving!* Mom finally got to the edge of the room and peered through the screen, scanning the edge of the woods for intruders.

"Mom!" Carolyn choked out. Mrs. Becker jumped in surprise and looked down.

Her reaction was nothing short of what Carolyn had expected. She gave a strangled cry and ran for the door, and in seconds, was at Carolyn's side, asking if she was all right.

Carolyn managed an, "I think so." Mom didn't even ask what she was doing out there. Carolyn noticed the board she'd been standing on had broken. The very ends of the board were still nailed to the supporting beams on either side of where she'd been climbing, but the middle of the board had splintered and fallen into the rose bush. Mom, however, paid no attention to the damage she'd done to the house. She made Carolyn get up very slowly to make sure she wasn't hurt.

"I think I twisted my ankle again," Carolyn grimaced as soon as she put weight on her left foot. Mom supported her back into the house and guided her to the couch in the living room. Carolyn sat down gingerly. "And I think I bruised my tailbone," she added.

"Poor baby," Mom said sympathetically. "I'll get you some ice…" And she was off, bustling around trying to make Carolyn as comfortable as possible.

Carolyn smiled in spite of the pain. Mom still loved her. Mom had always loved her. Mom didn't deserve to be snuck out on. *Never again*, Carolyn promised. Mom brought in an ice pack and some blankets and pillows. Carolyn snuggled in and thanked her.

"You're welcome, honey." Mom switched off the lights and started up the stairs.

"I'm sorry, Mom," Carolyn said quietly.

"It's okay," Mom reassured her, retracing her steps and taking a seat on the arm of the couch. "How was youth group?"

Carolyn almost jumped to her feet. "*What?*"

Mom laughed. "Did you think Mrs. MacMillan wouldn't call me and tell me you'd jumped out of a car so you could go to youth group with her son?" She stroked Carolyn's hair. "You've had a pretty crazy day, young lady. Go to sleep and we'll talk in the morning."

Message from: Leah Sorman <PussyCat240@aol.com>
To: Carolyn Becker <SkiBlink@aol.com>
Alive???

Yoo-hoo! You disappeared again. ☹ What is going on down there? Trouble in Paradise? You know I'll listen, and even make my best effort to give you sound advice.

Well, I hope things are okay. I would fill you in on the adventures of Leah and Church Boy, but I get the feeling you don't read your emails anymore. Well, I miss you. Bye.

CHAPTER NINETEEN

Instead of grounding Carolyn for another week, Mom revoked her computer privileges. "It's summertime. I don't want to keep you inside for two weeks with this beautiful weather outside," she had said. The one-week groundation would have been fine by Carolyn if she'd been allowed to surf the web, but since Mom had forbidden her to use the computer, all she had to do for the rest of the week was write and jam.

Sunday evening, Mom left quietly to go grocery shopping. Carolyn knew she'd been hoping to leave and come back without her daughter figuring out she was gone and taking advantage of the opportunity, but Carolyn wasn't going to be fooled that easily, and she needed to talk to Matt. Part of her couldn't believe she was sneaking out again. *One more time won't hurt,* she told herself, eyeing Buddy as he slept off in the corner, but he was too deeply asleep to notice her departure.

Carolyn knew she had about an hour and a half. She would have to move fast, but she *had* to talk to Matt. At the back of her mind, she'd always entertained a notion that Matt was just being hard to get or something, or that he just wanted to manipulate her into going to church with him and that once she gave in, he would finally take her back. Now it was time to find out for sure. Jimmie was playing video games in the family room, and Carolyn got out the door without a problem.

She found herself waiting nervously on Matt's doorstep again, wondering, as always, if she was doing the right thing.

Matt's little sister, Kelsey, answered the door. Carolyn hadn't seen her in a long time. Kelsey's blue eyes, the same icy shade as Matt's, widened and she ran back into the house to get her brother without so much as a "hello." Confused, Carolyn stepped over the threshold and shut the door behind her so the air conditioning wouldn't be wasted.

Matt appeared a few seconds later. "Hey," he said, his face brightening.

"Hey," Carolyn said back, shifting her weight nervously onto her uninjured foot. "Um. Do you think it's time we got back together?" she blurted.

Matt absorbed the question slowly. "I'm not sure that's a good idea," he said hesitantly. Carolyn was shocked.

"Why not? I went to church with you! I even kind of *liked* it! Isn't that what you wanted?" She'd been hoping he'd sweep her up in his arms and kiss her passionately, but once again, things weren't going quite as she'd planned.

"Carolyn," Matt chided. "I didn't decide not to kiss you because you don't go to church. I thought we'd been through this. This is my personal choice." His voice was gentle and sure.

"Matt," Carolyn said knowingly, sidling closer. "I know that was just your cover story. It's okay, you can drop it now." Matt opened his mouth to object, but before he could find the words, Carolyn cut him off by placing her mouth on his. *That should show him.*

Matt seemed indecisive. For an instant, he kissed her back, and Carolyn thought she felt the familiar sparkles she'd missed so much – but then, just as quickly, he was gone. Carolyn opened her eyes. Was it her imagination, or did Matt look… afraid?

"Go," he ordered, anger burning up the ice in his eyes. Like a chastened puppy, Carolyn obeyed and let herself out the door. She couldn't believe she'd been wrong. Matt was really serious about this whole thing. She shuffled down the sidewalk, humbled, humiliated, mesmerized by the cracks underfoot. She was surprised to find herself, not at home, but at the Donahues'.

In a trance, she knocked timidly at the door. She had to knock a few more times before Skitt came and opened the door. Carolyn caught a glimpse of him in his boxers before he shut the door almost all the way.

"God!" he said through the crack, hiding behind the door. "I thought you were my parents or something. Anne's not home."

"That's all right," Carolyn said, undaunted by his appearance. "Can I come in?"

"Can I put some clothes on first?" Skitt retorted.

"If you must," Carolyn sighed, sneaking one last peek at his bronze, well-defined abs before he shut the door all the way. *What am I getting myself into?* She wondered.

It's not 'into,' she rationalized. *It's 'out of.' I'm getting out of this horrible state where nobody except the kid I hate wants to lock lips with me. And that's assuming Skitt even would. Anne said he wouldn't. But what would she know? She wasn't in the attic the other night.*

The door opened, and Carolyn realized she'd been pacing. She stopped herself and strode into the kitchen, brushing up against Skitt as he held the door open for her. "Where is everyone?" she asked casually.

"Some official tour of Santa Catalina," Skitt said apathetically. He seemed really confused as to why Carolyn would be there when Anne wasn't around. "Can I, uh, get you anything?" he offered.

"I'm okay, thanks."

Skitt continued to eye her with that adorable, mystified expression on his face as he took a seat on one of the wooden stools along the countertop. Carolyn gave him her best smile, her heart pounding for more reasons than she cared to count, and seated herself on the stool right next to his. The wood was hard, and Carolyn's rear was none too happy about the bruise she'd gotten falling off the side of the house the night before. "How come you didn't go?" she asked in a soft voice, maintaining eye contact as best she could, though her instincts kept screaming, "Look away!" Eye contact wasn't one of her favorite things. Lip contact was preferable in her book.

Skitt looked back into her eyes and replied, "I was asleep when they left."

"Oh." Carolyn angled herself towards him, not quite allowing their arms or legs to touch but staying close enough to feel the warmth radiating off of him. Carolyn wasn't sure if it was intentional when Skitt slowly closed the distance, so that she could feel the skin of his arm brushing the skin of hers and the warmth of his leg mingling with the warmth of her own. Her heart beat faster, and she felt light-headed.

She was pretty sure it was intentional, however, when his face drifted towards hers. Her heart rate skyrocketed, and she closed her eyes, leaning towards him ever so slightly. As soon as their lips touched, it was like some sort of switch was flipped in both of their minds, and they kissed with unbridled passion.

"Drum lesson?" Skitt asked mischievously, lacing his fingers into hers and drawing her along up the stairs to the couch in the attic. Carolyn followed willingly. Skitt kissed her like no one had ever kissed her before. She couldn't forget that that was probably because he had years more experience than she did, but she chose to ignore that fact. Someone cared about her! It was enough to make her want to laugh and cry all at once. Someone wanted her around. Someone loved her! These were the only thoughts running through her head as Skitt pulled himself closer to her, though they were already as close as they could get. Carolyn let herself think it would never end and played along, pressing herself against him.

Skitt's watch beeped, and Carolyn suddenly remembered Mom, grocery shopping, with no idea where her daughter was or what she'd gotten herself into. If she didn't leave now, Mom would get home first and ground her for even longer, or worse, confiscate her guitar or something. "I have to go," she said. Skitt was reluctant to move. "Skitt, you have to get off me now," Carolyn said more forcefully. "My mom doesn't know where I am."

This statement seemed to serve as a reality check for Skitt, and he rolled off her, swearing. "Is this what you came here for?" he demanded.

"Yes," Carolyn admitted shamelessly.

Skitt groaned. "Carolyn, I'm going to *college* next year. You're not even in high school!"

"Yes I am!" she insisted. Would be, in the fall.

"The point is, if anyone ever found out..."

"Well, *I* won't tell," Carolyn promised.

"But the fact that it happened at all," Skitt said, his expression pained. "You'd better get out of here before anyone finds us."

Carolyn gathered what little dignity she had left and stalked out the door. It had felt so right when he'd kissed her, but the further she walked, the dirtier she felt (and the more her ankle throbbed). The things she kept doing to try and fix her problems only seemed to make everything worse. *I should just become a hermit. Or maybe Matt has the right idea. I could become a nun and never have to worry about this kind of thing again.*

Fortunately, there were no cars in the driveway when Carolyn got home. She listened at the screen door, and she could hear Super Smash Bros. music floating down from the family room. Buddy was still sound asleep in the corner. Everything was just as she'd left it, but she had changed – again. She slunk back up to her room and shut the door.

I should just let Mom ground me for life. I clearly can't handle relationships at all. I don't deserve the few friends I've got left. Oh, God, what will Anne think if she finds out about me and Skitt? But he won't tell her. Will he? I know I won't. I just don't think I can look her in the eye ever again. Or Matt either, for that matter, who probably would prefer it that way anyway.

It was just, I felt like he cared about me. Skitt, I mean. I felt like somebody loved me, or at least wanted something to do with me, which is more than I can say for most of my "friends." It felt good to be wanted (even if he just wanted to make out with me).

I'm starting to miss Dad. I sure don't miss all the fighting between him and Mom, but it's so weird not having him here. It's not like we were best buddies the way I used to be with Mom, or the way Jimmie and Dad were. Yeah — Jimmie's got the worst deal, now that I think about it. He and Dad were best friends. They played sports and video games; Dad was the one who was supposed to teach Jimmie everything because, you know, they're both guys. It's just not the same being a boy raised by a woman. You miss out on a lot. I hope Jimmie will be all right. He hasn't said anything to me since that night a long time ago when he broke down and cried — nothing about his feelings, anyhow. Come to think of it, I don't think I've heard him say much of anything to anybody since Mom and Dad started fighting in January. Not that I see him with his friends. But he seems to be trying to separate himself from us, and I don't really blame him. I guess it's not so different from my response. Emotional attachment can be dangerous in times like these. For a while there, I was trying to look out for him, but I guess I sort of forgot about that when things got out of control. More out of control than they already were.

I wonder what people would do if I just disappeared. Would anybody miss me? I doubt it. They'd probably be glad to see me go. They'd probably think, "Remember that crazy girl who used to rain on everybody's parade, and went around kissing all the boys because she had to be sure everyone didn't hate her, but they did anyway? It's a good thing she's gone." They're probably scared of me, like Tori. Well, good. I'd be scared of me, too. I kind of am

216

scared of me, and what stupid thing I'll do next. It probably would be better if I stopped myself before I got around to it, and just jumped off a bridge or something right now.

I think I need to sleep this one off.

CHAPTER TWENTY

Monday morning, the phone woke Carolyn at 10:30. Sleep hadn't improved her mental state. "Hello?" she said groggily.

"Morning," said a laughing Raven. "Sorry if I woke you up."

"S'okay," Carolyn said, sitting up and throwing the covers off. "What's up?"

"Do you want to hang out today?"

"I wish," Carolyn said dejectedly. "I'm grounded."

"For what?" Raven asked in surprise.

"Well, I wasn't really supposed to be out Friday, but as you know, I was at youth group," Carolyn explained, avoiding the real reason she was housebound. She winced just remembering what she'd done to Matt when she'd kissed Paul that day last week. "And my mom caught me sneaking back in because the thing I was climbing up decided to break."

Raven made a sound that could have been sympathetic or amused. "Aw. That's too bad. I was going to dye my hair today and, I don't know, I thought it would be fun if you came and dyed yours with me."

"That *does* sound like fun. I wish I could, Rae," Carolyn mourned.

"I can save my dye. When are you un-grounded?"

"I think I'll be free in time for youth group this week," Carolyn said uncertainly.

"I've got an idea!" Raven burst out. "You want to come sleep over my house after youth group? We can do our hair and jam and stuff!"

Carolyn couldn't help wondering why Raven was so eager to hang out with her, but she said she'd talk to her mom about it.

"Great!" Raven said exuberantly. "Are you... um... allowed to talk on the phone?"

"Uh..." Carolyn hadn't thought about it. "Probably. My mom just said I couldn't use the computer."

"Cool. I'll be your entertainment today," Raven volunteered cheerfully. She chattered on, and Carolyn listened in amusement and bewilderment as Rae told her about her favorite bands and the concerts she'd been to.

"Lucky," Carolyn said enviously. "I've never been to a concert, but since I started hanging out with Finn and borrowing his music, I've wanted to go to so many."

"Maybe we can all go to one this summer," Rae suggested eagerly.

"Yeah!"

"Speaking of Finn," Rae said, kind of uncomfortably, Carolyn thought. "Do you think he's cute?"

"Oh, my God!" Carolyn groaned. "Why does everyone think I like him?"

Rae laughed. "*That's* not why I was asking... why, do you?"

"No!"

"Oh. Well, that's good, I guess. I mean, I don't know. Whatever, right?"

"You like him, don't you?" Carolyn guessed.

Raven giggled nervously. "You caught me. But don't tell him, okay?"

"I hadn't planned on it," Carolyn told her. "Just because we play DDR together doesn't mean I tell him everything about my life." *Uh, right, except for the whole thing with Paul, and Matt, and me being such a drag – yeah, we don't talk about anything serious at all.*

"Good." Raven sighed in relief. "I don't want to make the first move, but I don't want *him* to feel forced into making it because someone told him to, you know?"

"Yeah," Carolyn said, quickly changing the subject. "So what color were you going to do your hair?"

"I can't decide. I've got red, purple, blue, black, and turquoise. What do you think?"

"Oh!" Carolyn said in surprise. "I didn't realize you meant *those* kinds of colors!"

Raven laughed. "Blue is way more exciting than platinum blonde, don't you think?"

"Absolutely."

Someone knocked at the door. "Lynnie? I need to use the phone!" Mom's voice called through the door.

"Okay!" Carolyn called back. "Uh, sorry, Rae, I have to go. I'll help you choose on Friday."

"Aww. Okay. It was fun talking to you!" Raven bubbled. "Bye!"

Carolyn opened the door and passed the phone out to her mom. "Thank you," mom said. "Since you're up..." Carolyn suppressed a groan. That was Mom's 'I'm going to put you to work today' voice. "I have to do some weeding. The whole walkway is overgrown... and the garden's a disaster... Throw on some clothes and come out and help me, okay?"

Mom was gone before Carolyn could object. *Man, being grounded sucks.* Weeding. *Could she have come up with a worse chore if she tried?* Carolyn doubted her twisted ankle was a legitimate excuse for skipping out on the chore, seeing as the swelling had already subsided and the pain was nearly gone. With a groan, she threw on some grubby clothes and popped an MxPx CD into her Walkman to help her stay sane. It was going to be a long week.

Carolyn jiggled her leg nervously as the car sped down the freeway. This was the first time she'd visited Dad since he and Mom split up. Dad had visited *them*, but until now, Carolyn hadn't seen the apartment he'd been renting. While they'd been weeding yesterday, Mom had announced that she'd just gotten off the phone with him and that he wanted to spend some time with the kids. "I figured the timing was great. It won't interfere with your social life since you're grounded this week, anyway. You can't possibly get into any trouble when you're half an hour away from home." Mom had gone on and on about the visit, trying to get Carolyn excited, but that wasn't the real problem. Carolyn looked forward to seeing Dad.

The problem was, she'd read so many books and watched so many movies where the kid had shown up at one of their parents' houses to find that the parent had started a new life or a new family or a new relationship. *What if Dad has a new girlfriend? What if he's already making plans to get an official divorce and marry someone else? He can't do that! ...can he? But he wouldn't! But what if he did?* The argument raged on in her head as Mom drove and Jimmie buried his face in a summer reading assignment in the back seat. The silence was growing painful when they pulled into a parking lot outside a multi-level apartment complex.

Carolyn reluctantly gathered her duffel bag and backpack from the trunk and followed her mom inside. Jimmie trailed along, his bag rolling along on its wheels and clicking loudly with every bump it went over. "Lynnie, let me help you carry something," Mom offered as they waited for the elevator.

"I'm fine," Carolyn said curtly. She couldn't help being bitter about this whole separation thing, and she certainly didn't want Mom thinking she approved.

Dad's room was on the fifth floor, all the way down a narrow, décor-free corridor with an ugly, stained, grayish carpet. Carolyn wrinkled her nose at the unfamiliar smell of the place. She couldn't imagine her dad being happy here. When they reached the last room in the hallway, Mom stopped and rapped on the door.

Dad answered a few seconds later, greeting the kids with huge grins and big hugs and all the excitement he'd always had. He didn't appear to be hiding anything.

"I just made some iced tea and lemonade," he said to Mom. "Would you like some?"

Mom declined and went on her way. "I want lemonade," Jimmie said, depositing his stuff on the floor just inside the door like he lived there or something. *And I guess, in some sort of twisted way, he does.* Carolyn adjusted the straps on her backpack but didn't put it down. She just couldn't think of this place as home, in any sense of the word. It was worse than trying to move into their big, modern house in Long Beach after spending twelve years in Alaska.

"How about you, Caro? Anything to drink?" Dad asked.

"Sure. Lemonade, please." Carolyn felt like a guest in a stranger's home. She looked around. The place was barely furnished. The couch that had once been in the garage because no one wanted to bring it to the dump slouched next to dad's bedside table, which was adorned with his reading lamp and a few books. One of Grandma's quilts that had found their home in the Beckers' attic was folded haphazardly over the top of the couch. Carolyn knew that was where her dad had been sleeping all this time – on a pullout couch with an old quilt and his favorite firm pillow – and felt a pang of guilt. Why should *she*, the kid, get a perfect room with more luxuries than she could imagine, including a desk, a stereo, curtains, a freaking *canopy* over her bed, and so many other things when Dad had barely enough, and certainly not enough to be happy or comfortable? *I guess I can understand why we've never been allowed to visit before. And I understand now why Mom had us bring sleeping bags.* She'd had to stuff hers into the bottom of her backpack, and had barely managed to fit all her clothes with it in there, but Mom had insisted.

Carolyn arrived in the kitchen just in time to see Dad put the pitcher of lemonade back in a mini-fridge that barely had enough room for it. Carolyn sipped from the glass Dad had handed her and tried not to grimace at the overly sweet concoction. Someone had added a little too much sugar. Jimmie was going to be off the walls in no time.

Dad wanted to know what they'd been up to lately, and Jimmie launched into a detailed report of the past few weeks. Dad nodded and snuck in a, "that's great, Jim," whenever Jimmie paused for a breath. "What about you, Caro?" Dad asked when Jimmie was finally done.

"She just plays her guitar all the time," said Jimmie quickly. Carolyn glared. Why was he suddenly talkative? "She got grounded, too!"

"Why don't you let Carolyn talk, okay, Jim?" Dad said amusedly. "What did you get grounded for?"

"I snuck out on Friday," Carolyn admitted guiltily. "I was at church, though! You'd think she'd forgive me after that."

Dad laughed, and Jimmie butted in, "Maybe she would have if you hadn't broken the verandah trying to climb in your window!" And then he proceeded to laugh so hard that he snorted.

How does he even know all this? Carolyn thought in disgust. "You broke the verandah?" Dad asked in concern. "Are you all right?"

"I'm fine," Carolyn said, sticking her foot out so he could see the Ace Bandage peeking out from under the Chucks she had on. "Just twisted my ankle. Again." She tried to laugh it off, but Dad's face was grim.

"I don't like the sound of that, Caro," he said sternly. "No more sneaking in and out."

"Believe me, I've learned my lesson," Carolyn said earnestly. "And by the way, I didn't *break the verandah*. I just snapped a board in half."

"Either way, Caro, it was dangerous trying to climb up the side of the house, and it was dishonest to go behind your mom's back like that. I hope it doesn't happen again." Carolyn dropped her eyes under his intent gaze.

"Yes, Dad."

Reassured, Dad pressed, "How *did* you pull that one over on her, anyway?"

"I went out the window in my room and jumped from that part of the roof down to the verandah roof, and from there to the ground."

Dad shook his head, trying to be the responsible parent but also, Carolyn could tell, trying to hide that he was impressed by her escapade.

"Anyway," Carolyn said quickly. She started talking about the end of school and mentioned the drama with her friends, but refused to go into detail.

"What about that boy – Matt?" Dad asked. "Are you still seeing him?"

"Sort of. It's complicated."

"You're too young for complicated, kiddo," Dad said fondly. "Take care of yourself, all right?"

"I will," Carolyn promised.

"So what do you kids want to do?" Dad asked. "It's a beautiful day."

"I guess it wouldn't make sense to drive all the way back to the beach, huh?" Carolyn joked.

"No, but there's a pool down on the ground floor," Dad suggested.

In the end, Dad took them swimming, mini-golfing, and shopping that week. They went to the movies one night, and Dad brought them on an expedition through the woods, where Jimmie climbed every boulder he saw like a monkey hyped up on too much of Dad's lemonade (which Carolyn couldn't help thinking Jimmie was.) They won thousands of tickets at the arcade on Friday afternoon, and Carolyn and Jimmie conspired to save up enough tickets to get a little TV for Dad.

"The TV is 20,000 tickets, Carolyn," Jimmie pointed out. "We'd have to be in here every day to win that many."

"No," Carolyn objected. "We've already got four thousand. Five visits and we should have more than enough tickets to win Dad his little entertainment system."

Jimmie wrenched his eyes from a wiffle ball set. "All right," he agreed. "I already have a wiffle ball bat that's better than that one, anyway."

"That's the spirit!"

As they were riding back to the apartment, Carolyn suddenly realized what time it was. "Dad!" she said. "I have to get home! I'm going to youth group with Matt tonight!"

Dad looked at the clock on the dashboard. "Well, I was going to take you two out to dinner..." he said.

"It's okay," Carolyn said quickly. "You've spent more than enough money on us this week." As an afterthought, to make sure Dad knew how much she appreciated it, she added, "It was great, though. I had a lot of fun. More fun than I would've if Mom had kept me home as her weeding assistant, that's for sure!" Dad chuckled.

"All right, if you're sure." Dad glanced in the rear view mirror to see if Jimmie had any objections, but he was lost in his Game Boy and had missed the whole conversation.

Chapter Twenty-One

Carolyn watched the clock the whole way home, and after thanking Dad with a fast hug, she dashed inside, packed fresh clothes, and grabbed her guitar gear. Two minutes to get to Matt's house if they were going to leave on time. She was never going to make it, not with a backpack, her guitar, and the amp. Still, she struggled to make her way out the door, fumbling to get it open because she had no free hands and hoping Matt would still bring her after she'd kissed him Sunday, when he so obviously hadn't wanted her to. "I'm going to youth group with Matt!" she called out for her mother's benefit.

"Hold up!" came the voice from the kitchen.

"I can't hold up any longer! I'm going to make him late!" Carolyn yelled. Then her heart sank. "I *am* ungrounded, right?"

Mom appeared in the doorway, drying her hands on a dishtowel and seemingly deep in thought.

"Remember, you grounded me Friday afternoon last week. A week is up now. Right? Right?" Carolyn pleaded.

"Oh, I guess so," Mom said grudgingly. "Just promise me you won't sneak back in tonight… especially not with all that stuff. Why do you need your guitar for youth group?"

"It's not for youth group. I'm sleeping over someone's house tonight. Don't worry though," Carolyn said, trying to avoid the inevitable confrontation.

"Do I know this person?" Mom asked suspiciously.

"Well, no, but-"

"I don't know if that's a good idea, then," Mom said.

"Mom! Come on!" Carolyn whined. "I already promised."

"I just wish I knew her parents."

"They're from the church!" Carolyn informed her. "They're good people! Honest! Mom, if you don't let me leave now, Matt's going without me." Carolyn rushed out the door before Mom could put her foot down and give her a definite "no," since that had clearly been the answer she was leaning towards. Carolyn walked down the sidewalk as fast as she could with all her equipment, the amp banging against the side of her leg and the strap of the soft guitar case digging into her shoulder.

Matt and his grandma were waiting by the car. Mrs. MacMillan glanced at her watch. "I'm here!" Carolyn called from half a block away. Both of them looked up, and Matt, seeing how much she was carrying, ran down the sidewalk to help.

"What's all this for? Have you joined the praise team?" he asked in shock, taking her amp and backpack. Carolyn wondered why he was being so nice after how she'd acted Sunday. *Probably just because his Grandma's watching. Or because he thinks Jesus is watching or something.* Carolyn stifled a laugh.

"No. I'm sleeping over Raven's tonight, and she said to bring my guitar so we could rock out."

Matt opened the trunk and hefted her things in. "I see," he said. Carolyn angled the guitar into the tight space and adjusted the backpack to act as a cushion on one side so the instrument wouldn't slide around. "Do you want shotgun again?" Matt asked.

"Oh, I don't mind," Carolyn said good-naturedly. "I'll take the back this week." Matt seemed surprised, but he opened the back door for her without comment. They stopped to pick up Finn on the way. Carolyn suddenly felt self-conscious. Sitting in the backseat of a car with a dude had such negative connotations. None of the others seemed concerned, though, and Carolyn let it go. She was trying to go with the flow rather than always being the sticking point. So far it wasn't working too well.

People were already playing Knockout and Ga-Ga when they arrived. Raven hurried over as soon as she saw Carolyn lugging all her stuff around, trying to figure out where to put it. "I had my mom wait so you could put your stuff in my car," she explained quickly, taking the amp from Carolyn and leading her over to her mom's station wagon. "Can you believe this is the car I'll have to learn to drive in in a few years?" she said, loading the stuff into the back. She rolled her eyes and giggled.

"Hey, my mom's SUV isn't much better," Carolyn said comfortingly. "Maybe I could drive my dad's car. It's a lot smaller. But it's a stick-shift..."

"Yeah, I know what you mean. It should be a rule or something that you get your own car when you get your license."

"Ha! Wouldn't that be nice," Carolyn agreed.

Raven shut the back of the car and shouted, "bye, mom! See you tonight!" They made their way to the basketball court. "I still can't decide what color to do my hair," Raven chattered, fingering a dark strand in contemplation. "I don't think red is really that original because, you know, *everybody* dyes their hair red..."

"Rae," Carolyn interjected. "Let's go play hacky sack." She pointed to where Finn, Drew, and some of the other skater kids were kicking a little red bean-filled bag around.

"Ooh, I'm so bad at hacky sack," Rae said. "I'll totally embarrass myself."

"That's okay. I suck at it, too." Suddenly, Carolyn remembered that Rae had a crush on Finn and said, "if you never hang around him, he'll never figure out you like him. And if you're terrible, he'll figure out pretty fast that you're not hanging around because you want to play hacky sack." *Wow. That sounded like something the old me would have said!* Carolyn felt a smile grow on her lips. She'd forgotten how good it felt to help other people with their problems instead of fixating on her own.

"I guess," Rae said slowly. Carolyn grabbed her wrist and dragged her over to the game. Someone kicked the sack way up in the air and completely missed everyone in the circle. Carolyn darted sideways and head-butted it back into play.

"Nice save, Caro!" Finn yelled. Raven eyed her jealously.

"If you get to know him, he'll talk to you, Rae," Carolyn said. "He's not a snob or anything. He just doesn't know you well enough yet."

Rae made a face. "I'm not sure *that's* the problem," she said, discouraged.

"What do you – watch out!" Carolyn warned as the hacky sack flew in Raven's direction. Raven shrieked and caught it. Carolyn shook her head. "You're not supposed to catch it," she said.

"I know," Raven said, laughing hysterically and throwing the sack back in. "I wasn't ready. Try me again." But the next time the sack came in her direction, Raven shrieked again and kicked at it wildly, barely even making contact with it. Carolyn quickly stuck her foot out and to save it from hitting the ground, but she, too, missed almost completely.

"Maybe we need to practice a little tonight," Carolyn suggested, a laugh in her tone. Raven laughed and agreed.

"But I'm having fun," she added. "I just suck at hacky sack."

"Pizza!" someone yelled. Finn caught the hacky sack in his beanie and everybody assailed the pizza delivery car. Carolyn made sure to let Raven slip in between her and Finn when they all circled up to pray. Raven squeezed her hand in thanks.

"And while we're all listening," Jiles said when he'd finished praying, "I have an announcement. If you're going into ninth grade, you're not in middle school anymore! You belong at the high school youth group now! It meets on Saturday nights, 6:30 til 9:00. You're welcome to keep coming here until summer's over, but you're also welcome to start showing up on Saturdays." The silence broke as excited ninth graders started talking about what high school would be like. "Okay," Jiles said with a grin. "Go eat your pizza."

Dinner and worship seemed to fly past, and in no time, Carolyn found herself in the same position she'd been in the week before: wedged in between Matt and Raven on the couch, wanting to keep talking to Raven but unable to say a word because Sgt. Matthew was watching and would shush her as soon as she opened her mouth. *He takes everything so seriously these days,* she thought resentfully. *Well, he can't* make *me listen, even if I'm not allowed to talk.*

Jiles was trying to prove that Jesus had risen from the dead, but Carolyn wasn't buying it. "Some people try to deny this truth. Some think that Jesus was only pretending to be dead, or that he fainted while hanging on the cross and the Romans just thought he was dead. But you know what? These executioners were professionals. They knew how to kill a man, and they could tell the difference between someone who was alive and someone who was dead. No one has ever survived crucifixion. It is impossible. Especially in this case, where Jesus had been severely flogged beforehand. Even if, by some strange occurrence, Jesus wasn't really dead when they laid him in the tomb, there is no way he could have moved the two-ton boulder they'd placed in front of his grave and snuck past the professional guards stationed outside. Not if he was an ordinary man, which skeptics who accept this theory assume him to be."

Just to prove that she didn't have to do what Matt said, Carolyn kicked Raven's foot. Rae looked at her in surprise. Using her eyes and eyebrows, Carolyn tried to say that she wanted to annoy Matt, but Raven wasn't getting it. Finn leaned over from the next seat and raised his eyebrows in question. Carolyn did her face routine again, feeling completely ridiculous, but Finn picked up on it. He grinned and snagged Raven's little memo pad. Raven blushed and turned her face away so he wouldn't see.

Jiles continued. "Others think that maybe Jesus' disciples stole his body and merely *told* the world that He had risen from the dead. But we're still faced with a few obstacles, the huge boulder and trained, determined Roman soldiers in front of the tomb being just the physical problems. The disciples were in hiding the night before resurrection day, out of fear of the Jews. Above all else, they were worried about their own safety."

Watching Matt, Finn tore the corner off a piece of paper and discreetly flicked it behind the girls' heads so it hit Matt's ear. Matt turned his head in annoyance, but Finn was innocently jotting down a note about Jiles' sermon in the notebook, and Carolyn and Raven were leaning forward, apparently listening intently as Jiles talked about the Resurrection but really just trying to hide their grins from Matt. This was too amusing.

"But for the sake of argument, let's say they got up their courage and went out, and defeated the guards, and moved the boulder, and took the body," Jiles narrated. "Now what? They're going to go around lying to people about how Jesus rose from the dead? If this kind of conspiracy had occurred, the disciples would have been going against everything they'd ever been taught, through the Law and by Jesus himself."

Matt turned back around, and as soon as he got back into the talk, Finn shot another wad of paper his way. Matt looked again, but Finn couldn't cover it up this time. He was laughing too hard. Matt scowled and stole the memo pad. Once he looked the other way, Finn mouthed, "party pooper" and turned his attention back to Jiles, as well. Carolyn didn't have any choice but to listen now.

"Jesus' resurrection proves that he was more than just a man. He was – is – the Son of God. He miraculously returned to life, and appeared to hundreds of people, including his brokenhearted followers and some stubborn doubters. His followers took heart and went out to spread the news: Jesus Christ is alive! They were persecuted, jailed, and even killed because of what they believed, but they would not waver from the truth. The doubters suddenly became Christians. Why the change of heart? Because they'd met with a resurrected Jesus!"

Carolyn stopped wishing for Raven's memo pad so she could doodle. What Jiles was saying actually made sense, unlike so many of the things that had happened to her lately. The logic was winning her over. Carolyn was caving, and she knew it. *But people can't just come back to life!* she told herself. *If you're dead, you're dead! That's it!* However, she had run out of excuses. *It's impossible! It's impossible!* her mind screamed. Yet her heart kept shouting, *it's true, it's true! Everything can change now!*

"Jesus led a blameless life," Jiles said, eyes brimming with passion. "He was tempted just like the rest of us, but he never sinned – not once. 'The wages of sin is death.' That means that every one of us deserves to die. I know it's hard to hear it. I know it's hard to believe that if you've told one little white lie, you're going to the same place as a serial killer. That's why Jesus *had* to die in our place, and by coming back from the grave, He conquered death once and for all, and anyone who puts their faith in Him will be saved." Jiles eyed the clock. "We'll talk about that more next week, but your parents are going to kill me if I don't let you go now." He smiled and paused to see if there were any questions. Carolyn had so many, but she bit her tongue and decided to ruminate on what she'd just heard for a while before saying anything. Torn, she left the church in silence once again.

June 2, 2000

I'm really confused. But I suppose that's better than where I was before that. Confusion's got hope at the end of it. Maybe I'll figure it out this time around. I don't really know what this whole God thing is about, but it sounds like it could be interesting. Hey, I'm not going religious on you or anything — hah, can you imagine? No thanks! But I mean, it IS interesting, and I'm not saying I totally don't believe it... I just don't totally believe it, either. This is where the confusion sets in. Part of me wants to believe it so badly. Part of me wants the hope it could give. But part of me is clinging to rationality (and even that part is being overcome somewhat) and to familiarity and habit, too, I guess. There was a time when I could say I'm doing just fine without God, but at this point in my life, if He's real, then I probably need Him. It doesn't look like I'm getting MYSELF out of this mess, at any rate. I guess time will tell....

233

Chapter Twenty-two

"You're kind of quiet," Raven commented, digging around in one of the drawers in her personal bathroom.

Carolyn shrugged. "It's two in the morning. I'm a little tired. Plus I don't want to wake up your family."

"Not *that* kind of quiet," Raven said knowingly. "You've been quiet since we left the church. Plus you were scribbling away like crazy in that notebook of yours." She lined up a few bottles on the counter and asked, "Are you thinking about what Jiles said?"

"Well, sort of," Carolyn admitted. "I mean, it's pretty crazy stuff."

"That, it is," Raven agreed. "Well, do you want to talk about it?"

"I dunno. Maybe when I'm more awake?"

Raven laughed. "I guess that's fair. But you know you can ask me anything. I might not have the best answer, but I'm here for you. I want to help." Carolyn thanked her, blinking back tears at the kindness Raven had always readily shown her. "So." Just like that, Raven was back to the hair dye conversation, as though talking about a guy who came back from the dead so the rest of the world could be – what had Jiles said? – saved was a perfectly ordinary, every-day occurrence. "What colors do you think?"

"I don't know. You've got blue eyes. How about blue, or turquoise?"

Raven nodded thoughtfully. "Good call. Now, for you…"

"I don't think I should do all my hair purple or anything," Carolyn said quickly. "If I show up at home with purple hair, I'm guessing my mom will never let us hang out again."

"Well, you could do just a *little* purple," Raven suggested. Suddenly, she snapped her fingers. "I've got it. Black with purple streaks!"

Carolyn tried to picture it. "Will it wash out?" she asked nervously.

Raven shrugged. "Yeah. It fades a lot in the first week, and by the end of the second week it's usually gone." She grinned. "It's great for those of us who can't keep one hair color longer than a week or so."

"All right, let's do it!" Carolyn said, before she could chicken out. The dye smelled funny, and made her choke a little.

"Yeah, I know, the kinds of chemicals they put in this stuff, right?" Rae said. Carolyn coughed and nodded. "Now put this towel around your shoulders so it doesn't get on your clothes…" Rae handed Carolyn a towel that was already stained with more colors than she had lined up on the counter, and Carolyn put it on like a cape. *Black hair. Who would have ever guessed they'd see me with black hair?*

Carolyn tried to keep the conversation going in spite of her tiredness, confusion, and the stench of the dye. "We need to get you a hacky sack," she said. "That way you can practice, and next time we play with Finn and the guys, you can impress him."

"I don't know if I should, now," Raven said sadly.

"Why not? I thought you liked him."

"I do!" Raven said fervently. "But it's just, I don't know. He seems to like *you.* I don't want to ruin that."

Carolyn actually laughed. "Keep still!" Raven ordered.

"Me and *Finn?* God, why does everyone say that? It's getting really old. Besides, that would have to be as bad as dating, like, my cousin or something. *Ew.*"

"What, you don't think he's cute?" Rae wheedled.

"I didn't say he wasn't *attractive.* I just can't imagine myself ever dating him. He's pretty much the best friend I've got now."

"Isn't that always the way?" Rae said knowingly.

"What do you mean?" Carolyn asked. Instead of answering, Rae told her to put her head in the sink. Carolyn followed her instruction, trying not to bump her head on the faucet. Rae rinsed the goop out of Carolyn's hair. "Now you're supposed to shampoo. You can use that shower, I won't look."

Raven occupied herself with the colors, still trying to pick which one would look best, while Carolyn stripped and leapt into the shower at lightning speed. "You're not getting off the hook that easy," she said through the curtain.

"What do you mean?" Rae asked innocently.

"You know what I mean. You and your little prophecies about me and Finn."

Rae laughed. "Forget it, okay? I didn't realize you were so against going out with him."

"I'm not," Carolyn insisted.

"Oh. Right. My mistake. Saying it would be like dating your cousin isn't being against going out with him."

"Well… People used to marry their cousins," Carolyn said. The shampoo she was using smelled really good, like fruit and flowers combined.

"So you *would* go out with Finn," Rae pressed. *Oh! That was tricky.*

"*No.*" Carolyn peeked out of the shower, and caught Raven smirking. "Just shut up," she said grouchily. "And look the other way, I'm getting out."

"I think I'm going for turquoise," Rae finally decided. "I was going to do some sort of combination, you know, with the blue, like you said, but I'm too tired." She started working the dye into her own hair. Carolyn offered to help, but Rae said she was a professional and she could do it really quick on her own, so Carolyn sat on the closed toilet and combed her damp hair while she waited. "By the way, am I allowed to look at you yet?" Rae asked.

"Oh, right," Carolyn said. "How does it look?" She avoided the mirror, afraid of her own reflection.

Rae turned to look. "Oh, my word! It looks amazing on you!" she squealed. "You carry it off really well. I think any color would look good on you." Carolyn blushed at the compliment. "You'll have to let me play around with your hair once that comes out, okay?" Rae rinsed her hair in the sink, and Carolyn turned her face so Raven could go shampoo in privacy.

"It looks excellent," Carolyn told her once Rae said she could look.

"Really?" Rae smiled. "Thanks. I've always been a fan of turquoise..."

Out in Rae's bedroom, they both climbed into sleeping bags ("it's not a real sleepover if one of us is in a bed," Rae had said) and chatted tiredly, avoiding the topic of Finn, and boys in general. However, Carolyn was quick to drift off to sleep. She'd been so tired lately, and she could really understand why. So much had been happening, so many things were on her mind. At least when she was asleep, she could dream that everything was okay, and imagine that life made sense – just for a little while. But lately, things were looking up for the very first time, and maybe she wouldn't have to kid herself much longer.

As soon as everyone in the house was awake, Carolyn and Rae hooked up their equipment and started jamming. "This is really fun!" Carolyn commented. "I've never played with another person before."

"I have, and let me tell you, it usually doesn't work quite this well," Rae said, glowing with excitement. "We must just be really compatible or something. Could you play that crazy song again? The really angry-sounding one? I want to try and come up with a bass line to go with that..." Carolyn played it again, and again, until Rae was satisfied with her creation.

"Listen to that!" she said when they were done playing the finished piece. "That is *music,* dude! We could, like, be a band or something."

"That would be super fun," Carolyn agreed. "We definitely have to do this again sometime. But for now, I think I'd better go home. I'm a little worried about what my mom will say if I'm not home by mid-afternoon."

It turned out that Mom had more to say about her hair than about her timing. "I'm not grounding you again, because it's got to be a sin to keep a kid indoors during the summer," Mom said when she was done ranting. "But that's another week without the computer for you." She shook her head hopelessly. "What am I going to do with you, Lynnie?" Carolyn bowed her head in shame. She knew what Mom was thinking: "you used to be such a good kid. What happened?" It was the same thing everyone thought. She shrugged it off with that practiced, cold indifference, thinking, *nothing really matters anyway.*

June 3, 2000

Last night at Raven's was really fun, and my hair looks really great black and purple, though mom flipped out about it — of course. Oh, and Rae and I are thinking of starting a band. For now it looks like it'll just be the two of us, but hey, it should be fun, especially since she's virtually my only friend right now — well, her and Finn and maybe Margo — so it will be good to have an excuse to hang out with her more often: we've got to practice. It would be so fun to make it big. Can you see us opening for, say, Blink-182? How rad. It's too bad I can't go live in that fantasy world until I can figure out how to make my friends not hate me.

Chapter Twenty-Three

Carolyn spent most of the week out of the house. She joined her friends on the rocks at the beach, and hung out with them on the boardwalk, though she didn't go surfing with them. It took enough energy just to make pleasant conversation with people she felt were complete strangers, especially when half of them hated her. *And if they don't, they should. Take Anne, for instance. How could I do this to her?* She had done her best to push the memory of Skitt and the guilt that came with it out of her mind, but seeing Anne was a constant reminder of what she'd done, and listening to Tori whine about how much she "looooved" Skitt definitely didn't help. The Gilmans had left for vacation on Sunday and planned to be gone for two weeks, leaving Carolyn without a real confidante. She supposed Raven would have been a good person to talk to, but Raven lived at the other end of town, and didn't know anybody Carolyn was talking about. She didn't particularly want to bring up the subject with Finn or Nick, so she kept tactfully silent.

Anne and Tori were shocked to see Carolyn's black and purple hair. "You really *do* look like a punk now," Tori said derisively.

"It's a big change," Anne said neutrally. "It's cool, though."

The guys even noticed it as soon as they all met at the arcade, though Carolyn had always assumed boys were completely oblivious to things like hair color. In shock, Nick stated the obvious: "Dude, you dyed your hair!" Matt looked dismayed and said nothing. Finn gaped and seemed unable to decide if he liked it or not, and finally just said, "wow." Carolyn smiled and gave it a flip, then proceeded to tie it back and take the guys on at DDR.

Finn picked up on her mood though, just like always. He had this scary sixth sense that seemed to tell him when Carolyn was really struggling with something. After destroying them all at DDR, he asked her what was going on now.

"What are you, my big brother?" Carolyn asked, annoyed.

"Well, someone's got to watch out for you," Finn said lightly.

"I'm just fine, thanks."

"Ha ha ha. Really. I won't tell anyone if you don't want me to."

"Yes, well, I said the same thing to someone else," Carolyn said. It was partway true, anyway. She'd told Skitt no one had to know about what they'd done. Something told her Finn would understand, but she wasn't letting anything out. "That's why I can't talk about it."

Finn looked somewhat impressed and let it go, heading over to the Jackpot game to win some big tickets.

"Okay," Tori said, coming up behind Carolyn, who jumped in surprise. "So there's this dude."

Carolyn wanted to scream, but kept her tone down to the best of her ability. "I *know*, okay, Tori? Everybody knows. The fact is, Skitt is eighteen. Even if he wanted, he really couldn't go out with you, okay?"

Taken aback, Tori persisted. "But it's not about Skitt," she said. "It's about this other guy." She should have known. With Tori, there was always bound to be "another guy."

"All right. Who is it?"

"It's this really cute lifeguard…"

"Oh, for Christ's sake, Tori!" Carolyn burst out. "The lifeguard is probably eighteen, too. Do you think you could maybe restrict yourself to the guys in high school?"

Tori looked hurt. "I should have known *you* wouldn't understand. I thought the old Carolyn might have re-inhabited your body, but I see I was wrong. My mistake… *punk*." Tori stalked off, and Carolyn glared after her.

"Drama queen," she muttered under her breath. If Tori was allowed to label her, Carolyn would label Tori right back. "I think I need some ice cream."

"Good, I was hoping someone else would decide they were hungry," Anne called from the ticket counter. "Let's get something to eat." At the word "eat," Matt, Finn, and Nick suddenly appeared nearby.

"Good idea. I need to fuel up for my soccer game later," Nick said.

"Soccer game?" Anne asked.

"Yeah. I'm doing the Summer Sports League this year," Nick explained. "They do a couple weeks of soccer, a couple weeks of baseball, and a couple weeks of football, plus some straight track and field training. It never hurts to be able to run a five minute mile."

"Wow. Sounds intense," Tori remarked.

"It is. Good intense, though." They made their way down the boardwalk, squinting through their sunglasses at the colorful signs by the beachside shops.

"I just want ice cream," Anne said. "It's too hot for real food." Carolyn agreed. The ice cream truck was parked a little ways down, and they made a beeline for it. Tori quietly refused to buy anything, and Carolyn figured she was still "health-kicking." Nick, on the other hand, bought several different snacks.

"Have fun trying to eat all those before they melt," Carolyn smirked, eyeing his armful of goodies.

"Watch me," Nick said, shoving a chocolate Popsicle into his mouth and pulling the stick out clean.

"Okay, I'm impressed," Carolyn admitted.

The sound of wheels on the boardwalk grew louder behind them, and Carolyn moved aside, looking to see who was coming. To her dismay, Mark and Jason, Paul's high-school cronies, were roller-blading right in her direction. They didn't stop, but Mark called out pointedly, "Hey, Carolyn! How's *Paul?*"

Carolyn retorted with a quick tongue. "Why don't you ask him?" She stuck up her middle finger as they passed, holding it at such an angle so that Mark and Jason could see it, but Matt couldn't.

"What was that about?" Matt asked.

Carolyn assumed he meant Mark's comment, and replied smoothly, "I'm thinking they just wanted to embarrass me."

Matt looked dubious, but swallowed the story credulously. Carolyn almost pitied him and his gullibility, but at the same time, she was glad he was so trusting of her, even though she'd given him no reason to trust her whatsoever. She supposed he would find out everything someday, but she didn't plan on telling him anytime soon. She didn't plan on telling *anybody* anytime soon. No, Paul – and Skitt – would have to stay her dirty little secrets.

At home, Mom announced that Carolyn and Jimmie would be spending the weekend with Dad. Carolyn couldn't decide whether to be happy that she got to see her dad, or disappointed that she had to miss youth group, but in the end it didn't matter – she had to go, either way. She called Matt to let him know he didn't have to drive her on Friday, and he actually sounded relieved.

Great, I'm such a burden to have around, she thought bitterly. *I mean, God, it's not like they even have to pick me up or anything. I just show up, jump in whatever seat's available, and ride along. Geez.*

Dad didn't seem too thrilled about Carolyn's new hair color, but he didn't object, either. Mom was the one who hated things like purple hair. Dad always thought of things like that as "expressions of individuality," as he liked to call them. Carolyn and Jimmie won more tickets for Dad at the arcade, and Dad brought them out shopping again. He was eager to buy them things, and Jimmie let Dad buy him video games and other toys, but Carolyn felt guilty having him spend his money when his apartment was still so bare. Finally, when Dad said they wouldn't leave the mall until she'd picked something out, she went into F.Y.E. and picked out a Five Iron Frenzy CD, since Finn liked them so much.

Back at the apartment, Carolyn moped around. Friday night, she missed middle school youth group. Saturday night, she missed high school youth group. Dad sensed her melancholy and asked what the matter was.

"I'm missing youth group right now," Carolyn explained.

"Oh, right," Dad said, remembering the last time he'd had to drive her home so she could get there on time. "Isn't that on Fridays?"

"The high school group meets on Saturdays."

"Oh. Well, I was going to ask your mom if these weekends could be a regular thing, but I don't want to interfere with youth group…"

"I still want to visit, though!" Carolyn said.

"We can do any days you want during the summer," Dad said agreeably. "I just have to know ahead of time so I can arrange my schedule at work."

"Okay." That made it sound like he'd be gone all summer, so Carolyn unleashed a burning question. "When do you think you're coming back?"

Dad pursed his lips. "I'm not sure, Caro. Not soon, probably." Carolyn's heart sank. "Your mom doesn't want me to talk to you kids about it, but I don't want to keep secrets when you're old enough to know that sometimes,

people just have to spend a little time apart to pull themselves together."
Carolyn nodded. She knew all about that. "But don't you worry, kiddo. You
and Jim keep visiting, and if you ever need anything – and that means advice,
too," he said meaningfully, "please call me up."

"All right, Dad. I just wish you'd come home."

"I know, Caro." Dad wrapped her up in a hug, and Carolyn hugged him
back, trying to hide the fact that she was crying. She hadn't had a good hug
from her Dad in a long time, now, and for some reason, it was just what she
needed.

June 11, 2000

I never realized just how much I missed having Dad around until we started visiting him so regularly. He's so much fun to be around, and I wish he'd realize that he doesn't have to spend money on us to be that way. He'd be fun even if all we did was sit around in his apartment and eat Goldfish all weekend. God, I sure wish he'd come home.... The sad thing is, I don't think Mom misses him that much yet. If she does, she's doing a good job of hiding it. I guess I should be glad she isn't all mopey about it. I don't think poor Jimmie could handle having two of us in one house; it's hard enough on him as it is. I don't think I could handle it, either. Although... Mom does spend more time than she used to in her room with the door closed. I like to think she's just watching TV, but she could be crying. That really depresses me. I don't want to know if she is. Parents are supposed to be the strong ones. Since when is it my responsibility to take care of them???

Well. On a brighter note, Five Iron Frenzy really IS as good as Finn keeps saying. I mean, I borrowed that one CD from him a while ago and thought it was pretty good, but I can't stop listening to this new one I just bought. Amazingness! You can't be unhappy while listening to guitars, trumpets, drums, and saxophones all at the same time. Sorry, just isn't happening. LOVE IT!

Carolyn, I'm really starting to worry here. Please just send something, anything, so I can relax a little. I'm not trying to be a nag, and I've been pretty good about not sending thousands of emails asking where you are, but this is getting out of hand. I feel so helpless! I can't do anything for you. There are a million miles between us! (Well, probably not QUITE that many, but it sure feels that way.) What can I do for you? Please trust me again. I miss being your confidante. Love always.

Chapter Twenty-Four

There was no way to avoid the confrontation. Even if they hadn't bumped into Kate, Erin, and Shawna, it would have come eventually. The usual crew was hanging around at the beach. Nick had gone off surfing, but the rest of them, out of boredom, had decided to build a sandcastle.

"I wish we had more tools," Tori complained. "This sand is so irritating. I don't like what it's probably doing to my cuticles." She shuddered.

"Speaking of tools," said a voice above them. A shadow fell over the sandcastle, and there they stood, bikinied, primped, and sneering. "I think Paul is missing his," Kate said. The other girls burst into laughter, and they turned around and left, just like that, barely able to walk because they were laughing so hard.

Carolyn's face was burning, and though she knew it was out of embarrassment, she reached for the sunscreen so she'd have something to do besides look at her friends.

"Carolyn," Matt said sternly. "I think we might need to talk." She got up and followed him over to the rocks, where they usually sat, and where they could have a little privacy. "What is up with you and Paul?" he demanded.

"Nothing!" Her voice felt high-pitched and false.

"Yeah, that's why people keep coming up to you and saying stuff about him," Matt said. "Carolyn, if there's something going on, I have a right to know. I'm supposed to be your boyfriend, but you never tell me anything." His voice softened, and he laid his hand on top of hers. This gesture, at one time, would have sent her heart off into flying trapeze stunts, but now it simply weighed her down.

Carolyn pulled her hand out from under his and said, slowly, softly, but distinctly, "I don't think we can go out again. Ever."

"Why not?" Matt asked, aghast. "There isn't *really* something between you two, is there?"

Carolyn sighed and buried her face in her hands. "It's a really long story."

"Well, I want to hear it!" Matt insisted. "I deserve to hear it!"

"Okay, okay, pop a chillaxative."

"Okay, my girlfriend is about to tell me about how she's involved with another guy who she supposedly hates, and I'm supposed to relax. Good idea, Carolyn," Matt said caustically.

"Just be quiet and listen, please," Carolyn begged. "It's hard enough for me to say this without your commentary." Matt apologized, and Carolyn began her story. She told about the first time Paul had kissed her.

"That was only a night after *I* kissed you!" Matt said indignantly.

"No kidding."

Something seemed to click, and Matt suddenly asked, "That's what all this has been about, isn't it? I thought I did something wrong. I was blaming myself for the way you were acting, and how much you'd changed – when all along, this was the reason, wasn't it?"

Carolyn nodded. "But that's not the end of the story."

"It gets worse?"

"It gets worse." Carolyn went on to say how she'd found out Paul secretly liked her, and how, when she and Matt had decided to "take a break," she'd let Paul kiss her because she thought Matt didn't love her.

"Carolyn!" Matt reached out and pulled her close in a comforting hug that should have set her nerves on end. She should have been fizzing, sparkling with excitement, but somehow the contact was flat and lackluster. "I never stopped caring about you, not for a second! Taking a break was your idea, remember?"

"But we had a fight, don't you remember?" she said mournfully. "We had a fight because I thought you were a Jesus freak and didn't want you to go to youth group, and you were mad I was being so narrow-minded, and, well, I felt like I'd lost *everything*."

"Carolyn, I'm not everything, you know. The world would keep spinning if we broke up for good. Not that I want that! But it's a huge burden for me to know that you're giving me that much weight in your life. Nothing should be that important except for God." She'd expected something like this, and didn't argue. He finally let go of her, and Carolyn took a deep breath.

"I still don't think we should keep going out," she said, not wanting to mention the incident with Skitt.

"I agree with you," Matt said, quietly so as to mask the quiver in his tone that Carolyn was able to detect even at such a low volume. "But *not* because of the thing with Paul. I can tell you regret that, and I forgive you, though I wish you'd spoken up sooner. The real issue is that we aren't seeing eye-to-eye anymore. We haven't since you decided I was a Jesus freak, and that you wanted nothing to do with that."

Carolyn nodded. They could have their own reasons for not staying together. He could want to stay apart based on a moral objection that was completely different from the guilt trip Carolyn was putting between them.

"I wish you'd just give this whole Christianity thing a chance, though," Matt said wistfully.

"I go to youth group!" Carolyn said defensively.

"Yeah, and pass notes to Rae and get Finn to throw things at me," Matt said with a bit of a smirk.

"Someone who was wise beyond his years once told me not to take things so seriously," Carolyn informed him.

"Oh, really? Well, there are some things I could take more lightly, I agree. But there are some things *you* have *got* to take more seriously. The Gospel is one of them. Relationships are another."

"Matt, if I take everything seriously, I'm going to have a mental breakdown before I graduate."

"Well, there are a lot of things you *do* take too seriously," Matt conceded. "There's a balance, and you're putting too much weight on the things that don't matter, and not enough on the things that do matter."

"Any other major character flaws you want to point out for me?" Carolyn asked sharply.

"I'm not trying to be critical," Matt said. "I'm trying to help, by giving you advice. See, there you go, taking things too seriously again."

"Well, thanks for the advice, but I think I can handle it on my own," Carolyn said defiantly. "I'm glad we've got everything out in the open." She got up and clambered down the rocks, Matt following close behind. They rejoined the rest of the crowd, and Carolyn once again put on her game face. Nobody ever had to see past it. No one had to know that she'd just died inside.

I'm sorry I haven't replied to anything in forever. I got grounded for two weeks, so at least I sort of have an excuse. But I guess it's sort of a lame one, since it's not like I couldn't have emailed you before then. Anyway, please forgive me YET AGAIN.

You would be proud of me. I've been going to Matt's youth group. I'm not saying I particularly like it, though there are some cool people there. But you know me. Religion is so NOT my scene.

My life is falling apart. My friends hate me. My boyfriend hates me. My family hates each other. My dad isn't even living with us anymore. I hate just about the only person in the world that likes me. Lots and lots of drama. It's way too complicated to go into details. Glad you had so much fun in Honduras and are having good luck with Church Boy Ian. It looks like it's my turn to live vicariously through you.... So give me all the details!!!

Chapter Twenty-five

Saturday night rolled around. Carolyn didn't really want to get in a car with Matt, but she missed youth group. Besides, she could usually count on Finn to break up any awkward silences, and if nothing else, she had another sleepover with Raven – this time at Carolyn's house – to look forward to.

Just as she'd anticipated, Finn helped keep the conversation going. They talked about Five Iron Frenzy for most of the ride, and Finn promised they'd go see them someday. Matt didn't seem particularly excited about this, but Carolyn wanted to shout. She'd never been to a concert before, and Five Iron Frenzy seemed like a good one to start with.

"Come on, Matt, where's your sense of adventure?" Finn said.

Matt just shook his head. "Concerts aren't really my thing," he said, dismissing the topic.

"Concerts are my thing," Carolyn grumbled. "Or would be, if I'd ever been to one."

Finn chuckled. "Soon enough," he said.

They pulled up at the church, and everything looked about the same as usual, except there were a lot of intimidating older kids playing Ga-Ga and Knockout. Fortunately, most of the other eighth graders had decided to go, so at least Carolyn knew someone. However hard she looked, though, she couldn't find Raven, so she did her best to stick with Finn and Matt. However, the latter didn't seem to want anything to do with her, and went off with some of his other friends, whom Carolyn didn't know particularly well.

"Well, this is grand," she complained.

"Don't be a downer," Finn warned. "Come on, let's go meet some of the high school kids."

"Why would we do that?" Carolyn asked, trotting along beside him.

"Because we're making the best of every situation," Finn said.

The high school kids were a lot more welcoming than she'd expected. Many of them attended the same high school she'd be going to next year, and Carolyn started looking forward to hanging out with them during the year – instead of her old friends, the ones who were afraid of her.

The pizza came at the same time as always, and just like the middle schoolers, everyone was eager to get first dibs on a slice. The guys she and Finn had met had a contest to see who could make up the craziest concoction of different sodas and who could drink the most. Carolyn, not usually a soda-drinker, tried someone's mixture of Mountain Dew, Sprite, root beer, and grape soda and actually liked it.

Raven showed up while they were eating, saying she'd gotten held up at the music store because the people there couldn't fix her effects pedal. "It looks like I'll just be playing my bass at your house," she said apologetically. "They have to ship it off somewhere to get it fixed."

"That's all right," Carolyn said cheerily. "I don't even *have* an effects pedal, so we're even." Rae laughed.

Upstairs, a different group of people played the music, and sounded even better than the middle school praise team. *I wish I had a band,* Carolyn mused as she watched them. *Rae and I need to get ourselves a drummer or something. How rad would that be?*

When they were finished with music, Matt turned to her and said seriously, "I know Jiles is going to give his testimony tonight. He always does when there are newcomers. Do you think you could *try* to listen?"

Carolyn nodded yes. Things seemed to get more and more interesting every time she showed up at this place. She could hardly *not* listen.

Jiles took the mic and prayed, as usual. Then he introduced himself. "For those of you who don't know me, my name is Jeff Riley, but everyone here calls me Jiles." With a jolt, Carolyn realized why he'd always looked so familiar. *Riley. Riley! He's related to Paul!* she thought. The idea sickened her. That was where she'd seen him before – in Paul, who had to be his brother, they looked so similar. She wanted to get up and storm out right then. What could Paul's brother possibly have to say that would be worth hearing?

"Did you know he was related to Paul?" Carolyn demanded of Matt.

"No," Matt said calmly. Carolyn couldn't tell if he was lying or not, and decided to believe him. Knowing Matt, he was doing his best to be completely perfect, and lying wasn't such a perfect thing to do. She knew from experience.

"I didn't want anything to do with people," Jiles was saying. Carolyn perked up. That sounded like her! "I hadn't realized yet that people will always let you down. I let people down all the time, myself. We've got to learn to forgive them, just as Christ forgave us." *Just like Matt forgave me when I told him about Paul!* Carolyn thought excitedly. He'd been so quick to let it go. Maybe this was why.

"In high school, things kept getting worse for me, even when I was sure I'd hit rock bottom. I used to blame God. I used to think, 'if He even exists, he must have it in for me. What did I ever do to deserve this?'" Carolyn clung to every word. She'd thought the exact same thing so many times!

"I finally realized that what I needed was *forgiveness*. I couldn't carry the weight of all the stuff I'd done, the people I'd betrayed, the girls I'd gotten too involved with, the drugs I'd stolen money to purchase." *Just when I was about to say no one could ever forgive me for all the stuff* I've *done lately.* "It was killing me. Figuratively, at the time. But it would have killed me for real eventually.

"And not only did *I* need to be forgiven," Jiles continued, his speech gaining momentum. "No, it's not enough to *be* forgiven. We must also forgive. The Lord's Prayer – you all know it: Forgive us our debts, as we also have forgiven our debtors." In her peripheral vision, Carolyn saw heads nodding, and wished she had a clue what Jiles was talking about.

"But you know what? It's a cycle. Being forgiven, it becomes that much easier for us to forgive others." Jiles gesticulated passionately, arms waving, hands weaving pictures so they could understand. "And having forgiven others makes it possible for God to continue forgiving us!" *I guess maybe I could use a little forgiveness, myself,* Carolyn pondered. *And I guess if I'm really honest, there are a few people I probably need to forgive, too.* "And once we are forgiven-" Jiles smacked his fist into the palm of his other hand for emphasis "-once we are forgiven, we can enter into heaven. That's what it's all about, folks.

"Let me share a story with you. If you have your Bibles, turn to Matthew, chapter eighteen." Jiles waited, and around the room, the kids who had Bibles with them riffled through the pages until they found the passage he'd mentioned. "This is the parable of the unmerciful servant." Jiles launched into a story in which an indebted servant begged his master to be patient, promising to pay back the millions of dollars he owed. Instead of selling the servant, his family, and all his possessions to cover the debt, the master was merciful and cancelled the man's debt. Moments later, the first servant, free of debt, encountered another servant who happened to owe him a few dollars. He demanded that the other man pay him back at once, choking the other servant and refusing to be patient, although the other man promised he would pay back everything in time.

"Geez," Carolyn whispered to Finn. "What a jack- er, jerk," she corrected herself. "If someone had just told *me* I didn't owe them a million dollars anymore, I'd be running all over the place telling everyone who owed me anything not to bother paying me back." Finn nodded in agreement, but even he was too enthralled to tear his attention from Jiles, who hadn't quite finished the story.

"The other servants couldn't believe what they'd just witnessed. They went and told their master right away. Then the master called the servant in. 'You wicked servant,' he said, 'I canceled all that debt of yours because you begged me to. Shouldn't you have had mercy on your fellow servant just as I had on you?' Then he turned the servant over to the jailers to be tortured, until he could pay back everything."

'Serves him right,' Carolyn almost scoffed. Jiles paused for emphasis.

'This," he said, and Carolyn could tell he had the verse memorized by the way he gazed so intently at each student in the room, "is how my heavenly Father will treat each of you unless you forgive your brother from your heart." *Does this mean I'm going to jail if I never forgive Tori for gossiping about me? Or Paul for everything he's put me through?*

"There are worse places you could end up than jail," Jiles said gravely, as though he'd read her thoughts. "Without forgiveness, in and out – without being forgiven yourself, and without forgiving others – you've got a one-way, no-stop ticket to hell." Carolyn jumped. *Are they allowed to use that word?* she wondered again. She unconsciously started biting her nails in distress. "That's why we should take heart from verses like Mark 3:28, which says that 'all the sins and blasphemies of men will be forgiven them.'" Jiles closed his Bible.

"Just because we're forgiven," he cautioned, "Does not mean we don't still have to pay the price for what we've done. I'm still suffering the natural, earthly consequences for my actions, five years later. No one can make that go away. But the difference is I know I'm clean, like I never made those mistakes in the first place. I'm forgiven, and no one can make that go away, either. Have you been forgiven?" he asked intently. "Let's pray."

Carolyn's mind was on anything but Jiles' prayer, though. *How nice would it be to have all my friends forgive me for how I've acted this year?* she mused longingly. *How nice would it be to stop holding grudges against everyone who's wronged me? How nice would it be to not be angry at someone — or everyone, is more like it — all the time?* She didn't want to wall herself into a narrow mindset. But she didn't want to lock herself out of the *right* mindset, either. She needed to talk to someone who knew what all this was about, and as much as she loathed his brother, Jiles seemed the best choice. When everyone had been dismissed, she told the others to go ahead of her, and promised to come down in a few minutes. Tonight looked like the night that everything would finally get straightened out.

"Can I talk to you?" Carolyn blurted, as soon as everyone but Jiles and the praise team had left the room. Her own actions and lack of self-consciousness surprised her, but it was like she had no control over herself.

"Sure," Jiles said eagerly, sitting down on one of the couches. Carolyn reluctantly sat at the other end of the same couch, remembering what had happened the last time she'd combined boys and couches. Somehow, though, in spite of everything his brother had done and in spite of all she'd gone through with Skitt, Carolyn was not afraid of Jiles or what he would do to her. "What do you want to talk about?"

"I don't really know," she confessed. "I guess I'm pretty confused. All the stuff you said tonight…. It's true?"

"Every word," Jiles promised.

"But how do you *know* God is real? How do you *know* you didn't just convince yourself He was and let it make you feel better?"

"That's faith," Jiles explained patiently. "'Being sure of what we hope for, and certain of what we do not see.' If you're looking for proof, the easiest thing

I can tell you is to look at the world we live in. How did it get here? Every planet and star in its proper place. The universe turns like a wheel. Every being down to the simplest single-celled organism functions beautifully and intricately. The things *we* create fall apart and break down, but the earth has endured for billions of years, in spite of us. These things couldn't just happen. Someone has to make them work, and I can tell you for sure that no human mind could have designed this world."

Carolyn turned this over in her mind. "What was the first thing you said? Faith is being sure of what we hope for? What's that supposed to mean?"

"It's a different kind of hope than you're probably used to. It's not like 'I hope we don't have homework tonight,' or 'I hope such-and-such asks me out.' This hope is a certainty that our eternal fate is sealed. When we die, if we have Christ in our hearts, we will spend forever and ever in heaven. If not, we go the other way. I don't want to go all fire-and-brimstone on you, though." Jiles smiled encouragingly.

"I appreciate it," Carolyn said in relief, trying not to act too excited – but she was. Just like it had for Jiles, maybe this would make all the difference for her. She hoped it would. Jiles was right – she was sick of rock bottom. She didn't want any more of the ground to crumble beneath her feet. She wanted to believe everything he'd said so badly, but how could she? Could any of this be possible, or was it a mass delusion? "So let's say God is real," she conceded. "Why would He ever want *me?*"

"Of course God wants you," Jiles said comfortingly. "Never think otherwise. You are His unique creation, His child. Right now He can't treat you like one because your back is turned. But if you turn and face Him, and allow Him into your life, and start building a relationship with Him, that will change."

"I didn't *mean* to shut him out! I didn't know," she protested. She blinked back tears and stared fixedly at the scratchy red carpet underfoot.

"That's okay," Jiles told her. "He can forgive you for that, too. I can see that you're sorry, and God can certainly see what's in your heart. So talk to Him. Ask Him to forgive you and take over your life."

"Is that all I have to do?" Carolyn asked. "It's that simple? And He'll do for me what He did for you?"

"Absolutely. Now, it's not an easy relationship to maintain," he cautioned. "Life won't stop happening, but now you've got the God of the universe on your side. Everything looks better from that perspective."

"It sounds so wonderful," Carolyn murmured. "I just wish I could be sure..."

"I'll pray with you," Jiles offered. Carolyn reluctantly consented, bowing her head and feeling her face heat up. *This is ridiculous*, she kept telling herself, but something was pulling her in the opposite direction. She resisted, tears of overwhelming confusion, frustration, and awe threatening to spill over. Everyone here cared for her and loved her so much, but it was a different kind of care than she'd ever experienced, and it was more fulfilling than any of the other kinds of love she had seen.

"Jiles," Carolyn said quickly, before he could start to pray. "Does God love me like you love me? Like everyone here seems to accept me and care so much about me?"

"More than we ever could," Jiles promised.

"Then maybe... I should pray," she volunteered.

"That's an excellent idea," Jiles encouraged her.

"But I don't know how," she faltered.

"Just talk to God like a friend. Tell Him what you're feeling," Jiles prompted.

Carolyn hesitated. "Okay," she began. "God..." *This feels awkward*, she wanted to say. "I'm not really sure you're there, but I wish I could be. I wish I could feel this love and forgiveness I keep hearing about. I wish I could trust you with everything and go to heaven. I wish you'd take away these doubts

I have. God, I want to know you." Her voice caught, and she quickly said "amen."

Jiles nodded in approval. "If you don't mind, I'd still like to pray for you," he said. Carolyn nodded, less hesitantly this time, but her mind was already elsewhere. It was filled with hope, an emotion that hadn't swept over her in a long, long time, and with peace, because suddenly she knew that everything was finally going to change. Before Jiles finished, she hastily brushed the tears from her face.

Jiles said "amen," and Carolyn echoed him. "Thank you," she said quietly, allowing herself to meet his gaze in spite of the tears in her eyes.

Jiles patted her arm. "God bless," he said. Carolyn got up and, as though in a dream, floated down the stairs and out the door. An ethereal halo seemed to surround everything she looked at, even the most mundane objects like parked cars. The sky and the little drops of rain seemed to glow with that otherworldly aura.

Back at the Smiths, Carolyn dazedly hugged Matt, his grandma, and Finn, thanking them all, and skipped off down the street. The sky still had that peculiar luminosity about it, and Carolyn slowed her pace, staring upward. She suddenly saw that the cause of that peculiar luminosity was not, as she had thought, her own ecstatic frame of mind, but a great rainbow that arced across the entire sky, casting light all around. Tears trickled from her eyes again. This *had* to be a sign. *God really is there, and He's speaking to me right now!*

"How did I ever miss You?" she whispered. "God, how did I miss You? Please forgive me! I know it now, I know it! I need You in my life more than anything! How did I get this far by myself? I won't go a step further without You. Take everything I am and make me like you, Jesus." She couldn't taste the difference between the rain and her tears of joy and relief as she gazed up at that proverbial symbol of hope, and knew that it was there for her. She was starting over, and deep down, she knew that she could count on God to right her wrongs, when everyone and everything else she'd ever counted on as rock-solid had evaporated. She'd always wanted and tried to fix everything herself, but now she was learning that only God could fix everything, and what's more, she knew, He would do a much better job of it than she ever could, even before she started messing everything up.

"Hey, Carolyn!" Raven's voice broke her concentration, and Carolyn turned around. She'd forgotten Rae was there in light of her new hope, but the poor girl was standing with a pile of stuff and needed a little help carrying it. Carolyn retraced her steps and took Raven's bass and sleeping bag.

"There's a rainbow," she said distractedly. "You can get a really good view of it from the corner." Rae followed her excitedly, and the two of them watched the streak of colors in the sky. Carolyn didn't know how long they stood there, but as the rainbow faded and the sun dipped below the horizon, she was startled by an ambulance screaming past, its lights imposing themselves on her retinas so she could scarcely see and its wail piercing her eardrums. It served as a reminder that she was not alone in the world, and all was not well – but even that knowledge couldn't shatter her mood. Still smiling numbly, she made her way lingeringly up the driveway under a sliver of a moon and a plethora of stars, Raven trailing behind her with an amp and a backpack.

Another ambulance – or maybe it was the same one – flew past in the other direction, lights and sirens blaring in distress, as she crossed the threshold, and Carolyn said a brief prayer for whoever was in it, but she couldn't be worried by it. God loved her. God wanted her around. Nothing could touch her now.

June 17, 2000

 Everything is all right now! I don't know how things are going to turn out with my friends or my family, or Matt, or Skitt, or Kate, Erin, and Shawna. I don't know if things can ever go back to the way they were before. No, that's not true. They WON'T go back to the way they were before, because just like Matt kept saying HE was different (and to think I thought he was crazy), I'm different too! God finally opened my eyes to EVERYTHING, and now I can see that He's in charge. I've got Him in my heart now, and I might not know what's ahead of me, but whatever it is, it's in His hands.

 Everything is going to be fine.
 EVERYTHING IS GOING TO BE FINE!

Chapter Twenty-Six

Sunday morning, Carolyn awoke bright and early with the strange intention of speaking to Paul. Despite her hatred for him, one thought dominated all others as she and Raven shuffled around, getting breakfast and finding clean clothes to wear, and that was that she *must* speak to Paul. Before the two of them could get their equipment set up, Carolyn said she had to talk to someone.

"Who?" Raven asked.

"You probably wouldn't know him," Carolyn said. "I kind of wish *I* didn't know him, but the point is, I have this bizarre feeling that I have *got* to talk to this kid, *now*."

Raven looked excited. "Then it's probably a God thing!" she exclaimed, pulling on her sneakers without bothering to untie and retie them. "Let's go!" Carolyn finished the knot in her own laces and led the way down the street to Paul's, splashing through puddles and nearly slipping more than once in her hurry.

When they reached the front walk, Carolyn became aware of someone else heading the other direction on the same walkway. It was not Paul, as she had hoped, nor his parents – but, to her surprise, it was Jiles.

He stopped dead in his tracks, looking puzzled. "Carolyn! Raven! Is everything all right?"

"Yeah, I just need to talk to Paul," she said uncomfortably.

"You and me both," Jiles muttered, starting to walk again. Carolyn jumped out of the way as he passed. There was an odd sense of urgency and distress about his rushed and clumsy movements.

"What do you mean?" Carolyn demanded, trotting along behind him.

Jiles punched in a code on a keypad outside the garage. "There are things I have to be sure of…" he began. The pad beeped, denying the access code he'd put in, and Jiles pounded his fist on the wall in frustration. Carolyn started to feel that something had gone horribly wrong, and her stomach knotted. Jiles typed the code again, more carefully this time, and the door opened infinitely slowly.

"There are things I have to be sure of," Jiles repeated.

"Did something happen to Paul?" Carolyn pressed, her voice a squeak, and in her own ears, barely audible over her racing heart.

Jiles nodded, gripping the steering wheel. Carolyn had left every inhibition behind as soon as she realized that things weren't right, and could possibly never be right again, if only Jiles would tell her what the problem was. Now she clambered into the front seat as if to say, "You're not getting rid of me." Raven seemed hesitant, but followed Carolyn's example.

"Is he going to be all right?" She was panicking, but she couldn't stop herself.

Jiles started the car, stabbing at the radio button to make it shut off. "I can't handle noise right now," he explained. Carolyn nodded in understanding and waited for him to answer her question. "I don't know if he'll be all right. My parents just called from the hospital to say to get there right away."

266

Carolyn couldn't speak. *The* hospital? *What could he have gotten himself into that would require a trip to the hospital?* She wrung her hands and almost without thinking about it began praying fervently in her head. Jiles was probably doing the same thing, and she hoped Raven, silent in the backseat, was also praying. It sounded like Paul could use all the prayer he could get. After the rush he'd been in moments earlier, Jiles seemed oddly hesitant to actually drive anywhere.

"Can I drop you girls off at home?" he asked after a moment.

"But I want to know what happens to Paul!" Carolyn objected.

"I'll fill you in as soon as I find out," Jiles promised, finally backing out of the garage.

"But I *have* to talk to him!" Carolyn persisted. "Please let me come! I won't get in the way, I promise. I just need half a minute to talk to him." It struck her then that she didn't know exactly what she wanted so desperately to say to him.

Jiles shook his head. "They won't let you in the room yet, anyway," he said. "I promise I'll keep you up to date, and I'm sure they'll allow visitors soon. Now, which way do I need to go to bring you two home?"

Carolyn pointed miserably. "Jiles, what does Paul know about Jesus?" she asked suddenly. "Have you ever told him what you told me?"

Jiles hesitated, looking hopeless. "I've told him," he said grimly. "I don't think he's ever accepted Christ as his personal savior, and that hurts. But he said something the other day that made me think he might have, and I need to know."

"What was that?" Carolyn prompted, tracing invisible patterns in the scratchy grey upholstery in the car.

"He came to me the other night and said he'd done something really bad. At first he wouldn't say; he thought I would be ashamed to be related to him if he told me. But I finally dragged it out of him. He said there was this girl, and he knew he'd hurt her. He said he'd always treated her badly, but he feels especially guilty because he took advantage of her even though she was dating someone else." The knots in Carolyn's stomach twisted painfully. She was that girl! Jiles paused and said, "I'm not sure I should be telling you this. It's his personal business."

Carolyn wanted to say that it was her personal business, too, but instead she simply said, "Well, I think you've gotten the worst out already. What did he say after that to make you think he knew Jesus?"

"He said he'd been thinking about all the things he'd done to her, and he wished he could make amends. He said he'd tried once, but she refused to even listen after everything he'd put her through. He said he could understand that." *If I'd known he was actually serious... oh, who am I kidding? I wouldn't have forgiven him. I can hardly see forgiving him even now, even after what Jiles said last night, and even now that I've got God on my side.* She inwardly asked for a forgiving heart, though it was against every instinct in her body to forgive this guy for the way he'd acted.

"I told him Jesus was the best place to start if he was looking for forgiveness, but I don't know whether he took that to heart," Jiles finished sadly. "He never does."

Carolyn turned her face to the window and allowed a sheet of freshly blackened hair to fall down like a curtain in front of it so Jiles wouldn't see she was crying. "Good for him," she whispered, tasting the saline pearls tumbling from her eyes.

"Are you all right?" Jiles asked, taking his eyes off the road for an instant.

"Fine," Carolyn said. "That's my driveway." Pulling up to her house, Jiles didn't appear convinced, but he didn't speak again. *He knows,* Carolyn thought miserably. *He knows I was the girl Paul was talking about.* It was evident in the glance he'd just thrown her, in the very fact that he had taken the time to drive her home on his way to the hospital to check up on his little brother. *Maybe he even knew it before I reacted, and was just carrying Paul's message to me now that Paul might not be able to. Maybe Jiles is challenging me, trying to get me to forgive Paul.* Frantic, hysterical, disjointed thoughts like this barraged her mind. "Thank you," she whispered as she climbed out of the car.

"You're welcome." They shared a tiny smile of understanding before Carolyn closed the door.

"Yeah, thank you for the ride," Raven said. "I hope your brother's all right."

"Thanks. Oh, here, write your phone number down...." He rummaged for a scrap of paper and a pen, which he passed to Carolyn through the open window. "I'll call you when I find out more, okay?"

Carolyn nodded and scribbled away. "Tell him... tell him...."

"I'll tell him you were worried," Jiles assured her, taking the paper and booking it out of the driveway. Carolyn watched the car peel out and sniffled involuntarily.

"Why are you crying?" Rae asked in hushed tones. "It was you he was talking about, wasn't it." It wasn't a question, and Carolyn confirmed her suspicions with a nod. Rae wrapped her in a comforting embrace. "I'm sorry you had to go through that."

"I am, too," Carolyn said, returning the hug. "But maybe it was just another challenge God had to put me through to push me in the right direction – towards Him."

They pulled apart, and Raven nodded as though Carolyn had just said the wisest thing she'd ever heard.

Carolyn laughed a little. "I don't know what to do with myself, now."

"You need to take your mind off things," Rae suggested. "Let's rock out."

They played for most of the day, and Carolyn managed to enjoy herself sporadically, but even rock therapy couldn't quell her anxieties about Paul. She could only hope and pray that he would be all right.

It was nearly a week later when Jiles phoned to say that Paul was going to live. Carolyn cried all over again in relief. "Praise God! Praise God." She sat heavily on her bed, trembling uncontrollably. "What happened?"

"We've spoken to the police and a few kids who were at the same party as him and Erin that night. I guess everyone was drinking–"

"Wait, *Erin?*" Carolyn interjected, the fresh shock knocking into her like a tsunami.

"Erin? She's Paul's girlfriend–"

"I *know* that!" Carolyn interrupted hysterically. "Is *she* in the hospital, too?"

"Yeah, why?"

Carolyn whimpered. "We're friends... sort of." She cut herself off. Could she call herself a friend after the way they'd turned on each other that year? "Sorry, sorry, what were you saying about the party?"

"They went out to Erin's sister's car," Jiles continued in a rush. "I guess that after having a bit to drink, a joyride probably seemed like a fun idea, but it's not like either of them knew how to drive, and the alcohol wasn't making things any better, and then.... I guess they ran a stop light.... They were hit in the passenger's side."

That's where Erin was sitting, Carolyn thought. "So will Erin be all right, too?"

Jiles hesitated. "She got the worst of it, but I think she'll pull through. I don't know as much about her condition."

"When can I visit?" Carolyn wanted to know.

"Not yet. Neither of them is strong enough for company yet. I'll let you know when the doctors decide it's okay."

Carolyn sighed. "Okay. Thanks for calling, Jiles."

Friends and enemies alike formed an endless procession of visitors to Paul's hospital room. Carolyn and her friends clung to each other for emotional support as they hustled down the hallways. The smell of disinfectant and the sickly green of the walls nauseated Carolyn, but the support of all her dearest friends was enough to make her giddy with happiness in spite of all stenches, and in spite of the daunting conversation awaiting her in Paul's room. It had hung over her head for another week before Jiles had called to say she could visit, so she had a decent idea of what to say when she got there, but it would be hard with so many people watching, and she didn't know how Paul would react.

The room was less drab than the corridors. The walls were pale yellow instead of that hideous shade of puke-green, and flowers and cards already decorated the flat surfaces of the room. Carolyn added a yellow rose to the window sill for each of the victims, and her friends placed their bright and fragrant offerings nearby. Nobody spoke; the journey through the corridors had subdued them all.

Carolyn rushed to Erin's side, taking her friend's limp white hand in her own. "I've been a terrible friend," she whispered, the words like sand in her throat. She could feel a flush coloring her own cheeks – embarrassment at being the only one talking, and talking, no less, to someone who was still on too many painkillers to remain conscious for long or understand what she was saying. Now that she had seen Erin's condition, Carolyn was tempted to hate Paul all over again. Plain, simple, naïve Erin, motionless and ghostly pale in a hospital bed – *she didn't deserve this.*

"When was the last time I even talked to you, Erin?" She touched the girl's ashen cheek, which nearly matched the white bandage around her head. Her dark eyelashes stood out like spiders on that porcelain face. "I'm sorry. Please get well," she pleaded, as though Erin could hear, and would respond at any moment. Carolyn almost laughed at herself. What had she been expecting? That Erin would magically awaken and say, "That's all right. We can be friends again now?"

Margo and Anne joined her, and they instinctively took each other's hands. Out of the corner of her eye, Carolyn caught sight of the boys hovering awkwardly near the door. Tori took a seat at the end of the bed and surveyed Erin's visage.

"We weren't very good friends to her, were we?" Margo commented.

"No, we weren't," Carolyn agreed.

"I don't think she really wanted to be Brat Queen with Kate and Shawna," Anne speculated. "She never quite seemed to fit with them, and she was too good for Paul."

Though she agreed wholeheartedly, Carolyn said quickly, "We shouldn't talk badly of Paul. I think he's seen the error of his ways."

Anne simply shrugged. Paul had only ever been a jerk in her eyes. Margo, on the other hand, knew the whole story and gaped at her. "You don't mean you... forgive him?"

Carolyn nodded slowly. "That's what I mean," she said.

"Wow," Margo breathed. "You're a stronger person than me, Carolyn."

Carolyn smiled knowingly. "I'm not a strong person. I couldn't have come around without God's help."

Now even Tori looked at her strangely, and Carolyn realized that her preoccupation with Paul's condition had prevented her from explicitly addressing her change of heart in the past two weeks. "That's right. I never told you.... I went to Matt and Finn's youth group a few times, and God finally revealed Himself to me."

Tori's nose wrinkled almost imperceptibly. "I never saw it coming," Anne uttered. Her tone didn't reveal whether she was supportive of that decision, but it didn't matter to Carolyn anymore whether other people agreed with everything she did, just as long as *she* knew it was right.

With another smile, Carolyn timidly joined Matt, Finn, and Nick around Paul's bed. His parents stood on either side of the bed, carefully avoiding each other's gazes, and Carolyn remembered that they were divorced.

She couldn't bring herself to look at Paul right away. When she did, she noted that Paul's head, like Erin's, was wrapped in a bandage. Various bandages dressed other parts of his body, and an IV ornamented one forearm. Carolyn winced. The words weighed on her heart, and she longed to let them spill out, but she couldn't utter a sound with all these people there.

Soon after, though, the boys drifted awkwardly away. Carolyn almost laughed at how out-of-place they seemed, but now was not the time for levity. The words were burning holes in her tongue. She didn't want to say them in front of Paul's parents, but she couldn't bring herself to ask them to leave, so she reached out and covered his hand with her own, kneeling as close to his head as she could. She spoke in her head, as though by some miracle of telepathy, Paul would hear her when the others couldn't.

"I guess the old me would have said you deserved this, or you had it coming. You always seemed to enjoy making my life a living – well, you made it easy to hate you. But you know what? I forgive you. For everything. And if you were awake, I hope you'd be able to forgive me for not believing that you were sorry when you said you were. I'm praying for you, and I hope you get out of here soon." Then, out loud, she whispered, "I forgive you" one last time before excusing herself.

They didn't linger. Mrs. Becker picked them all up in the SUV and drove them to the beach, where they made themselves comfortable in their usual spot on the rocks. No one had spoken in a long time, but Carolyn still had words ready to burst out of her.

"Guys," she said finally, nervously fingering the silver-and-garnet cross necklace Gram had sent for her birthday – the same one she'd sworn she'd never wear; and yet, there she was, with the delicate charm dangling at the hollow of her throat while the Swiss Army Knife from Gramps still lay untouched in the drawer of her bedside table. *It's funny,* she thought, *how differently things can go from how we planned.*

"I really messed up this year," she admitted. "I was a terrible friend. I was selfish. I never thought about anybody else. I just focused on *my* problems and how badly everything in *my* life was going, but I didn't care about *your* problems. At the time, I didn't care about *anything.*" The speech was a relief, yet it still pained her to say it. How could she have been so cold? "Looking back, I can't believe you guys still want me around, but I'm so thankful that you do, and I hope you can forgive me for the way I acted this year." She couldn't make herself meet their eyes. What if they didn't accept her apology?

Margo was the first to speak. "Of course we'll forgive you. That's what friends do!" Carolyn felt a small smile on her lips. Even her friends were proving what she'd already learned that summer: sometimes people don't always get what they deserve. *I deserve to be rejected and hated by them, and yet they still love me. This is grace.* Carolyn felt like she was sparkling all over again, this time without any help from Matt.

"Of course!" Anne quickly agreed. Anne still didn't know about Carolyn and Skitt, and Carolyn felt a pang of guilt. She'd already decided that Anne didn't have to know about that. She'd confessed it to God, and He'd forgiven her. Except between her and Skitt, it was as though the whole thing had never happened, and Carolyn planned to keep it that way.

"I'm glad you finally came around," Finn said with a grin. The comment was not scathing or bitter, but sincere and heartfelt, and Carolyn's smile grew.

"Yeah," Matt and Nick agreed.

"Though I can't say you didn't confuse the heck out of me at the time," Matt added. "I thought you hated me."

"I know!" Carolyn said sadly. "I'm sorry! I should have told you everything from the start!"

"But it's okay," Matt said quickly. "It's all in the past now."

"Exactly," Tori chimed in. "I only made things worse, but I'm not kidding. I was really scared of you."

Carolyn laughed. "You didn't need to be afraid of me just because I wore black, Tori. I should have been more afraid of myself than you were."

"But we don't have to think about that," Tori said. "Like Matt said, it's all behind us now. We can start fresh. Or at least pick up where we left off at the end of Christmas break."

"So you guys are willing to just forget about everything I put you through?" Carolyn asked incredulously. These guys were too good to be true!

"Well, seeing what happened to Paul kind of gave me a bigger perspective," Margo said thoughtfully. "Why hold grudges when something like that could happen? It's not worth it. He could have died. Life's too short for grudges."

Aisling piped up. "I haven't been around much this year, either," she admitted. "I let my busy schedule get in the way, and before long I was too busy working through lunch to even sit with you guys. If I could do it over again, I would. In a second! But this year I have to go off to freakin' Santa Catalina, so I don't even know when the next time I see you all will be. Except you, Anne."

"Well, hey, we can forgive you, too," Carolyn said generously. "You guys are the best friends anyone could ask for. What would I do without you? I've been so blessed and I never even realized..."

"All right," Finn said suddenly, pushing himself to his feet. "This is enough sappiness to last me the rest of the year. DDR, anyone?"

They all laughed, and as they made their way across the sand, the girls hugged each other joyously. These were the treasures of life. Worrying about Paul and Erin wouldn't heal them any more quickly; the best she could do was pray daily and continue to live her life to the fullest. It was funny, Carolyn thought, how their near-death experiences had done more than shock her and her friends. It had brought them back together when she had been so convinced that nothing ever could. Even through the tragedy, God was still at work, sending blessing after blessing her way, and Carolyn didn't plan to let anything pass her by. Every moment was a gift to be thankful for, and even when the hard times rolled around, like she knew they would, she would stand firm with a little help from her friends and a lot of help from her Jesus.

Message from: Carolyn Becker <SkiBlink@aol.com>
To: Leah Sorman <PussyCat240@aol.com>
Subject: New Life!

Guess what! I finally put my trust in Jesus! I can't believe I didn't listen to you when you used to tell me that was everything I needed. It is, and I know that now more than ever before. Everything is still crazy, but like Finn keeps telling me, I need to make the best of every situation. You (and everyone else) were right when they said it wasn't my place to solve every problem or fix every person. That's too much for a person to handle. So I'm learning to do what I can and leave the rest up to the only One who CAN repair everything that I mess up.

Paul, the kid I always told you I hated, and his girlfriend Erin, who I also hated, were in a car accident recently, and that came as a real shock for everyone. My heart was finally ready to forgive him, but he was unconscious when I told him, and I can only hope that God relayed the message. This is a hard situation to see the bright side of, especially when it's been so long since I've looked at anything optimistically, so please pray for me, and for everyone here, and for Paul and Erin to get well quickly.

Now that I've made this decision, I could potentially get back together with Matt, and I know you're wondering if I will – but I'm not going to. When something like a relationship gets broken as badly as ours, it's hard to repair it. At first I thought his stubborn faith and my disloyalty were the only things keeping us apart, but we've come so far we can never go back. And you know what? That's okay with me. It's time to move on, and I'm accepting that. I've learned from this whole mess, and one lesson that stands out is that we can not be static! Everyone, everything is changing all the time, and it's all out of my control – but God can handle it far better than I can. And as far as relationships are concerned, I've got this gut feeling that now is not the time for me to start a new one or rekindle the old flame I shared with Matt. I messed up all of that so badly that it doesn't really come as a surprise that God isn't about to stick me in any new romantic relationships for the time, and I'm learning to be content with that.

With all of that said, that doesn't mean there can't be some sparks between you and Church Boy........ ;-)

Things are finally looking up, Leah. Things are looking way up.

In Christ,
CIB

Printed in the United States
200314BV00005B/1-45/A